A Work of Art

Sidney B. Silverman

DEDICATION

Dr. Ernest Traad, a retired cardiovascular surgeon, served the South Florida community, and as his fame grew, an international clientele. He is loved by his patients, and honored by his fellow surgeons. During a period when my wellbeing hung by a slender thread, Ernie was at my side, as a friend and consultant. He oversaw my medical treatment, and steered me through to recovery.

ONE

I'm an artist. Not a good one, as judged by the marketplace. If I had to live off my earnings, I'd have starved to death. Far from starving, I live a life Aladdin's genie might have granted me.

I own a brownstone—it's actually a redstone—a block away from Gramercy Park. My gallery, The Michael Angelo Gallery of Contemporary Art, as well as my art hedge fund, occupy the ground, parlor, and second floors. A kitchen, dining room, and staff quarters are on the third. I employ a couple to manage the building, cook, and clean. My bedroom, library, and studio are on the fourth floor. An art school initially occupied the fifth floor. There, I had hoped promising young artists, all on scholarships paid for by me, would hone their skills under the watchful eye of instructors. The school didn't work. There were days when only students showed, and days when only teachers showed. I closed it and turned the fifth floor into offices. The basement is home to a swimming pool, gym, sauna, and massage room.

If I wanted to, I need never leave home, but I do. I'm invited to art, theater, and opera openings. I receive invitations, not because I'm special, but because I entertain lavishly. My guests are eager to reciprocate, hoping for a return invitation.

I'm a member of the National Arts Club, and on its Board of Governors. I was young when elected and imagined that someday I'd be Chairman of the Board.

1

How did I make my money?

I forged one of the great masterpieces of German expressionist art and sold it for a price beyond the dreams of avarice.

My accomplice in crime was Adolph Hitler.

How did he help me? In 1937, Hitler seized fifteen hundred paintings from federal and state museums. He branded the works Entartete Kunst (degenerate art) or unfit for viewing by the German people. About a third of the paintings were sold outside Germany; a third were burned in the main fire station in Berlin; and the remaining third inexplicably disappeared in the chaos of World War II. The painting I forged was one of the lost works.

I learned about Hitler's campaign against modern art when I was twelve. I asked my grandfather, an art teacher and scholar, what Hitler had against art, any art. Good paintings or bad.

"Michael," he said, "Hitler had weird views about almost every aspect of life. He tried to exterminate the Jews, and murdered six million of them. Why? In his opinion, the Jew was not a pure German, the only race entitled to inhabit the world. Hitler's skewed view of people carried over to art. He believed a portrait should portray the stereotypical German, the Nordic type, free of scars and blemishes and healthy, happy, and strong. If a landscape, it should depict a scene from everyday life."

"Hold it, Grandpa. You're going too fast. Show me an example of a painting Hitler despised and why."

My grandfather left the room and returned with a catalogue of German expressionist art. He showed me a portrait by Ernst Ludwig Kirchner of the artist Oskar Schlemmer. He asked me what I saw.

"Well, Schlemmer has huge ears and a twisted nose. Nobody looks like that."

"Kirchner," Grandfather said, "took a subjective approach. He searched below the surface to reveal the soul of his subject. The artist saw his subject tormented by his outsized ears and disjointed nose. Schlemmer suffered and his suffering was captured by Kirchner. What he painted was not a mirror-image of Schlemmer.

"An artist is not a photographer. He uses his imagination. There's a famous landscape in which a pasture is painted blue and the sky green. Have you ever seen a blue pasture or a green sky? Van Gogh did."

Grandfather turned to two paintings: one a triptych by Max Beckman, and the other a triptych by Adolf Ziegler. "One hung in the 1937 Munich Degenerate Art Exhibition. At the same time and in the same city, Hitler staged a second exhibition, The Great German Art Exhibition, which showed what the Nazis believed was great art. Both paintings depict the same theme. Can you tell which painting hung in which exhibition?"

"Well, it's clear. I like the Beckman a lot better. Hitler, I'm sure preferred the Ziegler."

"You're a smart young man. The Beckman is powerful, biblical, and political; the Ziegler is airless and inertly realistic."

"Did the experts in Germany speak out against Hitler?"

"No Michael, Germans were too frightened. But, before Hitler came to power, curators, critics, and connoisseurs lauded the paintings of the German expressionists. Today, museums and collectors do everything possible to acquire them. The leading artists of that period would be enshrined in an artists' hall of fame, if only there were one."

The High School of Music & Art is located at West 135th Street in Harlem on Hamilton Heights near the campus of the City College of New York. The building was originally used as a training center for teachers, but a surplus of teachers during the Great Depression made the center unnecessary. In 1936 the mayor of New York, Fiorello H. La Guardia, converted the building into a public school for gifted students in the arts. At the dedication of the school, he called it "the most hopeful accomplishment of my administration." Judging by the fame of its alumni and their contributions to the world of art and music, even for a mayor highly regarded for his progressive programs, it may well have been his outstanding achievement.

My grandfather, Michael Angelo Lombroso, was the first art teacher hired at Music & Art. He taught at the school from its inception until he retired in 1972. He was more than a teacher; he was a critic and an adviser to collectors and museums. My grandfather lived for art and inhabited its world. So did his wife, Maria.

Of all the married and unmarried couples I came to know, my grandparents were among the few happy ones. They met in Brooklyn in1925 at an artists' flea market. They confessed: both were addicted to secondhand markets. At first, they haunted sales in the five boroughs. After they married, they traveled in search of art treasures throughout the six New England states and eastern Long Island. They bought paintings, rolls of linen canvas, stretchers, artists' tools, paints, and brushes. Supplies my grandfather acquired during his service in Europe in World War II augmented their purchases. "The Germans," he said, "were rightly famous for dyes and pigments made in the 1920s. In Hungary I discovered a treasure trove of several hundred tubes. They are valuable."

My grandfather did not live long enough to see how valuable the paints turned out to be.

When their acquisitions overflowed their small apartment, they rented storage space in the basement of their apartment house. After they died, I inherited their treasures. I made good use of my inheritance.

My grandparents were separated only once, and that was as a result of World War II when my grandfather served in the army. He was too old to be drafted when the war began and did not enlist as he was disinclined by nature to engage in combat. An opportunity arose in 1943. In that year, as the Allied forces began planning for an invasion of Europe, the Monuments, Fine Arts, and Archive Section (MFAA) was formed, known colloquially as the Monuments Men. It was made up entirely of volunteers, drawn from the US and Great Britain, all experts in art and antiquities. Its task was to preserve Europe's castles, palaces, cathedrals, and other grand buildings from the pillaging and destruction of the Allied invading forces. They did so by obtaining orders barring troops from using palaces and castles as billeting quarters. They also tried to influence military leaders to avoid bombing ancient buildings. Some buildings were spared, but too often military tactics trumped cultural interests. As the war was drawing to its close, the focus of the division shifted from protecting monuments to recovering art stolen by the Nazis.

In 1943, at the age of forty-one, my grandfather joined the Monuments Men.

Grandfather's unit was charged with the task of reclaiming the thousands of paintings and sculptures looted by the Nazis. Under his guidance, many works were recovered. Grandfather had them removed to three collection points in Munich, Wiesbaden, and Offenbach. The Monuments Men searched archival records, and when the rightful owners were identified, they returned the works to them.

Roosevelt, Truman, and Churchill awarded citations to Grandfather. European museums and collectors paid tribute in the form of goodwill and long-lasting friendship. During his lifetime, he was a guest at Europe's major art festivals and frequently asked to recount his adventures in World War II. Grandfather was a star in the United States, but in Europe, he was a superstar.

My father, also named Michael Angelo, was born in 1930. Growing up in a household in which art was the lingua franca, he turned his back on art and anything related to it. When it was time for high school, he applied only to Stuyvesant, an all-boys school with an emphasis on math and science. From Stuyvesant, he went to City College and then to Columbia Law School.

In law school, he met my mother, Isabella Lovato, a Floridian and one of only a handful of women in his class. They graduated in 1957 and went their separate ways. Michael and Isabella met again as opposing lawyers in a real-estate transaction. Shortly after the deal closed, they married, left their law firms, and formed their own, Lombroso & Lombroso. They struggled at first, but by the time I was born, they had a successful real-estate practice representing local developers and brokerage firms.

I was born on February 15, 1960, and christened Michael Angelo. To avoid confusion within the family and friends, my grandfather was referred to as "senior," my father "junior," and I the "second."

After my birth, my mother worked part time as a lawyer and spent the rest of the time taking care of me. We lived on Riverside Drive and 111th Street, a block away from my grandparents. I don't remember my mother very well because she died when I was six. My father did not remarry. I thought it strange that he didn't remarry. He was handsome, urbane, and in great demand. I once asked him why he didn't.

"Michael," he said, "I have the best of both possible worlds. I choose my companions and am free of entangling relationships. Many of my friends have been divorced, others remain shackled and suffer. I married once. It was a good match. Why take a second chance?"

I did my father one better. I never married.

My grandparents raised me. When my father had to work late, was away on business, or on "vacation" with one of his women, I stayed with them. They taught me to paint, encouraged me to study art history, and took me to museums and galleries.

My grandparents admired all art, from the old masters to the modern artists, but they were particularly fond of the German and Austrian artists of the early twentieth century, particularly the art of the Weimar period. The school was known as German Expressionists

I, too, favored that school. By the time I was thirteen, I was painting in the style of the expressionists. When I was ready for high school, I applied to Music & Art. My grandparents looked upon me more as a son than a grandson.

My father encouraged me to follow my passion for art. "We pass this way only once," he said. "Might as well spend your life doing what you love." He added a caveat. "Of the thousands of painters, only a handful make a living. If you become a lawyer, you'll have a safety net. You can work in my firm. You won't have to slave away. I'll see to it there will be plenty of free time to paint. Until your paintings gain recognition, your salary will support you. Having my son at my side will make me happy, and to boot, your salary will be a tax deduction for me."

My father and grandparents were obsessed with taxes, or rather ways to avoid paying them. My dad delighted in describing real-estate tax shelters. "You get to deduct depreciation, a non-cash item based on the assumption the property has declined in value. In fact, the property has appreciated. So, you get a tax deduction without paying a penny, and what you own has appreciated. What a loophole."

My grandparents kept records of every penny they spent at yard sales, including travel and lodging. They deducted the expenses from their income contending the costs were part of an art-related business. Fortunately for my grandparents, they were never audited.

I inherited my grandparents' and father's dislike for paying taxes. When I made my fortune, I put half in a Swiss bank account and paid no taxes on the money this vast sum returned. I thought my grandparents and father would be proud of me for finding the ultimate tax shelter.

I thought about my father's advice about going to law school. I was aware the odds for success as a painter were against me. While law was not my passion, as the child of two lawyers, it was part of my DNA. After Music & Art, I attended Columbia College and Columbia Law School. After graduation I worked in my father's firm. I had ample time at night and on the weekends to take art lessons and paint.

My teachers liked my technique, but said there was no market for my work. One summed up the consensus. "Art is in flux. Abstract replaced expressionism, and pop replaced abstract. Artists should seek to be original, not copy the style of past masters. You have to find your own style. Instead you're mired in the work of the German expressionists. Collectors want original work, not knockoffs. The expressionists got tired of their work and broke new ground with Dadaism, Cubism, and Futurism. If you continue to paint in the style of Otto Dix and company, you'll never sell a painting."

I paint out of passion, not to make money, but I have an ego. I want to be recognized. I faced a dilemma. Unless I abandoned my style of painting, I'd die a lawyer.

In a perfect world, art should be judged on aesthetics, not provenance. If a painting is grand, why should it make a difference that it was painted by me and not Otto Dix? The art market, however, is imperfect. There's a raging battle over whether a painting is by Jackson Pollock, or by his lover and student, Ruth Kligman. If a Pollock, it's worth millions; if a Kligman, it's worthless. What's the painting worth *qua* painting? The market doesn't care until it knows who painted it.

I grew bitter as gallery owners—many friends of my grandparents—refused to show my paintings. How could I sell if no dealer would display my works? I concealed my anger, maintained a friendly demeanor, and obtained solace by thinking about my revenge.

Here was the plan I conceived. I paint in the style of the German expressionists. No one wants my paintings. Well, I'll forge works confiscated by the Nazis and numbered among the missing. I'll pass the paintings off as originals, ones I found in my grandparents' basement storage room. I'll put the forged works in art shows, lend them to museums. Maybe even rent them to the superrich to show off at parties. My forged paintings will be prized, while my original work is neglected. What exquisite irony! If I'm discovered, it will shock the art market. What, there are forgeries undetected for years and traded in the market for millions of dollars? The collectors who buy for investment will withdraw. Prices will nose-dive. That's good for the public. People who have a limitless sea of money buy masterpieces today. They outbid museums, enclosing priceless art behind moats and rendering them inaccessible to the public.

The barbarians brag. "Look at me! I've got everything, including priceless art. I'm a cultured man. Right?" Wrong. You're a mean-spirited, materialistic, evil person who has plundered many times, and deserves to shell out millions for forged paintings. Maybe fear of buying phony works will keep you out of a market for great works of art that you really care nothing about. Then museums will be able to buy, and the public permitted to see, great paintings.

I'll protect my ass from criminal charges. I'm a lawyer. I'll build my defense in anticipation of being nabbed. I'll use the millions gained by fraud to help artists. I'll turn into Robin Hood. I'll steal from the anesthetized privileged and give to the starving artist. I'll tithe. I'll double tithe. My crime will be victimless, in the sense that the ones shelling out the millions won't miss it. I'll be redistributing the wealth from the unworthy to the worthy. That's no crime.

Fantasize, fantasize, fantasize.

I had to stop dreaming and start doing.

TWO

I wrote two words on a scrap of paper: *strategy* and *tactics*. I placed the paper in a drawer in my desk. I sat down and thought about the words. Strategy was my overall plan; tactics, the steps to effectuate the plan.

Using my grandparents' supplies, my talents, and a reproduction of a great painting, I should be able to copy it. What I couldn't do is create a record of its whereabouts from 1937 until today, a period of sixty years. No matter how good a job I did, if the painting lacked a provenance, no one would buy it. *Fool, you're not there yet. That's why you wrote strategy and tactics.*

First, select the painting. Copy it. Then throw yourself at the mercy of the nine muses, the goddesses of art. The odds are against you, but if you win...Keep thinking about winning and get to work. Right now you have to pay a visit to the library of Heinrich Robert "Harry" Fischer.

Fischer was a rare book dealer in Vienna until 1938 when Hitler annexed Austria. He was a Jew, saw no future in a Nazi-run country, and immigrated to Great Britain. When World War II erupted, he, like other immigrants from Germany and Austria, enlisted in the British Army's Pioneer Corps. When the Monuments Men was formed in 1943, he transferred to that unit.

After the war, Fischer, together with fellow Austrian immigrant Frank LLoyd, founded Marlborough Fine Art in London.

The gallery dealt in paintings from the Weimar period, as well as modern and contemporary art. It became the leading postwar gallery.

Grandfather had met Fischer while both served in the Monuments Men. They bonded. Their friendship continued after the war. Grandfather served as an adviser to Marlborough and attended art festivals in Basel and Venice in which Marlborough was a participant.

Fischer was an expert on German art. He owned many rare art books, journals, and auction catalogues published in Germany between 1910 and 1939, and *catalogues raisonné* of the leading German and Austrian expressionist artists. He also owned a two-volume document started in 1942 by the Reich Ministry for Public Enlightenment and Propaganda; it ended in 1945, with the demise of the Third Reich. The document listed sixteen thousand paintings, sculptures, drawings, and objects d'art confiscated by the Nazis from federal and state museums and private collectors. It identified the owners and traced the fate of each work—which ones were sold, which destroyed by fire, and which were unaccounted for. The document consisted of two hand-written volumes. Fischer joined them with his collection of rare books and catalogues.

Grandfather was a frequent visitor to London and a guest at Fischer's home, in Hampstead Heath, a neighborhood populated by German-Jewish refugees. I accompanied my grandfather on several trips to London. Fischer's home fronted on the Heath and was within walking distance to Buckingham Palace. I'll never forget the wry look on his face when he said to me: "I can walk from my humble castle to Buckingham Palace without crossing a street."

A library on the second floor, adjacent to the bedroom occupied by me, housed Fischer's treasures. I had spent many hours reading the books and catalogues, but only glanced at the volumes on the confiscated art. What I had earlier ignored was to become my Rosetta Stone.

Fischer died in 1977, eighteen years ago. He was survived by his widow, Elfriede. Was she alive? Was the library in her possession? Pierre Levai, Frank Lloyd's nephew, was in charge of the Marlborough Gallery in New York, one of several branches of the original London Gallery. I called Levai.

He said Elfriede was alive and living in the same house in Hampstead Heath. He had seen her just last year. As far as the library was concerned, she intended to give it to the Victoria and Albert Museum, and was negotiating with the museum at the time of his visit. He was unaware whether the gift had been made. He gave me her phone number.

I telephoned Elfriede. She remembered me. "You were only a little boy when you came to our home with your grandfather. I was stunned by your behavior. You loved art books and spent all your free time in Harry's library. I'm not surprised you want to see the library again. Well, you're in luck. I haven't sold it. No, I'm only kidding. I would never sell Harry's treasures. I'm donating the entire collection to the V&A. Soon, but not yet. It's hard for me to part with them."

I said I would need a week or two to pore over the library collection and would stay at the King Solomon Hotel in Golders Green, close to her home. She insisted I stay in my old bedroom. "Our life was full. So many friends came to visit. No more. I'm lonely. Please stay with me." I agreed and said I would arrive toward the end of May, beginning of June and would give her an exact date when I made my plane reservation.

The telephone calls to Elfriede and Levai revived memories of my grandfather's relationship with Fischer, Lloyd, and the Marlborough Gallery. My grandfather had encouraged Fischer and Lloyd to open a gallery in New York, to promote the new movement in abstract expressionism, a form of art centered there and referred to as the "New York School." Grandfather told them that so important were the new works, New York would soon eclipse Paris as the art center of the world. In 1963, Lloyd left London to open and run the Marlborough Gallery in New York.

Almost overnight, Marlborough was a success. It made a nearly clean sweep of the artists of the New York School. It represented Robert Motherwell, Barnett Newman, Mark Rothko, Adolph Gottlieb, and the estates of Jackson Pollock and Franz Kline.

Frank Lloyd began his career in glory and ended it in disgrace. He was the chief architect and beneficiary of a fraudulent, evil, and greedy scheme that attempted to rip off the estate of Mark Rothko, who had committed suicide in 1970. Rothko had left behind 798 paintings and drawings. Marlborough entered into a contract to sell the paintings with the executors of the Rothko estate—one of whom was an accountant employed by Marlborough, another an artist represented by the gallery, and the third, a false friend of Rothko. Under its terms, Marlborough acquired one hundred Rothko paintings for $1.8 million, payable in twelve years without a penny of interest during the period. The remaining 698 were consigned to Marlborough for sale at commissions as high as 50 percent.

Rothko's daughter and son challenged the contract in Surrogate Court, the court having jurisdiction over the property of deceased New York residents. The Surrogate found the contract was conceived in fraud, and constituted a clear case of overreaching. The contract was cancelled and Marlborough fined $9.2 million. In a related criminal action, Lloyd was convicted for violating a court order, falsifying documents, and tampering with evidence.

Lloyd showed no contrition. He openly proclaimed that he "collected money, not art," and that the only measure of the success of a gallery was "the amount of money it made."

Lloyd's greedy, evil actions served as a rationale for my contemplated crime. Lloyd plundered the estate of his former client, robbing Rothko's children of their inheritance. Rothko's life was his paintings; they were the essence of his existence. Lloyd stole Rothko's life. In contrast, I would be recreating works of art lost to the world. I would not be robbing artists or their children. Further, I intended to use 20 percent of the profits to help my fellow artists. My crime was noble, Lloyd's larcenous.

As a lawyer, I was aware that the law would consider my socially desirable act a crime. I wanted no witnesses. The most likely was my girlfriend, Delores Lorenzo. I had met her at Music & Art, where she had been two grades below me. She was my date at my senior prom, and when she was a senior, I was hers. Delores was a mezzo soprano, and at twenty-eight, was in the chorus of the Metropolitan Opera. She also understudied major roles, but had yet to perform the role on stage.

In the summer of 1995, she was under contract to The Santa Fe Opera. The company performed five operas between its opening in late June and its closing the third week of August. *Madama Butterfly* opened the season. Delores's role was Suzuki, Cio-Cio-San's (*Madama Butterfly*) maid. *Der Rosenkavalier* was the final opera, in which Delores was booked for the "trouser role" of Octavian. It was certain Delores would be in Santa Fe from late May through the middle of August.

When Delores was in New York, she spent her free evenings with me. If she were aware I was forging paintings, and I got caught, she could be criminally liable as an aider and abettor, or possibly as an accessory after the fact. She might also be compelled to testify against me.

There was a second reason to keep my plan hidden from Delores, based on the assumption I would not be caught.

Delores and I planned to marry. We kept putting off the date. Delores was on the road to success in her field. I was a failed artist holding down a job as a lawyer at the sufferance of my father. I'm Italian and a man. Italian men are the masters of their family. If we got married, I'd be the understudy. If, however, my scheme worked, I'd sell the painting for millions of dollars.

If, after I became a multimillionaire, we then married, I ran the risk that in the event of a divorce, she might expose me. *Why am I thinking of divorce before I'm married?* In our case, the possibility of a divorce was a real risk. We fight a lot.

When she's rehearsing an understudy role, which involves a sexy scene with a male singer, the man occasionally gets aroused.

She claims she did nothing to excite him, except as she was obligated to do in following the libretto. "It's not uncommon," she said. "Maybe my singing aroused him?" She knew how to arouse me from the time she was sixteen, and it wasn't by singing.

Italian men are high spirited and jealous. We flirt a lot but expect loyalty from our women. Delores's relationship with male singers has always been a bone of contention. And that is why when I think of marriage, I also think of divorce. When I think of divorce, I think of my father's client, Irving Gross.

Gross maintained a Swiss banking account through which he traded stocks based on inside information. The account concealed his unlawful trading from SEC scrutiny; it also hid his profits from the IRS. Gross's wife knew everything. When she filed for divorce, her lawyer threatened to inform the US Attorney's Office of Gross's Swiss bank account, unless he agreed to extortionate terms. What could Gross do? Go to jail or agree to the outrageous offer? He paid the price. I didn't want to open myself to the same kind of treatment and decided to keep Delores in the dark. While she was in Santa Fe, I'd complete the painting. When she returned, I'd tell her the same story I told others, "I found the painting in my grandparents' storage room."

Delores left for Santa Fe on May 25, 1995. I departed the very next day for London.

The exterior of Fischer's house was much as I had remembered it. The brick-and-limestone façade and the Spanish-tiled roof were unchanged. The interior, however, had suffered. It was formerly a showcase, in near-perfect condition; now it was shabby and in disrepair. Paint peeled from the walls, doors, and ceiling. The furniture in the drawing room, dining room, and downstairs library was stained and in need of recovering. Elfriede's appearance matched the interior of the house. She was disheveled, her hair unkempt. When she greeted me, she was dressed in baggy worn-out slacks and a moldy old sweater, a uniform she wore throughout my visit.

Elfriede was short. When I first met her, I was twelve, and we were both about five feet. She said she had shrunk over the past twenty-five years. "I was always short, but now I'm under five feet. To be exact, I'm four feet, nine inches."

The walls were bare. I remembered paintings hanging on every inch of space. I asked what had happened to the art.

"Frank, that horrible man—I still cringe every time I think of him—had a falling-out with my Harry. What had started as a partnership between two friends, both Viennese art dealers living in London, turned into a constant squabble between two enemies. The spats were over money and ethics.

"Frank claimed he was responsible for most of the profits, which would have been even greater if only Harry had not interfered in the gallery's dealings with artists and clients. Harry accused Lloyd of crossing the line between sharp practices—which Harry objected to—and outright dishonesty, which he refused to tolerate.

"I urged Harry to end their relationship. I feared the worst. In 1973, the two went their separate ways. Lloyd stayed with Marlborough and Harry started Fischer Fine Art. The paintings belonged to the gallery. At the time of the split, they were sold."

I guess she noticed my dismay as I looked at the decay, because she said, "Harry was busy running Fischer Fine Art, and then a few years later, was sick, very sick. I took care of Harry and neglected our house. He died on April 12, 1977. After Harry died, I lacked motivation to do anything, even to make minor repairs. I exist here and nothing more. Two months ago, I celebrated my ninetieth birthday with my friend, companion, and caretaker, Bertha Schleger. She has prepared tea for us. Would you care for some?"

On cue, Bertha entered the room. I rose and introduced myself. She was rotund. Her breasts were humongous and her legs elephantine. I judged her to be in her fifties, which she confirmed in her opening remark. "I'm sorry for you, you're such a handsome young man, to see me looking like this and in a uniform. Elfriede told me you were arriving today and asked me to dress like a servant. In truth, I'm a companion-nurse-cook. Thirty years ago, I was beautiful. Wasn't I, Elfriede?' Elfriede confirmed the fact and added, "You still are."

Over tea, Elfriede asked about the purpose of my visit. I decided to tell her the truth. She would not believe me, and if she did, my plan was not endangered. She was a recluse. "Elfriede, I am hell bent on returning to the world one of the great German paintings destroyed by Hitler." She must have missed the thrust for she replied: "I knew you were embarked on a noble mission, one that would make your dear grandfather proud of you." The subject never arose again.

It took me five days to select possible paintings to be forged. The Reich's minister's document listed sixteen thousand art works, of which the missing, marked with an "X," numbered fifteen hundred. I found 506 on the first go-around and an additional forty-six on the next round. I didn't bother with a third round. My group was large enough. I put aside the two volumes and opened the art books, auction and museum catalogues, and *catalogues raisonné* to search for photographs of the missing painting. It took several days for me to find fairly good color high-resolution images, dimensions of the works, and descriptions for the nine most celebrated of the missing paintings: George Grosz, *The Boxer*; Otto Dix, *War Cripples*; Franz Marc, *The Tower of Blue Horses*; Oskar Kokoschka, *Declining Girl Reading*; Tony Klee, *Winter Garden*; Lasar Segall, *Widow and Child*; Lyonel Feininger, *Vollersroda III*; Emil Nolde, *Man and Woman*; and Oskar Schlemmer, *Three Women*.

I photographed each of the nine high-resolution images three times from different angles with my Nikon F3 camera. I took the film, Kodachrome 64, to a same-day photo shop in Golders Green. I examined the photographs and believed I could paint reproductions closely resembling the originals. There was no need to decide which ones would be forged—that could wait until my return to New York

I bought Elfriede a dozen roses, and Bertha a box of marzipan. I said I was leaving tomorrow, eight days after I had arrived. I invited both women to dinner. Bertha suggested a restaurant in the neighborhood. At dinner, the only reference to my stay was Elfriede's remark: "I can tell from your handsome, smiling face that your visit was successful." She asked me to stay in touch, and I promised I would.

THREE

Before my forged painting transformed my life, I lived in New York on West 19th Street, far west, within hearing distance of the traffic on the Westside highway. My building was formerly an abandoned five-story warehouse. My father and several of his clients purchased it in 1988 and converted it into residential condominiums. At the gala opening, not a single apartment was sold or even drew an offer. The developers were nervous. They wanted to break the ice, and I was elected the ice breaker. In September, 1988, I bought the first apartment. I got an inside price and funds from my dad to purchase seventeen hundred square feet on the fourth floor facing north. I divided the space into three rooms: a kitchen, bedroom, and a studio filled with northern light. Before leaving for London, I stocked my studio with the material I would need to forge the painting. Most was taken from my grandfather's storage room

To get the material to my apartment, I rented a car and carted off a large roll of Belgium linen canvas, the very fabric used by the great German painters. I also brought in the fine old German pigments my grandfather had brought back from Hungary, old brushes, and six pre-World War II paintings from the storage room. Canvas is a fabric and needs to be attached to wooden braces, called stretchers, to hold it taut. I detached the wooden supports from all six paintings and saved the tacks. I planned to reattach my painting to the old stretchers and then reuse the tacks. The stretchers were old, as were the tacks, but probably made in America. I doubted whether an expert would examine wooden braces and tacks. If he did, most likely, he'd assume the original painting had been detached from the stretcher and rolled up to make it easy to transport. The expert would surmise that different stretchers and tacks would be affixed when the painting reached its destination. If its new residence was the US, the stretchers and tacks would be of American origin and date from the time the painting was carted off. I planned to reconfigure the old stretchers to fit my new paintings. I was confident an expert would place no weight on an archetypical stretcher and tacks.

I had black paint and a single-hair brush. When my work was done, I planned to artificially age the work by painting a black line along the edges. A canvas, over time, will reveal stress marks around the edges where the canvas has been stretched. The marks on old paintings are called *craquelure*. My new paintings would bear that mark.

My forgery, if held out as genuine, would be priced to sell for a lot of money. I could anticipate the most exacting scrutiny. If it passed the test, I'd be rich; if it failed, I would not have committed a crime. I'd maintain that the painting came from my grandparents' storage room. Is it a crime that my grandparents purchased a forged work of art? That I had no idea it was a forgery? I'm a lawyer. I thought not.

Suppose, however, it could be established that I painted the artwork? Would that be a crime? In criminal law, an attempt to commit a crime can itself be a crime. Was attempted forgery a crime? Artists often copy the work of others. The crime lies in passing off your work as another's, not in copying. In law school, we studied the classic example of when an attempted crime is not a crime. A pickpocket attempts to pick the pocket of a statue. A cop observes the act and arrests the thief. The offense is dismissed because it is impossible to commit the crime in question. My situation is different, but I could maintain that scientific advances have made forgeries readily detectable. My crude attempt was doomed to fail much as the pickpocket's attempt. Frequently, in the course of painting the forgery, my mind turned to criminal law and what would happen if I were discovered. I didn't want to go to jail. No amount of money was worth being imprisoned. I'd have to plan a defense in case I got caught.

Arlene Spiegler, my law school classmate and a specialist in criminal law, had worked in the US Attorney's Office before going into practice for herself. I'd have to speak to Arlene and pick her brain. Not now, but soon.

On my return from London, I selected the painting to be copied using the photographs I had taken of the reproductions. It was difficult. All nine paintings were important works—ones that had not been seen since the end of World War II. The process was so difficult that I thought about copying several. Then, I dismissed it. Finding one lost painting was a strange enough coincidence, but having more than one would make art critics scream the one word I feared: "forgery!"

Back and forth I went. Hours passed before I decided upon Franz Marc, *The Tower of Blue Horses* (1913). The photograph of the original showed it was neither signed nor initialed by the artist.

That the original was unsigned was important. In the event I got caught. I couldn't claim that all I was doing was copying another artist's work, if I had, in addition, forged his signature.

The Tower of Blue Horses is a large painting, six feet seven inches by four feet three inches. Large paintings are easier to copy than small intricate ones. I returned to my father's law firm in July, but continued to paint on weekends and at night. I finished late on Saturday, August 5. Perhaps, because this was my first attempt at forgery, it took longer than anticipated. I admired my work. The blue horses seemed alive, ready to jump off the canvas. I wondered what the painting might bring if I declared it mine. I knew the answer: nothing, the same as all my other works. I set the painting aside to dry

The next morning I examined it for flaws. I found none. Perfect. I thought, *looking at it, you can't tell it's freshly painted. I'm happy. I haven't done anything wrong. I've returned to the world a magnificent painting that, but for my efforts, would be lost forever. I'm not a forger, but the creator of a masterpiece. I wonder what Franz Marc would say if he were alive, standing in my studio and looking at my copy of his work. I can hear him saying: "Well, it's not original work, which a true artist would do, but thanks for returning my work to the world."*

I showered, shaved, and got dressed. I hadn't made love since Delores departed for Santa Fe. It was time for me to celebrate the end of celibacy. I'd bet all summer she had been fooling around with tenors, baritones, and basses. Let's face it. I was a cheater. Cheating on Delores was nothing compared to what I had in store for the art world.

My stomping grounds are museums. On a Sunday, they're filled with young, nubile, culture-hungry babes. I amaze them with my knowledge of art. When they're under my spell, I'll suggest they sit for a portrait.

Better get the studio ready. I stowed the painting in a closet, cleaned the old brushes, put them and the old paints away, adjusted my easel, and moved my own paints and brushes to my work table.

Something looked wrong. The studio was cluttered. Also, I didn't like leaving what might be, if authenticated, millions of dollars of artwork in my apartment. I decided to return what was left of the goods I removed from the storage room and store my painting there. Safe from Delores's eyes and from the beautiful young thing I was likely to pick up in the museum.

I also put in plain view several paintings of nudes I had done in art school. The paintings should bait the trap and encourage the young innocent to pose bare. From there it's a short hop, skip, and jump to my bedroom.

I rented a car and reversed my previous mission. People saw me, but, as is typical in New York, nobody paid any attention. After my mission was completed, I returned the rental car and hopped a subway to the Museum of Modern Art.

I was on the fourth floor of MoMA when I spied her. She was standing in front of a richly colored canvas by Hans Hofmann. "Do you know," I said, "in 1946, Robert Coates writing in *The New Yorker* first used the term 'Abstract Expressionism' to describe that very painting you are so intently admiring? The movement arose in the 1940s and 50s in the aftermath of the horror of war, the bombing of Japan, the Nazi genocide. The artists sought to create a new culture, a new civilization. They were a small band of painters who knew each other. They met in bars, cafeterias, cafes where they talked and talked and talked. Their works appear to have nothing in common, but yet stem from a common theme. Come with me and we'll look at the works of the other members, Jackson Pollock, William de Kooning, Mark Rothko, and Barnett Newman."

When she nodded in agreement, we introduced ourselves. Her name, Pamela Walker.

We looked at the other works. "They're so different," she said. "I can't find a common theme. Please tell me."

"The paintings all express a profound and urgent expression of self. A transformation of themselves and society into an expression of their souls."

"Oh, you're so knowledgeable. What do you do?"

"I'm an artist."

She reached out and grabbed my hand. "No wonder you know so much."

Just then Anthony Aritta appeared. We were classmates at Music & Art. He was the class valedictorian, studied art history at Harvard, and was working as an assistant curator at MoMA. Tony, Delores, and I had remained friendly, and seen each other at parties and art openings.

He knew Delores and I planned to marry, but he, nevertheless, flirted with her. She claimed he was a snob and not her type. Yet, when they were together, she laughed and talked a lot with him. I even saw them kiss. I couldn't understand it. He liked her. That was obvious. If she didn't like him, why was she kissing him?

I introduced Pamela to Tony and told her that he was an assistant curator at MoMA. To Tony I explained Pamela and I had met looking at the Hans Hofmann on the fourth floor, and now on the second floor, looking at other works from the Abstract Expressionist School.

After greeting me and assuring Pamela she was in good hands, he said with tongue in cheek: "The museum likes Michael's work. We've been collecting him for several years. He's a great guide. Oh, by the way, how's your sister Delores? Don't tell me she's with the opera company in Santa Fe? I'll call her, and tell her I ran into you and Pam." Aritta can be outrageous.

I quickly changed the subject. "What are you doing here on a Sunday?"

"I'm working on an exhibition of German expressionists scheduled for a post-Christmas opening. No firm date has been agreed upon. Art dating from 1910 through the 1930s is the hardest period to get collectors and foreign museums to loan paintings. They fear Holocaust victims will come out of the woodwork and lay claim to the paintings. It's difficult even though we agree to pay the costs of the lawsuits and indemnify them against loss by agreeing to give them paintings of equivalent value. I have to meet with two potential donors this afternoon and try and convince them to lend their paintings. They're not only worried about claims being filed, they want to know where their paintings will be positioned and whether their works will be discussed on the audio guide. All these variables and a lot more are made part of the lending agreement. Life in the New York art world used to be simple. No more.

"In the years of the birth of Abstract Expressionism, there were only a handful of galleries and slightly more collectors. It was easy to arrange an exhibition. The art world today is vast. Collectors live in Europe, Russia, China, and Japan. No matter where they stem from, they have one thing in common: huge egos. Two collectors insisted on meeting me this afternoon. I didn't want to be here, but I'll do anything to make this exhibition a success. It's my first."

You could have knocked me over with a wet noodle. A German expressionist exhibition with Aritta in charge? The gods had heard my prayers. I was out of my mind with joy. If I could get in the exhibition, I'd have made the first step, and an important one on the road to legitimacy. First I'd have to sell Tony. That would be difficult, but on the plus side, he was the only one I'd have to sell.

I wished Tony luck and said I might have something to show in the exhibition. Tony thought I was trying to impress Pamela and said: "Give me a call anytime. We need more paintings."

I shifted my attention to Pam. "How about coffee and a sweet bun in the café?"

"Meeting Tony sure put you in a good mood. Coffee with an artist whose work MoMA collects? Today's my lucky day."

Over coffee, I remarked on Pamela's interesting face, and how I'd like to paint her. "You're sure it's my face that interests you? If that's true, then why are you constantly staring at my breasts?"

"The human body is always of interest to an artist. You have a harmonious body as well as a lovely face."

"I'm flattered to be painted by a famous artist, but I'm not taking my clothes off. We've just met."

I assured her that sitters must be comfortable. If posing nude created anxiety, she should not. "I'll use my imagination to sketch your body."

We hopped the E train at Fifth and Fifty-Third Street and got off at 14th Street and Eight Avenue and walked to my apartment on 19th. She was nervous and showed it by talking incessantly. At times, she rambled. "I've never been in an artist's atelier. I hope I can trust you. No funny business, though you are cute. And talented. And smart. You know so much about art."

When she entered my studio, she saw the drawings of nude females. "Do you only draw nude women? Do you have any paintings of women fully clothed?"

I laughed and said, "Those paintings are in MoMA's hands."

She took a seat facing me. I placed a sheet of paper on my easel and went to work with pen and ink. I drew her face realistically, but not her body. I drew her breasts to resemble Delores's, large and floppy, and her mons veneris, also like Delores's, almost bald. When I stopped drawing, Pamela walked to the easel and stared at the sketch. "You miserable man! To think I almost liked you. My tits are high, firm, and my cunt covered with silken pubic hair. That's not your fault. I refused to take off my clothes. Well, I'm going to take off my clothes and you had better adjust the sketch or I'll bop you on the bean."

She took off her clothes standing right next to me and placed them in a neat pile on a chair. In doing so, she violated two rules adhered to by models: 1) they never get within striking distance of the artists; and 2) never undress in front of them.

She sashayed back to her chair. She was proud of her figure and had every right to be. She was that rare female who looks wonderful in clothes and even better naked. I reworked the sketch to reflect the fine tones of her body. She looked at the revisions. Smiled. We kissed and kissed before retreating to the bedroom.

Afterward, I gave her the drawing, which she refused. "Keep it so you'll remember me. In case there are days when you want to look at more than a drawing, here's my telephone number."

We ate an early dinner at a neighborhood restaurant. She grabbed a cab and said, "Promise to call soon." I called many times.

Then finally one day, Delores and I were finished. Twelve years of Sturm und Drang was enough. I had had it with an unfaithful girlfriend—which I had found out she most definitely was. I wrote saying our relationship was over, but placed the blame on me. "You are an extraordinary woman, talented, beautiful, and loving. I do not deserve you. If you have not yet arrived at that conclusion, you will soon. It's best our relationship ends at a time when our hearts are full of beautiful memories."

She did not respond.

FOUR

I called Aritta on Wednesday, October 18. Before I could say a word, he told me his news. "Delores and I are engaged. You're an idiot. She really loved you. Your letter saying 'thanks for the memories' really hurt. I caught her on the rebound, but she quickly got her sea legs back. We are really and truly in love. I was a cynic when it came to emotions. No more. Michael, I owe you."

I made a false comment about how much I miss Delores and then got right to the point. "Is your Expressionist Exhibition still on track?" When he said it was, I asked him to do us both a favor and suggested he meet me at my grandfather's former storage room. "There's a painting I'd like to show you."

Knowing Aritta, as long and as well as I did, before agreeing, he would have asked a lot of questions, some I would not have wanted to answer. Instead feeling sorry for me, over l'affaire Delores, he said: "Tell me when and where and I'll be there." We agreed on the next day at noon.

Before my meeting with Aritta, I met with Arlene Spiegler. I asked: "Is everything I tell you confidential even if I have not retained you and may never do so?"

"Of course. From the moment you park your *tuchas* in my office and seek legal advice, everything you say is privileged. The privilege is yours. You can disclose what you said, but not me, with one exception. Remember Professor Young? He preached there are no rules, only exceptions. Well, if you turn against me, I can use what you told me as a shield, that is, as a means to defend myself against your egregious, wrongheaded, mean attack. What do you want to tell me? Keep it clean."

"Arlene, I committed a crime. I forged a painting with the intent of passing it off as an original. I need your help in preparing a defense in case I get caught. Will you help me?"

"A lawyer cannot assist a client in the commission of a crime. Otherwise, the lawyer becomes an aider and abettor and a criminal along with her client. You have already forged the painting, but that is only part of the crime. The next stage is passing it off as an original. I will not offer any advice on that score for two reasons: one, I would be implicated in the crime, and two, I know little about the ways of passing off forgeries. What I can advise you on is a means to avoid a charge of criminal fraud. I am not going to moralize and try to dissuade you. I'm not your father confessor. I'll help but only in the limited area of constructing a defense."

"Arlene, I want to pay you for your time and to retain you as my lawyer in the event I get caught." She uncrossed her legs. I got a peek at her thighs. Heavy, like Delores's. My thoughts sprang to what was above the thighs. *Curious. Even in a tense situation my libido is front and center. Is it just me, or all Italian men?*

"No charge for this meeting. I won't agree in advance to represent you. If you do get indicted and you do want to retain me, it will cost you big bucks. I require payment in advance in full. You know why? When a grand jury returns a true bill, ninety percent of the time, the defendant is convicted or enters into a plea deal. In both cases, the client ends up in the slammer and the lawyer can forget about getting paid. That's why criminal defense lawyers insist on getting paid in advance.

"Here's my advice. Carry a tape recorder with you to every meeting in which you might be asked how you came into possession of the forged painting. Don't let the other party know you're taping the conversation."

"Hold it. I thought a lawyer—and I'm a lawyer—can't tape a conversation without obtaining consent?"

"That's true. The rule, however, is interpreted to prevent the lawyer from using the secret tape as a sword, but not as a shield. Let me give you an example." She uncrossed her legs again. This time I didn't look. I'm lying-- I did. I wondered if she saw me. If she did, she showed no sign. She continued: "Let's say a witness claimed you represented the paintings as genuine when you had said nothing of the kind. You could use the tape to defend yourself. That's the only circumstance in which you can use the tapes. A bit of a nitpick? I agree, but nits are not uncommon in the law.

"One other piece of advice. A half-truth may be the blackest of lies, but it's not chargeable under the criminal law. You know what a half-truth is? A statement that's literally true, but omits relevant facts, which if disclosed, would make the half-truth false as hell. Better than a half-truth, if it's possible remain silent. That's all I'm going to say. I hate criminals."

She held out her cheek. Instead, I kissed her lips.

"Pig! And don't you ever try to look up my dress again. It makes me nervous to be behind closed doors with a pervert. "

"Good-bye, gorgeous. I hope I see you only at class reunions."

When I met Aritta, I concealed a very small tape recorder in the breast pocket of my suit. Aritta was nonplussed when we entered the storage room. He changed when he saw the painting: "That's Franz Marc!" he exclaimed. "Where did you get the painting?"

I was now embarked on the first stage of deception. I had to be careful to tell only a half-truth, "I found the canvas," I said, "right here in my grandparents' storage room." That was literally true. I did find a roll of canvas in the storage room. What I didn't add was that the canvas was blank, and I copied the Marc painting on it. I knew my remark was misleading, but so are all half-truths. I had to walk a fine line. Was I careful enough? Only time would tell.

"I know how your grandfather got the painting," Tony said. "He was one of the Monuments Men. He regaled us in class about his efforts to recover looted art during World War II and afterwards. I think...I'm not sure...a high Nazi owned it. One of the blessed casualties of the war. There was no one alive to return the painting to. It was flotsam and jetsam. So, your grandfather kept it. He appreciated a great work of art. I don't blame him for keeping it. I'd have done the same thing myself. Your grandfather's no crook. It's old. Look at the cracking around the edges." I, of course, had painted the cracking but couldn't think of a half-truth, so I followed Arlene's advice and said not a word.

"I could include the painting in the exhibition, but couldn't say it was by Marc. The most I could say is that it's attributed to Marc. The museum may insist on saying the painting is of the school of Franz Marc. On the scale of authentication, 'of the school' is lower than 'attributed to.' The only way to authenticate the painting, since it has clouded provenance, is to hire experts to determine its genuineness. Too expensive for my budget. You might do so after the exhibition. If you got it authenticated, it'd be worth millions. Now I feel bad about stealing Delores from you. She could have married a millionaire."

I thought, *there's a half-truth if ever I heard one. He stole Delores from me? Nah. I ditched her. He's a worse liar than I..*

"I need to get professional art movers to take the painting from here to the museum. You'll have to sign an agreement to let the museum exhibit the painting with a limited note of attribution. I hope my boss approves. He might say no. He's a stickler for details. He may not want to include a painting that has no provenance. I'll do my best, but no guarantee. For what it's worth, I want to include the painting, but it's not my call." Once again, I chose to remain silent.

Aritta pulled out his cell phone and called Art and Antique Movers, Inc. "They'll be here in about twenty-five minutes. Let's wait for them outside. It's a nice day."

The movers enclosed the painting in a wooden crate. We followed their truck in a cab. Aritta signed and filled out the printed receipt: "One painting purportedly by Franz Marc, called *The Tower of Blue Horses*." Aritta handed me the receipt. He stared at me for a few seconds. "I have my work cut out for me."

Two weeks later, Tony called. "Bad news. Based on the advice of our attorneys, the museum will not include your painting. Now don't get insulted. There are a lot of forgeries around. Nobody is saying your painting is a forgery, but the circumstances are suspicious. A painting sitting in the storage room of an art teacher and scholar suddenly surfaces. Why did your grandfather keep it hidden during his lifetime? Our lawyers suggest something unpleasant: your grandfather feared he would be exposed as a thief. One of the lawyers suggested we imply as much and state that the painting was recently discovered by you. Another lawyer suggested you'd be a damn fool to agree. That's a red flag for every Holocaust victim to claim the Nazis stole the painting from their grandparents. Even if you agreed to admit you recently discovered it, we still might not include it. The lawyer said nasty things about stolen artwork and exhibitions. It's a target for a lawsuit.

"This is my first solo run at staging an exhibition. I'd love to include your painting, but I have to follow legal advice."

I said I'd call back. I called Arlene. Before I could say a word, she said, "Don't tell me. I'm not getting involved. You, Mister Mafioso, are on your own. I've recorded our previous conversation—and I am recording this one."

I thought about what I could say that would be believable, and if not true, at least a half-truth. I dismissed altruistic statements such as: "If the painting were taken from Holocaust victims, it should be returned to them or their descendants." Such crap. Nobody would believe it for a good reason: anyone owning the painting would not only lie, but kill to keep it. I had written a script and read it aloud to Aritta, holding the tape recorder against the earpiece of the phone: "Tony, I'm not afraid of lawsuits. My painting was not stolen from Jews. I don't care if you say it was newly discovered. If the museum is so afraid of strike suits, that the mere thought makes it shit in its pants, then return the painting. You want the painting in the exhibition then stand up for what you believe is right. Tell those chicken-shit lawyers to go back to chasing ambulances. What do they know about art?"

Aritta said, "We showed the painting to an expert on German art. Those guys are so spooked. They're afraid to say a painting is genuine for fear they'll be sued if it turns out to be a forgery. This guy was a master of double-talk."

He said, "The painting has been missing for fifty years. I can't say its genuine or a forgery. The pigments and canvas are from the period, but not the stretcher and the tacks. They're later, and what's more, American. It's likely that whoever swiped the painting, removed the stretcher and furled the painting to smuggle it out of Germany. Once back in the US, a new stretcher was attached. I place no weight on the origin of the stretcher and tacks. Your interest is in the painting itself, not some wooden braces or metal tacks. I can't give a definite opinion one way or the other."

I thought to myself, *the guy's a wimp, but he has impressive credentials. I'm still fighting.*

Aritta said, "Do I have your approval to make any disclosure we feel is appropriate?"

"No, you do not. If I don't like what you say, you can send the painting to another museum, one that doesn't need a phalanx of experts for approval before it exhibits a painting."

"Why the hostility, Michael? We're Music & Art buddies. I'll write something that will pass muster with the two prima donnas, you, and my boss. Give me your fax number and I'll send it to you before I show it to him."

When the fax arrived, it made me shudder. "*The Tower of Blue Horses* was painted in 1913 by Franz Marc. It has been missing for more than fifty years. Michael Angelo Lombroso recently discovered the painting in his grandfather's storage room. He believes the painting is the original."

I discovered the painting? I believe the painting is the original? Those statements, obviously false, would wreck my defense. I reworked the fax: "*The Tower of Blue Horses* was painted in 1913 by Franz Marc. It has been missing since 1945. The museum believes this painting to be the missing one."

Aritta called, and in an angry voice, said: "What do you think I am—a living example that evolution can run in reverse? You want to obtain the museum's imprimatur. Well, why should the museum believe anything about your painting? It has no knowledge one way or the other. If it impliedly authenticates the painting as you wickedly plan, and it turns out to be a forgery, the museum would be made out to be a fool. MoMA is not your stalking horse. You're the guy who's holding out the painting to be genuine. Why are you afraid to say so? What is it, Michael? The hat burns on the head of the thief."

I ignored his retort, although it hit me in the gut. "In the skewed art market in which you and your museum thrive, its word carries more weight than mine. You bet I want the museum to authenticate the painting. That's only fair. It's putting on the exhibition. It should believe the painting is genuine and put its mouth where its show is."

About a week later, Aritta sent me another fax: "This is all we are going to say. In my judgment it's too much: '*The Tower of Blue Horses* was painted in 1913. It has been missing for fifty years. The museum has not had the painting tested for authenticity. From observation, it believes the painting to be of the school of Franz Marc, or attributable to the artist.' No more negotiations. Take it or leave it."

Tony is stubborn. The museum's disclosure was a lot better than the truth. I accepted.

I was invited to a preopening party for donors and the opening night gala. I refused the invitations. Too many questions to answer.

FIVE

The museum opened at 10:00 a.m. I got there about 11:00. For a subfreezing January day, there was a good crowd in attendance. I went straight to the exhibition. There I was. Me, Michael Angelo Lombroso hanging in the same show with George Grosz, Oskar Kokoschka, Tony Klee, Lyonel Feininger, Max Beckmann, and Emil Nolde. My grandfather would have been proud of me. Or would he. "Look Grandpa, my technique is so good, MoMA believes my painting is attributable, or of the school of Franz Marc."

I tried to imagine my grandfather's response. There was not a hint of approval. Over and over again, I heard him say, "An artist is original. Creates his own work, not copies, or worse, forges the works of others. What you did is not art; it's theft of property."

To change my mood, I got an audio guide and viewed the exhibition. My painting was not included. It was the last one displayed—off in a corner by itself. People were massed around all the paintings, except for one. Mine. Nobody, but nobody, not even a straggler was looking at it.

Several art students were sketching paintings. When I was a student, I did the same thing. I wanted to ask them what they thought of my painting, but was frightened. Suppose they said it was a forgery. I was depressed.

I left the museum determined not to return until the exhibition ended. I put it and the painting to one side and worked long hours in my father's law offices.

I told my father that I had found the canvas in grandfather's storage room, and that it was in MoMA's retrospective. He asked if it was worth a lot of money. "It is, but only if authenticated by an expert. Experts are loath to give favorable opinions on paintings lacking a provenance. If the expert proclaims the work to be genuine and it turns out to be a forgery, the expert can be held liable for the difference between the price paid and zero. So they play it safe and refuse to certify. In its present state, unauthenticated, the painting is worth very little."

In early February, I was served with a summons and complaint and a motion brought on by order to show cause for injunctive relief. The plaintiff was Gertrude Lemberg. MoMA and I were named as defendants. Lemberg claimed her grandparents were Holocaust victims. *The Tower of Blue Horses* hung in their living room until a squad of SS troopers stole it along with other paintings and antiques. The order to show cause was signed by Justice Harry S. Edelman, a judge of the Supreme Court, New York County. The Holocaust National Victims Association, a not-for-profit organization, filed supporting papers and was granted leave to participate in the action. Lemberg, the sole surviving heir—all other family members having died in concentration camps—sought possession of the painting.

I called Aritta: "Yes, MoMA has been sued too. I told you back then, if you openly declare that a valuable object formerly in Germany has been missing since the Nazi era, Holocaust victims or their descendants will pop out of the woodwork and claim ownership. We have a good lawyer, Tom Bryant. He's working on the case. You can hire your own lawyer. Under our agreement we pay your legal expenses."

"I don't want to sit in the bull pen, nor do I want to hire my own lawyer. I'll represent myself and help Bryant. I've done some research. In the best tradition of the law, I'll represent myself free of charge so your penurious employer can conserve its pennies."

My intent was not to save the museum money, but to avoid testifying. As a lawyer representing a client, even though the client was me, I couldn't be compelled to be a witness. One can't be a lawyer and a witness in the same case. My status as a lawyer takes precedence over that of a witness.

Aritta suggested I meet with Bryant.

I had heard Tony and Delores had split and wanted to confirm the rumor. She had been my woman for twelve years. I didn't love her anymore, but in a strange, perverted way, I didn't want anyone else making love to her.

"When are you and Delores planning to get married? Under the circumstances, I should have *droit du seigneur*. For us it will seem like happy days are here again."

Aritta's Italian like me. I'm sure he wasn't happy knowing I had made love to her ever since we were teenagers. "Delores and I have split. She's always on the make. Flirting with every guy. Even married ones. It bothered me so I called it quits."

I needed Aritta. I took his side. "We Italian men can flit from one pot of honey to another, but we expect our women to be faithful. It's a matter of pride. While we were together, Delores's arms were open to every male singer and some monotones as well."

That afternoon I met with Bryant. He was tall, thin with only a few strands of the blond hair that in earlier years had covered his head. His jaw was pointed, his eyes bulged, and his nose was tinged with veins from, I suspected, too much alcohol. On his office wall were three certificates, one from Harvard College, another from the law school, and the third attesting to his service on the Law Review. Based on his diplomas, I made an educated guess that

Bryant was about the same age as my father. His corner office and its lavish furnishings indicated that he was a senior partner, and from personal knowledge, I knew his firm was a prominent one.

Bryant shook my hand, and went right to work. "As you probably know, there are two kinds of injunctions. The usual one prohibits the taking of a specific act. Lemberg is seeking the other kind, a court order requiring the museum to perform affirmative acts. She asks for a court order requiring the museum, at the conclusion of the exhibition, to turn over your painting to her. She also asks the museum to credit her for loaning the painting during the pendency of the exhibition. The schedule is tight. We have five days to prepare our response. The amicus filing by the Holocaust Association recounts the horrors of the concentration camps, Kristallnacht, and includes grotesque photographs of Nazi brutality. What the hell has that to do with whether Lemberg's grandparents owned the painting? I'll tell you. It will predispose the judge to be sympathetic to the plaintiff. We're going to need hard evidence of the history of the painting. With all due respect, the story of how it somehow ended up in your grandfather's storage room is worse than nothing."

"Some months ago, I did some research, Hitler hated modern art, called the works 'degenerate.' He seized modern art owned by federal and state museums, and showed them in an exhibition called 'Entartete Kunst,' or degenerate art. The exhibition opened in Munich in 1937 and toured other German cities and Vienna. Marc's *Tower of Blue Horses* was purchased by the Berlin National Gallery in 1921, remained there until it was removed from the museum by the Nazis in 1937, and included in the degenerate art exhibition.

"A veterans group persuaded Hitler to remove Marc's painting from the exhibition. They pointed out that Marc had died fighting for Germany in World War I, and argued that a war hero should not be dishonored by including his painting in the degenerate exhibition. The group prevailed. The painting was removed from the exhibition and offered for sale. In a strange twist of fate,

Hermann Goering, second in command of the Nazi party, purchased the painting. It stayed in his possession until 1945 when it disappeared.

Unless Lemberg's grandmother lived in a museum, or later with Goering, the painting could not have hung in her living room."

"How do you know this?"

"My grandfather, whom you made fun of just a few minutes ago, served in the Monuments Men during the war. His job was to find art looted by the Germans and return it to its rightful owners. He told me about a record maintained by a Reich minister listing all the looted works, the prior owners, and the fate of the works up to 1945. When his division uncovered art, they used the document to locate the owners or their heirs and upon doing so, returned the paintings. The document was taken back to London by my grandfather's friend Harry Fischer. He's dead, but his widow is still alive. I've been in touch with Pierre Levai, the nephew of Fischer's former partner, Frank Lloyd. He told me Fischer's widow donated the document to the Victoria and Albert museum. My grandfather never mentioned the painting to me."

Bryant dialed an internal office number and asked the person to come directly to his office. Bryant introduced the young man as Stephen Grossman. "I want you to call the Victoria and Albert museum and find out if it has available for public inspection a document donated by the widow of one Harry Fischer, dating from World War II, and containing information on art looted by the Germans. If so, get a full description of the document and whether it's available for public inspection. Come back as soon as you have an answer. Put aside everything else. This gets priority."

Bryant buzzed his secretary. He asked her to get him Richard Lowey on the phone. "Lowey," he said to me, "is the Chief Executive of MoMA. I'll need a liaison with the V&A. Museums come to the aid of other museums. An officer of the V&A will have to bring the document to New York and testify."

When Lowey got on the phone, Bryant asked if he could put him on speaker as he wanted me to hear the conversation.

"Mr. Lombroso has loaned a painting to the museum's current exposition on German expressionism. A Holocaust survivor claims the painting belonged to her grandparents. The Victoria and Albert has a document that will prove she's wrong. We need a friend in high places at the V&A to come to New York immediately with the document and testify in the case."

Lowey said, "The chair of the V&A is a good friend. London is five hours ahead of us. It's 3:00 p.m.; that means it's eight in London. Can it wait until the morning?"

"We were served yesterday. A motion is returnable in five days. We can't wait. Get me a name and I'll call. He can start work tomorrow morning. If he finds the Hope Diamond, he has to be willing to come right away to New York. It's that important."

Grossman came in as Bryant was talking to Lowey. Bryant cupped the phone and nodded for Grossman to speak. "It's in the V&A."

Bryant ended his phone call and turned to Grossman. He looked at his notes while speaking. "Elfriede Fischer, the widow of Heinrich Robert Fischer, donated his library several months ago to the V&A. The library contains rare books and catalogues as well as a two-volume document listing the paintings and sculptures looted by the Nazis. The document also records the owners of the works and their fate up to 1945, the year the document ends. The collection is open for inspection during regular business hours."

"Grossman, have you ever been to London? Go to the travel desk. Pack fresh linen, and get on the next plane to London. Have the desk book a room near the V&A. Photostat pages of the documents bearing on a painting by Franz Marc called *The Tower of Blue Horses*. Fax the photostated pages to me. Before you leave, I should have the name of our liaison at the V&A who will open doors. If I don't have a name before you embark on your odyssey, the office will get the info to your hotel. If you fail, you're fired!" Bryant said the last comment with a smile. "Good luck, Stephen, you're the best paralegal we have. If you can't do it, nobody can."

Lowey called back with the name and home phone number of the V&A contact, Gareth Keats. Bryant called Keats and told him a young man named Stephen Grossman was on his way to London and would call him on arrival. "He's going to need lots of help. The document in your museum's custody is in German, and young Stephen can neither speak nor read German."

Keats said Grossman would receive "expert help." He also agreed to come to New York with the document and testify.

Bryant leaned back in his large swivel chair. "Documents are frigid pieces of evidence. Pitting a document against a weeping Holocaust victim is a script for disaster. We need to put a flesh-and-blood witness on the stand if we have any chance of winning. Not just any old witness, but an international expert on German expressionist paintings who happens also to be a Jew. We can't draw the lines with Jews on one side and *goyem* on the other and expect a Jewish judge to decide the case for us. How are we going to find our expert?"

"Anthony Aritta, the museum's curator who organized the exhibition, was a classmate of mine at Music & Art. He graduated from Harvard with a degree in art history. He might know the right person."

Bryant's secretary placed the call to Aritta. "Mr. Aritta," she said, "Mr. Lombroso would like to talk to you." Aritta screamed into the phone so loudly that Bryant and his secretary heard him. "What are you, some sort of a fucking big shot you can't call me directly? I hope for your sake you're not going to ask me for a favor because it will be *denied*." I explained I was in Tom Bryant's office, and his secretary had access to a telephone directory and telephone. "Had I been in my own office, my liege, king of the world, my humble fingers would have dialed you directly." I then explained the purpose of the call.

Tony had just the man for us: Floyd Gruenfeld, a professor at Harvard who has written extensively on German expression-ist art, and, to boot, is a Jew. Aritta volunteered to call Professor Gruenfeld. He called back to say the professor was all ours at the bargain price of $200 per hour plus expenses. Bryant called Gruenfeld and the two agreed to meet the next day. Bryant invited me to attend the meeting, but to come an hour earlier. He said, "By that time we should know about the V&A, and start drafting our answering papers."

When I got to Bryant's office the following day, he handed me a set of papers. "This is a rough draft of our answering papers and a brief. We'll add an affidavit by our German-Jewish professor after we hear what he has to say. Read the papers in my conference room. When Herr Professor comes, we'll meet in the conference room along with the two lads who helped me put our papers together."

The draft was full of holes. Paragraph after paragraph ended with a warning "need citations or references to evidence." I thought, *this is how litigators prepare affidavits and briefs? These papers stink. I'm going to lose.* Bryant entered the room escorting two men. One was Floyd Gruenfeld and the other Gareth Keats. They differed radically in appearance. Gruenfeld was short, fat, and bald; Keats was tall and slim with a full head of gray hair. There were two young men, whom Bryant introduced as the "whiz kids who produced a working draft of our answering papers without the benefit of hearing our evidence." He continued, "At this session, we're going to prepare our witnesses, and at the same time provide the supplemental material to put the excellent draft in final shape."

We spent three hours in the conference room. Bryant was the conductor. As he worked with Keats and Gruenfeld, the evidence was overwhelming. A museum in Berlin acquired the painting in 1921. The Nazis seized it in 1937 and exhibited it in the Degenerate Art Exhibition in that year in Munich. Thereafter, Hermann Goering, Commander of the Luftwaffe and Hitler's designated successor, purchased the painting from the state and hung it in his living room. It remained there until 1945, when the Soviets overran Goering's home. The whereabouts of the painting have been unknown from 1945 until now, fifty one years later, when MoMA included the painting in its exhibition.

Bryant cautioned his lawyers: "We have to treat Gertrude gently. She has made a mistake, given what we have learned. Franz Marc made several paintings of horses, a subject he was fond of. Perhaps Lemberg has confused the *Blue Horses* with another painting by Marc."

The next morning I received a set of our final papers. My copy showed that a copy had been served on the plaintiff's lawyers, Bernstein & Bernstein, and the original and an extra copy delivered by hand to the judge's chambers. Our answering papers were excellent. I couldn't see how we could lose. I called Bryant and congratulated him on putting together an air-tight case in the few days allotted.

He said he thought about asking for an adjournment, on the ground there was vital evidence in England. "I decided against begging for more time. It's a sign of weakness. Even though our defense is powerful and bulletproof, I'm not sanguine. A lot of unexpected twists happen at trial. Nota bene. The judge is most likely on Gertrude's side. The injunction hearing is scheduled for tomorrow at 10:00 a.m. I'll be in court thirty minutes early. It's a good idea for you to be early too. We'll be ready to go before the judge arrives. Think of it as raising the flag."

SIX

The State Supreme Court building located at 60 Centre Street in lower Manhattan is imposing. On three sides of the massive, hexagonal structure are forty outsized stone steps leading to the entrance. On top of the six doors is a 140-foot pediment containing three large statues: Law, Truth, and Equity. A frieze along the fringe of the pediment bears the inscription: "The True Administration of Justice is the Firmest Pillar of Good Government."

Despite the noble sentiments, the court's reputation for fairness is uneven. One of my father's classmates, a litigator quipped: "It's possible to get a fair trial but only if both sides have a fix in." He provided an example. "Judge Rogers called the lawyers on opposite sides to his chambers. 'Max,' the judge said, 'you expect me to decide the case for you, and if I don't your family will not speak to me again. Phil, you want me to decide for your side. I know. Your father gave strict instructions to my father. I'll tell you what I'm going to do. I'm reassigning the case to Judge Levy whom neither of you know, and you'll have a trial on the merits.'"

The interior of the courthouse contrasts with the temple-like exterior. It resembles a low-income tenement. The elevators are old and slow; several are always out of service and the working ones are overcrowded. The bathrooms, when you can find them, are filthy and stink. Garbage litters the hallways. The courtrooms, once grand, have aged badly. Obscene words scratched into the wood scars the furniture.

Our team met in the rotunda and made our way to the courtroom on the fourth floor. Henry Bernstein and his client Gertrude Lemberg arrived shortly after us. Bernstein wore a snappy double-breasted blue suit and a bright yellow bow tie. His client was dressed in black. Upon entering the courtroom, she removed her black hat and veil.

A court stenographer was the next to arrive. She asked for a caption for the case and prepared her machine to transcribe the trial.

A few minutes after 10:00, the court clerk announced court was in session presided over by the Honorable Harry S. Edelman and commanded us to rise. Judge Edelman waved to us as he raced in through a back door then assumed a high-backed chair sitting on a raised platform. Once on his throne, he signaled for us to be seated. The clerk called the name of our case and asked whether both sides were ready. The clerk, having concluded his duties, sat in a chair next to a small table directly below the judge.

The judge looked at Bryant and then fastened his gaze on Bernstein and Ms. Lemberg, and winked. "Let's get on with the case. Mr. Bernstein, do you wish to make an opening statement?" When Bernstein said no, the judge asked him to call his first witness.

Bryant jumped up. "Mr. Bernstein has decided not to make an opening. In his place, I, too, would not wish to say a word about my client's delusionary claim. I, however, do not waive my right to an opening."

"Mr. Bryant, I cannot and will not prevent you from speaking as long as you wish. I would be less than candid, however, if I did not advise you that I, like most judges, prefer to hear the witnesses testify than listen to their lawyer characterize their testimony. Do you still wish to make an opening?"

Bryant made no direct response. He gathered his notes and strode to the podium, before which the lawyers would stand when making formal arguments or examining witnesses. Before Bryant began, I turned toward the spectators, a number of whom had just recently flocked to our courtroom and taken seats in the spectators' section. As I later was to learn, courtroom buffs and the press seek out hot controversies. When word got around about a trial on the fourth floor involving the theft of a major work by the Nazis and its sudden reappearance, attendance at our trial grew exponentially.

Bryant laid out our defense in all its stark significance. He read from documents tracing the history of the painting up to 1945 when it was last seen in the home of Hermann Goering. He pointed his finger at Bernstein and questioned how any attorney admitted to the bar could lend his support to a baseless, extortionate claim. As Bryant spoke, Judge Edelman made plain he was not paying attention. At one point, the judge swiveled his chair so that his back was turned to Bryant. Bryant thereupon departed from his prepared remarks and said: "Let the record reflect that Judge Edelman throughout my opening has been distracted and rude. He has turned his back on me."

"See here, Mr. Bryant, I'm paying rapt attention to your most interesting presentation. How much longer do you anticipate taking the court's valuable time? I don't mean to put restraints on you. It's just that the court has other business."

Bryant replied that he believed he could bring his opening to an end within the next fifteen minutes. He was as good as his word. He concluded by warning Bernstein that unless he withdrew Ms. Lemberg's claim, MoMA would seek to recover its legal expenses from both Mr. Bernstein and Ms. Lemberg. He then read from a law granting a party that very right.

Judge Edelman advised Bernstein "not to be intimidated by Mr. Bryant's threat. Any post-trial motion in this case will be decided by me. I assure you regardless of the outcome, neither you nor your client will be subject to sanctions. I also assure Mr. Bryant that sanctions will not be assessed against him or his client. I don't take kindly to any threats inhibiting a trial. Mr. Bernstein, please call your witness."

Gertrude Lemberg slowly ambled to the witness chair. On instructions from the clerk, she raised her right hand and placed her left on the Bible. After she swore to tell the truth, Bernstein began his questioning. She testified that her "great grandfather owned a bank headquartered in Katowice, in Upper Silesia, and that there were branches in principal cities of Germany including Berlin. Katowice was part of Germany until 1922 when it was turned over to Poland."

Bernstein asked her to name some of the famous clients of the bank.

She said, "Among the many important clients was Germany's greatest prime minister and diplomat, Otto von Bismarck. Together with Bleichröder, another German-Jewish banking family, my family's bank financed the Austro-Prussian war. It was also rumored that King Wilhelm, the sovereign ruler of Prussia, was a client."

"How do you like that," Judge Edelman interposed. "I thought Bismarck was an anti-Semite, and so were all Prussians, especially the King. Now I learn they did business with Ms. Lemberg's great grandparents and were probably social friends as well."

Bryant objected. "The family history has nothing whatsoever to do with whether the *Blue Horses* hung in Ms. Lemberg's grandparents' home."

Judge Edelman denied the motion, saying that this background information was relevant and asked Mr. Bernstein to continue with his client's "compelling" testimony.

Bernstein asked about the circumstances under which Ms. Lemberg's family left Germany.

"Two events in 1938 motivated my family to emigrate from Central Europe. One was a personal affront to my grandfather. A gentile, a long-time employee who was almost as dear to my grandfather as a son, threw a telephone book at my grandfather. It hit him in the face. The words said as the book was hurled stung more than the book. He called my grandfather 'a dirty Jew.' The employee was fired. My grandfather attributed the assault to the force of Hitler's anti-Semitic tirades. If they could provoke an attack by a dear protégé, what impact might they have on the unschooled masses, who, even before Hitler, hated the Jews? My grandfather did not have long to wait.

"Kristallnacht provided the answer. In two nights in November 1938, Jewish-owned stores, businesses, and shuls in Germany and parts of Austria were ransacked. Broken glass and other debris lined streets. Jews were beaten and killed for no other reason than that they were Jews. Hundreds of thousands were arrested and carted off to concentration camps.

"My father and grandfather acted promptly. Within a month of Kristallnacht, they had liquidated the family's property and moved to France. When the Germans conquered France, my family moved to Cuba. We stayed in Cuba until 1948 when we emigrated from Cuba to New York."

Bernstein followed up: You have informed me that before leaving Berlin for France, your family liquidated the family property. What property was included?

Ms. Lemberg: Yes, that is correct. We sold the banking business to a cartel and we sold our home in Berlin and our country home in the Black Forest region near Baden-Baden. They were distressed sales. We did not sell our furniture or our collection of paintings or sculptures.

Mr. Bernstein: What happened to the artwork and furniture?

Ms. Lemberg: We placed them in the custody of a dear friend, a Christian. He had helped us and other Jewish families to obtain exit visas. While we were in France, we learned that the Nazis seized our artwork and furniture. We later learned our friend and his family were interned in a concentration camp where they were gassed to death. It was not only Jews, although we were the overwhelming majority, but righteous Christians as well, who ended their lives in the infamous camps.

Judge Edelman: The wonderful thing about being a judge is that you learn something new every day. Please continue this interesting history lesson.

Mr. Bernstein: Ms. Lemberg, as Mr. Bryant keeps reminding us, this case is about a specific painting: Franz Marc's *The Tower of Blue Horses*. What paintings, if any, do you recall seeing in your grandparents' home?

Ms. Lemberg: I was a little girl of ten when we left Berlin in December of 1938. I don't remember specifics except for one painting. I was taking riding lessons, and like many young girls of my class, I had my own horse. It came from Poland. I named him Polonaise. I was in love with him. When I visited my grandparents' house, I always spent time admiring the *Blue Horses*. They reminded me of my own horse. So full of life and breathing flames. Although my grandparents had many fine paintings, the *Blue Horses* commanded the position of honor, above the fireplace. It made an indelible impression on me. I could never forget it.

Bernstein ended his examination. Judge Edelman called a fifteen-minute recess.

When court reconvened, Bryant was at the podium and Ms. Lemberg was in the witness chair. Under Bryant's questioning, the witness said the Lembergs' fireplace was large, standing five feet high "about as tall as I was at the time," and that the ceiling was about ten feet. Since the *Blue Horses* was more than six feet high, Bryant pounced: "The painting, Ms. Lemberg, contrary to your earlier testimony could not have hung over the fireplace."

She then claimed it hung in some other place, "it was surely in my grandparents' living room."

Bryant asked her if, when she was growing up in Berlin, she had spent time in the Berlin museums, particularly the Kronprinzenpalais, an annex to the Berlin National Gallery. She said, "Most Berliners visited the Kronprinzenpalais. It was a landmark and the first museum in the world to devote an entire floor to paintings by modern artists."

Bryant showed her a catalogue dated January 1936, listing the museum's extensive collection of expressionist art. *The Tower of Blue Horses* was included twice. Once on the front cover and again on an interior page shared with two other Franz Marc paintings.

She suggested that her grandparents might have loaned the painting to the museum. Bryant showed her another catalogue from the Kronprinzenpalais dated September 1921 depicting the painting and disclosing that it had been purchased that very year by the museum.

The judge remained eerily silent throughout the cross-examination. When Bryant said "no more questions," and Bernstein said he had no questions in reply, the judge held forth. "Mr. Bryant, what happened to the painting between 1936 and 1938? Perhaps it was purchased by the Lembergs? Museums have been known to sell their works. It's called deaccession."

Bryant assured the judge that defendants had a witness, "a renowned art historian who would trace the provenance of the *Blue Horses* up to 1945 seven years after the Lemberg's emigrated from Germany. It was never owned by the Lembergs."

The judge adjourned the case for the day. He asked Bryant for an estimate as to how long his case would take. "I'd say a day and a half, but to be safe, because it's hard to estimate how long cross will take, say two days."

We walked back to Bryant's office in the Chase Manhattan Bank building in lower Manhattan. Bryant explained his reason for feuding with the judge. "I want to make a record that will show the judge is prejudiced, in the unlikely event we lose and have to take an appeal. We'll have an easier time getting him reversed if the record smacks of bias. The judge knows I'm drawing him out, but he keeps fueling the fire."

Bryant seemed pleased with the evidence we would present to disprove the plaintiff's claim. "It all hangs on her testimony. There's no corroboration of the Lemberg family's ownership." He said he wanted to add drama to our presentation and had arranged to bring the actual *Blue Horses* to the courtroom. "Nothing so impressive as demonstrative evidence." The meeting concluded with Bryant's advice to our two witnesses. "Get a good night's sleep. No need to go over your testimony. You have it down. I don't want to throw our best pitches in the bull pen."

Bryant opened the wet bar in his office and offered us a drink. He poured a glass of scotch for himself saying, "I never drink until my work is done, and I never hurry my work to get to drink. I am partial to scotch."

The two witnesses joined Bryant in a drink. I declined to join them. I was fearful the conversation might come round to how I "found" the painting. I did not have my tape recorder with me. I bid good-bye to our team and made a silent vow on the next day to bring my recorder with me.

SEVEN

When court opened, the judge asked Bernstein if he had another witness or any trial exhibits. Bernstein said no and added "plaintiff rests." The judge turned to Bryant and asked him to call his first witness.

The judge's demeanor had changed. Yesterday, he had made some comments he would certainly come to regret. Today he seemed unsurprised when Bryant moved to dismiss Lemberg's claim. "It must be as clear as a fire on a hill at night that the *Blue Horses* was never owned by the Lembergs."

The judge said he would take the motion under advisement and rule after Bryant's case was completed. "We're here for a trial on the merits. It would be a monumental waste of the parties' and the court's time if I were to grant your motion, Mr. Bryant, dismiss Ms. Lemberg's case, and then be reversed on appeal. Please call your witness unless you wish to rest on the record."

Bryant recognized the deferral of a ruling was within the court's discretion. He called Gareth Keats, the chief administrative officer of the Victoria and Albert Museum. Bryant introduced Keats to the court and said his task was a limited one: to authenticate the many exhibits the defendants proposed to move into evidence. "The documents, as Mr. Keats will affirm, are in the custody of the V&A."

"I have a question for you, Mr. Bryant," Judge Edelman said. "Where did the documents come from? How did a museum in London come into the possession of these German documents dating from 1920 to the end of World War II?"

"If Your Honor please," Bryant said, "Mr. Keats will answer your question."

Bryant instructed Keats, who was already sworn in, to answer the judge's question. "Heinrich Robert Fischer was a naturalized citizen of Great Britain. He emigrated in March 1938 from Vienna to England after the Anschluss, or the union between Austria and Germany. He was a rare book dealer in his homeland, but saw no future for a Jew in Austria. He enlisted in the British Army when the war broke out. He valiantly served his adopted country. Mr. Fischer had a vast collection of art catalogues, books, and other material, which he brought with him. He died in 1977. His widow donated his library this very year to the Victoria and Albert Museum."

Judge Edelman smiled. "Mr. Fischer led a charmed life. He was able to escape from the Nazis, fight them in the war, and make a lasting contribution to society. I wonder if he knew Ms. Lemberg's family?"

Bryant moved the documents into evidence. Then he waited, staring at the judge.

"If you, Mr. Bryant, will represent that the exhibits are relevant to the case, and Mr. Bernstein has no objection, I will admit them into evidence," Judge Edelman said. Upon Bryant's representation and Bernstein's mumbling that he had no objection, the exhibits numbered one through fifty-five were admitted.

Bryant introduced his next witness Floyd Gruenfeld to the judge. "Since Mr. Gruenfeld will be called upon to express opinions on the provenance of the *Blue Horses*, it will be necessary for me to review his credentials." Bryant was invoking the exception to the rule that a witness may only testify as to facts and not express opinions. The exception allows an expert to express opinions in the area of his expertise.

"I understand," the judge said. "I'm sure his credentials are impressive."

Gruenfeld graduated from Princeton in 1960, was a Rhodes Scholar, and studied art history at Oxford. He stayed at Oxford for three years and received a PhD. He taught at Princeton until 1970, when he left to accept a chaired position at Harvard. He identified several articles he had authored on German expressionism, including one entitled "What Hitler Didn't Like About Modern Art." He served as an advisor to the Los Angeles County Museum of Art's 1987 exhibition "Fate of the Avant-Garde in Nazi Germany" and was the author of the exhibition catalogue. In 1991, the LACMA exhibition traveled to the Art Institute of Chicago, and in the same year to the Smithsonian in Washington. "In order to advise the museums on the exhibition, as well as prepare the catalogue, I reviewed all available information on the paintings and sculptures seized by the Nazis from federal and state museums in connection with the Entartete Kunst exhibition that opened in Munich on July 17, 1937. The LACMA exhibition was based on the original Munich exhibition."

Bryant said that the credential segment of Professor Gruenfeld's testimony was concluded and moved for an order certifying "Professor Gruenfeld as an expert on the art Hitler labeled 'degenerate,'" and "entitled to express opinions on the acts, circumstances, and aftereffects of the Entartete Kunst exhibition."

The judge said, "Of course your motion is granted. No sane person could question the Professor's learning in the field of German art in particular and art history of all periods. At the back of the courtroom, four burly men were balancing a large crate on a mover's wagon. Bryant turned to the rear and said, *The Blue Horses* has been moved to the courtroom, and with the court's permission, the painting will be unveiled for demonstrative purposes during Professor Gruenfeld's testimony."

"I welcome this great work of art to my courtroom. I ask the men to take their time in uncovering the masterpiece. The court doesn't want the painting to be damaged."

When the painting was displayed on an easel catty corner from the judge's bench, a gasp was heard throughout the spectator seats. "This is a stunning work. And to think that Hitler called it 'degenerate.' Please begin your examination in chief of the witness."

Mr. Bryant: What was it that Hitler disliked about modern German art?

Professor Gruenfeld: Hitler had a monolithic view of life. There was only one race, one people good enough to dominate all the others. He transposed his racial view to art. A painting, he believed, must capture a scene exactly as it appears. The artist must ignore what his brain tells him lies deep down in the heart and soul of the subject; he must render only the surface.

Look at this great painting. Has Your Honor or anyone else ever seen a blue horse? Franz Marc, the genius who painted this great work of art, saw not one, but four. The horses appear to be alive, ready to jump off the canvas and prance around this courtroom. Notice the horse in the foreground. He faces the viewer but his head is turned to the left. On his chest appears a crescent and crosses resembling stars. Is the horse celestial? He is what you see he is. What did Hitler see?

He saw a delusionary and depraved artist who painted animals that don't exist in real life.

Mr. Bryant: We know Hitler's solution for those who were not members of the master race. How did he deal with art that did not conform to his view?

Professor Gruenfeld: Hitler's concern was directed at the German public. He did not want them to be exposed to art he considered degenerate. As a first step, he seized all paintings not conforming to his views and removed them from all federal and state museums. Most of the paintings were from an annex of the Berlin National Gallery, formerly the palace of the ruling Hohenzollern House of Prussia. The Hohenzollern king abdicated the throne after that nation's defeat in World War I. Ms. Lemberg correctly identified the Kronprinzenpalais, as it was called in German, as the hall dedicated to all forms of modern German art, including Dadaism, Cubism, Futurism, and of course, expressionism. There were about four hundred and sixty paintings housed in the former palace.

Mr. Bryant (pointing at the *Blue Horses* on display in the courtroom): Was this monumental work of art on display in the Kronprinzenpalais?

Professor Gruenfeld: All the paintings could not be on constant display since the space in the Kronprinzenpalais, vast as it was, could not accommodate all. The curator determined which paintings should be displayed and changed the selection every several months with one exception. *The Blue Horses* was on display from the day it was acquired until that dark day in June when it was seized by the Nazis, removed from the museum, and forfeited to the state.

Mr. Bryant: When and under what circumstances was the *Blue Horses* acquired by the museum, and how long did it stay in the museum?

Professor Gruenfeld: In 1920, the Berlin National Gallery purchased the painting from the estate of the artist. There it remained until June of 1937, when it and about fifteen hundred other works of art owned by federal and state museums were removed from walls and storage racks. Of the confiscated art, six hundred works were displayed in the Archäologischen Instituts in Munich in the Entartete Kunst exhibition, which opened on July 17, 1937. The very next day, in the very same city, a second exhibition opened called the Great German Art Exhibition. On display was the art Hitler favored: naturalistic, following the classical models of Ancient Greece. In an ironic twist, over two million Germans visited the despised exhibition, and only a few hundred thousand saw Hitler's-.

Mr. Bryant: I show you Defendants Exhibits 15 and 16 received into evidence. With reference to these exhibits, can you tell the court whether this painting on display here in our courtroom was confiscated by the Nazis or allowed to remain in the museum?

Professor Gruenfeld (looking at Exhibit 15): This is the catalogue of the Entartete Kunst exhibition. It states that the *Blue Horses* was shown in the Degenerate Art exhibition in Munich. Exhibit 16 also affirms this fact. Exhibit 16 is a two-volume document prepared by the Reich Minister of Propaganda. It reveals that this very painting in this courtroom of great artistic and historical value was removed from the Berlin National Gallery and shown in the Munich exhibition. The document also reveals that the *Blue Horses* was not included when the exhibition moved to Berlin and Vienna.

Mr. Bryant: What happened to our illustrious painting, and what were the circumstances under which it was removed from the Degenerate Art exhibition?

Professor Gruenfeld: Franz Marc fought and died in World War I. Veteran groups protested the inclusion of his works in the Entartete Kunst exhibition. We have an exhibit—I believe it is Exhibit 17—a series of letters protesting the inclusion of Marc's works. The thrust of the letters: Marc was a war hero who sacrificed his life for the "Fatherland"; his memory should be respected along with his works. Hitler relented. *The Blue Horses* was removed from the exhibition, and purchased by Hermann Goering for twenty thousand Reichsmarks.

Mr. Bryant: What a downward progression. From the King's palace to the Entartete Kunst exhibition to Hermann Goering. What happened next?

Professor Gruenfeld: Under Goering's direction, Germany acquired one hundred thousand acres in the Schorfheide Forest north of Berlin, which was set aside as a state park. In the park, Goering built an elaborate hunting lodge named Carinhall after his first wife, Carin. The lodge featured an art gallery in which many works of art, including the *Blue Horses*, were displayed. Goering ordered Carinhall dynamited on April 16, 1945, in the face of the advancing Soviet army. Our painting was probably removed before Carinhall was blown up. Although the painting has not surfaced until this year's MoMA exhibition, there have been sightings. One art historian claims to have seen it in 1977, in the Haus am Waldsee in Zehlendorf Berlin, then under Communist control. Another historian claimed to have seen it in a youth hostel adjacent to Haus am Waldsee. In 1986, a third art historian organizing an expressionist show in Soviet-controlled East Germany put the *Blue Horses* on the cover of the catalogue. He was quoted as saying, "I hoped a little old lady would walk in, unfurl the canvas, and the rich blue paint would spill out." Others speculated the painting had been placed by Goering in a vault in a bank in Zurich, Switzerland.

"I was astonished," Gruenfeld continued, "when I learned the painting was in the MoMA exhibition. I thought that if the painting survived the destruction of Carinhall, it was hidden deep in the bowels of the Soviet Union."

Bryant shortly thereafter completed his direct of Gruenfeld. Bernstein's cross was perfunctory except in one respect. He asked Gruenfeld whether the painting in the courtroom was the "original, authentic one painted by Franz Marc."

Gruenfeld said exacting tests would have to be made before a conclusion on authenticity could be reached. Then he added: "To the naked eye, this looks very much like the original. I'd be surprised if it turned out to be a forgery."

I prayed Bernstein would let the matter rest. My prayers went unanswered. Bernstein asked whether Gruenfeld knew where the painting had been for fifty-one years. When Gruenfeld said no, I started to sweat. "Well then," Bernstein asked, "where was the painting before it was placed in the MoMA exhibition?"

Gruenfeld looked at me and said, "It was in Mr. Lombroso's grandparents' storage room in the basement of the apartment house in which they lived."

Bernstein said "no further questions". Judge Edelman called a recess, but before he adjourned court, he asked whether Bryant intended to question me. When he said no, the judge said that when court reconvenes, "The court intends to question Mr. Lombroso. Something smells fishy. Mr. Lombroso, you have been quiet. I suppose you have every right to rely on Mr. Bryant, but on the point of the whereabouts of the *Blue Horses* and its almost magical reappearance, the buck stops with you. Since neither trial attorney seeks to raise the issue, I will take matters into my hands and see if I can resolve the mystery."

I have smoked pot to excess, gotten drunk on beer, vodka, gin, and scotch, but never have I achieved the high I attained during the second day of the trial. My painting referred to as a "great work of art." Gruenfeld claiming to the naked eye it was the original. The gasp that echoed throughout the courtroom when the painting was unveiled. I thought about my grandfather and wondered what he would think of all this. *Michael,* a voice within me reverberated, *the genius lies in the origination of the painting, not in copying it. Any technician trained in art can forge a painting; only an artist can create one.*

During the recess, Bryant said he could not object to Edelman questioning me. "It would look like we have something to hide. You have no personal information on the one issue germane to the case: whether the *Blue Horses* hung in the Lembergs' living room. Nothing you say can affect the case. Give the judge long-winded answers. Have fun."

When court reconvened, I headed to the witness chair, but the court told me to remain seated at counsel table. "As an attorney, you are an officer of the court. No need to swear you in. You are obligated to tell the truth, and I'm sure you will do just that.

"Mr. Lombroso, how did this magnificent painting come into your possession?"

I accepted Bryant's advice to make "long-winded" speeches, anything to deflect telling the truth. So I told the story of how my grandparents met, their strange fascination with artists' yard sales, their weekend trips throughout New England, and the thousands upon thousands of artists' tools, canvases, and paintings they had purchased. I discussed how the acquisitions overwhelmed their apartment and the move of most of the purchased items to a storage room in the basement of their apartment building. I mentioned my grandfather's enlistment in the Monuments Men and his work in uncovering German looted art and his efforts to return the works to the rightful owners. I discussed his decorations, and the way Europeans had acknowledged his service. I recounted his meeting with Fischer who also served in the Monuments Men and that their friendship continued until "Mr. Fischer passed in 1977." I told how my grandfather was the first art teacher at Music & Art. I said my mother died when I was six, my father never remarried, "I was raised by my grandparents." I recounted how my grandfather, who had survived my grandmother, handed me the key to the storage room and said: "I have paid in advance five years of rent on the storage room. The contents are my gift and your grandmother's gift to you. What you do with the contents is your decision. My grandfather died two years later." Approximately thirty minutes after the judge had asked his question, I had answered it. I am sure of one thing—no one was paying attention to my answer except for me. I said, "I found the canvas in the storage room."

The judge observed the hour was drawing late. He wistfully looked at his watch and asked how the painting got to MoMA. I explained that I met Pamela and bumped into Anthony Aritta, a former classmate and now an assistant curator at MoMA. "He informed me he was organizing a retrospective on German expressionist art. I introduced him to Pamela. This time I took only fifteen minutes before I answered the question, which I was sure everyone but me had forgotten. "I called Tony. We met at my grandfather's apartment building on Riverside Drive. We went together to the storage room. I showed him the painting. He identified it as the missing Franz Marc masterpiece and arranged to have it crated and taken to the museum." This was the one time I felt safe mentioning the word "painting." It was not a half-truth but the whole truth. I had showed Tony the painting.

The judge was thoughtful, sinking back in his chair, and then he exploded: "I've figured it out! Your grandfather, while he was serving in the Monuments Men division, found the painting.

Goering was dead, and your dear grandfather would never have given it back to anyone connected with him. Instead he took it with him to America and gave it to his adored grandson."

"My grandfather was a thoroughly honest man. He never stole a thing in his life."

"I have no further questions for Mr. Lombroso. Instead of coming to the courtroom tomorrow, I invite the attorneys to meet with me at 10:00 a.m. in my chambers."

As we left the courtroom, Bryant congratulated me on my testimony. "I didn't understand a word you said. You know something, Lombroso, you're a master of double-talk."

When we were all in the judge's chambers the next morning, we could see that he was not happy. I must now decide Mr. Bryant's motion to dismiss, which I had earlier deferred ruling on. Mr. Bryant, with a heavy heart, I grant your motion. The injunction is denied and the case dismissed. Mr. Bryant, you may present an order in accordance with my ruling and I will sign it. I thank both parties for their excellent presentations."

MoMA's press officer issued a release focusing on my painting, the court proceeding, and the judge's ruling. It came close to authenticating my painting when it said: "Based on the expert testimony of Floyd Gruenfeld, *The Blue Horses* has returned to the world after a fifty-year absence."

The newspapers and monthly art journals covered the "historic" return of the *Blue Horses*. MoMA moved my painting from its former isolated position at the end of the exhibit to a prominent place in the center of the exhibition. The publicity from the case fueled interest in the exhibition. It was extended for two months. When I returned to the museum, there were crowds admiring my painting and several students sketching my work.

I was faced with a new dilemma. How could I sell it without subjecting it to tests that would surely reveal its true identity? In my present financial condition, I couldn't afford to pay the insurance premium on the painting. I thought, *one step at a time. You can sell the painting as is at a discount. Or can you? Probably not. In the art market there is nothing in between. It's either authentic and worth millions or it's worthless.*

I called Aritta about my insurance problem. "Under the museum's umbrella policy, you're covered for six months after the close of the exhibition, but only if you leave the painting in our custody." I liked the idea of leaving the painting with MoMA, where it would be safe and insured and added: "Six months will give me time to sell the painting." I wanted to put the idea of a sale in Aritta's head in the hope he would let people know.

EIGHT

Shortly after the court case had concluded, Aritta called me. He said his mother's favorite poet, Mary Oliver, had written a poem published in this week's *New Yorker* entitled "Franz Marc's Blue Horses."

"My mom says the poem is a polemic on war, but also praises the painting. I showed it to the curator. He got permission to hang a copy alongside the painting. He asked me to get your approval."

I raced to the newsstand and bought a copy of the magazine. As I strolled on home, I read the first two lines of the poem aloud. Paused, and then read two more lines

> I step into the painting of the four blue horses.
> I am not even surprised I can do this...
> Franz Marc died a young man, shrapnel in his brain.
> I would rather die than try to explain to the blue horses
> what war is.

The poem is antiwar, but in my ears it sings the praises of the painting, my painting, my work. I looked toward the heavens and heard my grandfather: "Don't be a fool. Marc is the artist. Your work was mechanical; he had the vision."

Alright Grandpa, I don't deserve all the credit, but I did bring the painting back to life. The poet saw my painting and was inspired. I did not hear anything further.

I got lots of calls from friends congratulating me. I also received two calls from strangers. Jay Winston, the well-known philanthropist, real estate tycoon and chairman of the board of the Metropolitan Museum of Art, invited me to lunch at the Trustee's dining room. The second caller was Cecil Ray, the general partner of a $6 billion hedge fund—Ray 2. He invited me to lunch at the University Club. My first date was with Winston.

I got to the Met early, about thirty minutes early. I strolled through the museum and landed at the restaurant exactly on time. When I told the maitre d' my name and that I was Mr. Winston's luncheon guest, he bowed so low his nose almost touched the ground. "Right this way Mr. Lombroso. Mr. Winston is expecting you." He took me to a private room adjoining the main dining room. As we entered, Winston rose, greeted me and extended his hand. He was tall, slight of build with a sparse head of blond-gray hair. He looked a lot like Prince Philip. I didn't care how regal he looked, I was taking no chances. I reached into my pocket and turned on the tape recorder

At lunch, he talked about the privilege conferred on those who own important works of art and their duty to the public. I knew where Winston was going. He had donated his collection valued at over a billion dollars to the Met. I was, therefore, not at all surprised when he said: "A museum is the best place to repose art. It's unfair for one person to keep great works for his own enjoyment. They should be shared with the public. A museum is an equalizer. Open to all. It's tough medicine for a collector to turn over a prized possession. I swallow hard every time, but do it again and again and again."

He asked whether I had any interest in donating my painting to a museum, and if so, whether I would consider the Met. "The Met has much more exhibition space than any other US museum. I will guarantee it will show your painting at least one month every year. Try to get any other museum to match that offer."

I said I could not afford to donate the painting since it was the only valuable thing I owned.

Winston spouted the conventional wisdom about Franz Marc. Then about his death at thirty-six while serving in the German Army in World War I and his important position within the ranks of German expressionist artists. He said, *"The Blue Horses* is one of the best examples of German expressionism and Marc's masterpiece." He asked whether I was willing to sell. When I said yes, he said it was difficult to put a price on priceless art, but the painting should sell at the high end for works of that school and period. "$50 million seems about right."

"Sold for $50 million dollars to Jay Winston."

"Not so fast. *The Blue Horses* has been missing for fifty years. Only a damn fool would buy your painting without putting it through an authentication process. It consists of tests and expert opinions based on the test results and also subjective judgments of experts. The procedure is expensive and time consuming. It might take as long as sixty days. You should bear the cost since you as the owner are benefitted by a favorable outcome. To show my good faith, I'll pay all the expenses and turn over the results to you. Now you must show your good faith and grant me a ninety-day option to purchase the painting at $50 million."

I said I would consider it and get back to him. On my way home, I thought, *I now know the price. Next, I'll have to find the damn fool. Was Cecil Ray my damn fool? I'd find out at lunch the very next day.*

Along with his invitation to lunch, Ray offered a word of caution about the University Club's dress code: "Be sure to wear a jacket and a tie. It's not necessary that the jacket match the pants. I'll meet you in the reading room to the right of the lobby, as you enter. Don't worry about my recognizing you. I've drawn a full report down to the kind of underwear you wear."

The University Club, is on the northwest corner of 54th Street and Fifth Avenue. It is an architectural landmark designed by Stanford White and completed in 1899. The reading room looks as if it were once part of an eighteenth-century London club that had been picked up and moved to New York. I had only a moment or two to look around when a giant of a man grabbed my arm and introduced himself. We took the elevator to the formal dining room on the seventh floor, a large room with elaborate appointments, the most notable being a hand-carved Italianate wooden ceiling. As we entered the room, I stopped to admire several paintings. They were very good. Cecil walked right by them. When I mentioned the club had fine paintings, some of museum quality, he said, "None are the best. I only want the best. I've done my research. *The Tower of Blue Horses* is the finest example of German expressionist art."

My tape recorder was on during lunch with Winston, and it was on again from the moment I entered the University Club. Cecil Ray was a financial whiz on trading securities but a neophyte when it came to buying art. I let Ray do all the talking.

He ordered a bottle of Chablis. I said I wasn't drinking and questioned buying a bottle rather than a glass. "I only want the best. A glass of wine comes from an opened bottle. It may have been opened days ago. By ordering a bottle, even if I drink only one glass, I have the best of the bottle."

I asked what he didn't have. "Art, my friend, the best painting in the world. What you own and what I crave."

"Jay Winston," I said, "who I recently met, said the *Blue Horses* would likely sell for fifty million dollars. He asked for a ninety-day option to buy my painting at that price."

"Winston's a shrewd businessman. A ninety-day option on a $50 million object is worth about $5 million. What did Winston agree to pay?"

"Nothing."

"Winston will string you along. At the end of ninety days, he'll ask for another ninety. He'll take your temperature. If he senses you're running a fever, he'll drop the price. I'll make you a fast deal. You sign a contract my lawyers prepare and I'll wire $50 million to your bank account."

My genetic antipathy to paying taxes rose to the surface. "Fast is a definite advantage, but you're going too fast. I agree to $50 million, but only if I receive it tax free. If the purchase price includes the capital gain tax of fifteen percent, the additional $7.5 million will increase my gain by that amount. If, however, you pay the tax on the $7.5 million, (an extra $1.25 million), I won't have to pay any taxes at all, except of course to turn over the $8.75 million to the IRS."

He agreed, but said he'd have to discuss it with his lawyers.

I said, "It's OK for me to say this because I'm a lawyer. Lawyers have a way of fucking up deals. We have agreed on the price. I'll draw a contract obligating me to direct MoMA to deliver my painting to you after the exhibition closes, and for the remaining period of the exhibition to list you as the donor. Upon written notice to you that the museum has accepted my direction, you will wire the money to my bank."

"We trade a $100 million dollars of stock practically every day without a contract, based solely on a call from my trading desk. We're not allowed to do business in the club. It's a farce. Everybody does. Even the president of the club. What you can't do is flaunt it. If you pull out a legal pad, I'll get reported. What are you going to write on?"

I raised my cloth napkin and said "on this." He laughed. I asked the waiter to borrow his pen and wrote:

> "On this third day of March, 1996, Michael Angelo Lombroso (hereinafter referred to as Lombroso) agrees to sell his painting in the MoMA exhibition on expressionist art titled in the museum's catalogue *The Tower of Blue Horses* (hereinafter the Painting) to Cecil Ray (hereinafter referred to as Ray) on the following terms: Lombroso shall direct MoMA to list Ray in lieu of Lombroso as the donor of the Painting, and upon the conclusion of the exhibition deliver the Painting to Ray at an address designated by him within the City, County, and State of New York. Upon written notice from MoMA to Ray that it accepts the direction, Ray shall forthwith make three wire transfers to the account of Lombroso to a bank as identified by him. The

first wire shall be in the amount of $50 million dollars; the second in the amount of $7.5 million representing the capital gains tax on the purchase price of $50 million dollars; and the third in the amount of $1.25 million representing the tax on the tax."

I had opened the napkin and written on both sides. I barely had room for our signatures. We both signed the napkin. I suggested that I keep it "as the party to be charged. You have no obligation until your name is up in lights at MoMA and it has agreed to deliver the painting to you."

When he agreed, I motioned to the waiter to pour a glass of Chablis for me. I proposed a toast: "Here's to Franz Marc, the creator of *The Tower of Blue Horses*. May his soul rest in peace." We clinked glasses.

I asked Ray why his fund was called Ray 2. "What happened to Ray 1?"

"It never existed. By calling my fund Ray 2, I create the impression that I've been in business for longer than I actually have. When potential investors ask about Ray 1, I say it was so successful, the limited partners voted to close it. In order to take on new money, I gave birth to a second fund.

"I thought if I came into money to start an art hedge fund, I'd call it M.A. Partners II."

Lunch with Ray provided a golden opportunity for me to gain information from an insider on how a hedge fund works.

"You checked on me. I checked on you. Ray 2 has net assets of six billion. You started four years ago. How did you grow so fast in such a short time?"

We had finished the bottle of wine. Ray ordered two glasses of brandy. I asked why he didn't order the whole bottle. "Maybe we'll get the dregs,"

"I like you, Lombroso, even though you may be taking me for a ride. Waiter! Bring us an unopened bottle of Rémy Martin. You pour and charge me by the glass.

"I started as a money manager at Morgan Stanley. I out-performed most managers and acquired a reputation as a gunslinger who knew his way around the street. What I did was unlawful under the National Securities Laws. I didn't get caught because no one got hurt. That's the trick of a perfect crime—no victims.

"I worked with friends from money managers employed by different firms. We picked stocks we thought were undervalued, and then bought a lot of them, quietly without ratcheting the market. Once we had our fill, we traded small lots among our-selves at ever-increasing prices. On these trades we made a lot of noise. We used other means too. When the stock prices reached a predetermined level, slightly below what we thought was fair market value, we sold. We always left money on the table for the next owner."

"Hold it. You're covering too much ground in too short a dis-tance. How does 'trading the stock' raise the market value and what other tricks did you use?" I opened a clean napkin and started to take notes.

"Don't you dare take notes, or I'll start talking about the Knicks."

"OK, no notes." My tape recorder was running. I had no need for notes. I folded the napkin and asked him to answer my question.

"Our back-and-forth trades are publicly reported even though in economic effect they're washes. They set higher bid and ask prices for the stock, which are artificial because we set them. The rising prices attract the attention of buyers outside our ring. We suspend our internal trading when the stock price reaches a pre-determined level. We then unload our holdings. The price is still low enough for the new buyers to sell later on at a profit. That's what I mean when I say 'no victims.'"

"You mentioned 'other tricks'? What are those?"

"We plant bullish stories about the companies in the *Wall Street Journal* and in business magazines, like *Barron's, Fortune,* and *Forbes*. The tales are true, but polished. They stimulate public interest in the stocks of the companies.

"If we played according to the rules and didn't manipulate the stocks, we might have sold out at the same price, but it would have taken years. By playing our little game, we advance the time of our reward *and* please our clients by making handsome returns over a short period of time."

"Do you still do that today in your hedge fund?"

"In the world we live in, performance is everything. If my fund stops performing, my investors will switch to another fund. There's no such thing as loyalty. My goal is an annual return of twenty percent. The Rule of 72 determines the number of years it will take to double the sum invested. All you do is divide the return into 72. If the average return is twenty percent, the sum invested will double in about three and a half years. That's good enough for the greedy bastards who invest with me."

"Wait a minute. If I turned my, or rather your fifty million back to you, and you earned an annual return of twenty percent, in three and a half years I'd have $100 million?"

"No, because there're expenses, including my take."

"What do you get?"

"I get two percent of the net assets and twenty percent of the profits. Last year, we did great. I grossed $300 million. My net was less because I have expenses. On the negative side, I also have to pay taxes. On the plus side, my compensation is taxed at the capital gains rate of fifteen percent rather than the much higher ordinary income rate."

"Do you get flak from your investors over the rate of your compensation?"

"Nah. One guy summed up the sentiment of all: 'I hope you make more money next year.' You see. The more I make, the more they make."

"In my next life, I want to come back as a hedge fund manager." In fact, I had no intention of waiting. Once I had my clammy paws on Ray's money, I intended to set up my own hedge fund. It would hold, not securities, but paintings. I'd follow Ray's path. I'd gather a circle of friendly dealers and manipulate the art market. Unlike the stock market, there will be no SEC looking over my shoulder. It was me against the buyers. Caveat emptor.

I called Aritta and told him I had sold my painting. "In order to complete the sale, MoMA must change the name of the donor to the new owner, Cecil Ray, and agree to deliver the painting to him at the end of the exhibition."

"I hope you got a big, fat price. Don't tell me how much. I'll be so envious, I won't sleep for a week. I can see my future. It's just like my past. I'll be a factotum plodding along all my life."

"Tony, you are the archetypical graduate of Music & Art. An assistant curator at MoMA and on your way up. Our classmates would kill for your job."

"Michael, you don't know what I'm up against. The bureaucracy is stifling. It will take another ten years for me to move up a notch. You think being an assistant curator is a great job? It stinks. It sounds great at parties, but try to pay the rent with prestige. I'm not alone. I've got two friends, one at the Met, the other at the Whitney. We'd like to quit, but don't know what to do. Sorry to cry on your shoulder. This call is about you, not me. I'll call Tom Bryant and let him know you'll be calling. He'll be helpful. His firm got a big fee for the case. By the way, he likes you. Give me a few hours to reach him and then call. Hotshot lawyers don't return calls quickly from assistant curators."

"Thanks Tony. Don't change jobs. When I get my money, I plan to start an art hedge fund. I'll need lots of help. Who could be better than the valedictorian of our class? Let's have lunch soon. This time at 21."

"I've walked past it dozens of times and stared in. Never thought I could afford it. What is an art hedge fund? I'm not sure I know what a plain-vanilla hedge fund is, but the powers that be seem to think the honchos running them have lots of wampum. How's that for a mixed metaphor? Let's defer my education on art hedge funds until lunch at 21."

Bryant was all smiles when we met. "How many millions did you get for that phony painting?" I told him $50 million tax-free and showed him the napkin. "Many centuries ago, pen and paper were invented. What the hell made you use a napkin? I've heard of Cecil Ray. He's a big hitter and wise as an owl. Did he buy without putting the painting through the mill?"

"The University Club where we lunched has strict rules about conducting business. We avoided detection by using a napkin. The maître d' thought I was wiping my nose or another part of my anatomy. As far as inspection is concerned, Ray's a sophisticated buyer. Read the handwriting on the napkin. What's there is all that's there. If testing is not mentioned, then it was waived."

Bryant read the napkin, stared at me for a few seconds, and said: "You think you're smart but you're not. Neither signature is acknowledged. He could renounce. Claim it was an outline only, not a binding deal. Claim your overall understanding was subject to many conditions too complicated to fit on the napkin. I'm not saying he'd win, but it's enough to raise an issue of fact. You want to hold Ray's feet to the fire. Act fast. Make him the donor. That's partial performance. Once he accepts that, he's stuck. I'll dictate a letter right now and have it hand delivered to his eminence, the pope of Wall Street. Michael m'boy, we'll give that smart ass no time to suffer buyer's remorse."

Bryant called in his secretary. "A letter to go out immediately by hand to Mr. Cecil Ray. Check his business address. 'Dear Mr. Ray: My firm represents the Museum of Modern Art in the City of New York, parenthesis MoMA. Paragraph. Pursuit to the terms of a written contract dated March 3, 1996, between you and

Michael Angelo Lombroso, parenthesis Lombroso, Lombroso has instructed MoMA to list you as the donor of the painting loaned to MoMA for the duration of the current exhibition on German expressionist art and entitled, single quote, *The Tower of Blue Horses*. At the conclusion of the exhibition, MoMA will deliver the painting to a destination designated by you within the City, County, and State of New York. Very truly yours.' Have our messenger wait until he receives in his hot little hands a stamped receipt on a copy of the letter. Tell the messenger to come directly back. When you get the copy, make a copy and send it directly by hand to Mr. Lombroso. No. Fax a copy to Mr. Lombroso. Michael, give her your fax number.

"Michael, as soon as you get the fax, send the wiring instructions to Ray and hope the money winds up in your account. Why the three wires? And for my edification, how did you decide on the three amounts?"

I explained that my father and grandfather were obsessed with minimizing the tax hit even though neither had any taxable income to speak of. "I inherited the adverse tax gene. Ray pays the tax on the $50 million. That's the second wire of $7.5 million and the tax on the tax. That's the $1.25 million wire. I pay the IRS $8.75 million and get to keep the $50 million clear of taxes."

"I'm not a tax or trust and estate expert but assuming the painting came from your grandfather's storage room, an estate tax or gift tax is due. I'm not sure who has to pay—your grandfather's estate or you. If it's your grandfather's estate, and it has no money, I'm not sure whether the IRS can chase you. A word of caution: seek expert help. The IRS loves to put tax evaders in the slammer, especially rich ones."

I wondered what I would do if the IRS sought an estate tax. Would I claim I inherited nothing since I forged the painting? Or would I pay the tax. Intent is an essential element in tax fraud.

I had no intent to evade taxes. I made a mental note to consult Richard Marx, a law school classmate and tax specialist. I thanked Bryant for his help and folded the napkin.

"Better let me get the napkin Xeroxed," Bryant said. "I'll retain a copy. Good luck, $50-million-dollar man."

NINE

I bank at First Federated Bank of Switzerland, FBS, the closest bank to my father's office. Several hours after Ray told me he had wired the funds to my account at FBS, they were not there. I called Ray. "Everybody cheats everybody. Fraud makes the world go round. The money is out of my account the minute I request a wire. Your bank holds on to the dough for a day, earns interest on the funds, and then deposits it in your account. If the funds are not there by tomorrow afternoon, call me. I'll threaten to report the scam to the Federal Reserve Bank."

The next afternoon, $58.75 million was added to my bank account. I did a jig while singing a song composed in the heat of the moment. It begins and ends with three words: poor no more. I kissed my hand, professed my love for myself, and resigned from my father's law firm.

My dad said he, too, was quitting. "I want to retire. I've got my eye on a sweet home outside of Stockbridge in the Berkshires. It's secluded on ten acres. There I'll write novels. I have a creative urge buried all these years under a pile of real-estate closings. There's a sexy, sixty-year-old woman who has agreed to be my muse. What are you going to do?"

My dad knew by now that I had forged the painting and sold it to Ray. He called it the perfect crime. "You said if I could earn a living as an artist, I could devote my life to my love. Well, in one fell swoop, I earned a fortune, enough to last one hundred lifetimes. I'm going to paint and spend the rest of my life in the world of art."

My dad was moving to the country; I, too, needed to move. I picked the neighborhood around Gramercy Park. Why Gramercy Park? It's off the beaten track, but convenient to most city attractions.

I was a member of the National Arts Club, located in the heart of Gramercy Park, between Park Avenue South and Irving Place at 20th Street. Its official address is 15 Gramercy Park South. Membership in the club is a family legacy. My grandfather was a member and so is my father. It's a club for artists, writers, and aesthetes—not rich businessmen and yuppies like the University Club.

Property located directly on Gramercy Park sells for a premium, as it comes with a key to the only private park in the city. I didn't need to pay for the elitist key. My club fronts on the park, has a key, and loans it to members. I wanted to put my money in bricks and mortar and turn a down-on-the-heels building into a gracious living and workplace.

I lunched at my club and strolled around the area. On Twenty-First Street in the 200th block, I found my building. It was a forty-foot wide, five-story tenement with twelve apartments. An unsightly fire escape was draped over the façade. A sign implanted in the scrubby garden announced that the building was for sale.

Artists see things invisible to mere mortals. The building had potential. What it needed was an architect with an Italian hand, a top-notch contractor, and my money. With effort, the building could be transformed into a palace. I rushed back to my club and called the broker. She answered my only reservation affirmatively: Could the building be delivered vacant?

We met that afternoon for a walk-through. There was no elevator. The apartments were in terrible condition. I was irritated by the broker's upbeat chatter about how beautiful the apartments could be made with a small investment. The building appeared to be structurally sound but nothing inside was worth salvaging. If ever there were a candidate for a total gutting, this was it.

I'm not the "damn fool" Cecil Ray was. Before going any further, I hired an engineer, Robert Livingston, to inspect the building. I told him my plan to gut it and turn it into an art gallery, art school, and living space. His verdict: "The structure of the building is as sound today as the day it was completed in 1921. The conversion will take lots of money, but the building has good bones and could support its new use, including a gym and a swimming pool in the basement."

It is *de rigueur* for a prospective buyer to counter the offering price with a lower bid. Professional realtors know better. If they want the property and believe the fair market value is equal to, or in excess of the offering price, they will not make a bid below the asking price. Instead they offer the asking price to make sure they buy the property. Among the pros, it's called "sealing the deal." I bid like a professional and offered the asking price. My dad represented me at the closing.

I needed an architect. I called one of my Music & Art classmates, Henry Greenberg. He graduated from Princeton, where he studied architecture under Charles Gwathmey. Upon graduating, he joined the firm of his former teacher, Gwathmey Siegel & Associates. The firm received a singular honor when the trustees of the Guggenheim Museum hired them to build an addition to the Frank LLoyd Wright-designed building. As work commenced, the critics were ready to pounce, but deferred comment until the addition was completed. Then, they agreed it was in harmony with the original design.

I could have called Charles Gwathmey. He would, however, have turned the day-to-day work over to a junior. By calling Henry directly and telling him the job was his, he got a leg up in the firm by bringing in my business, and I got an architect out to prove my confidence was not misplaced.

The Gwathmey firm wears two hats. To ensure its design is faithfully executed, the firm serves as general contractor. It employs a staff of expert workmen, mostly Italian artisans. The heavy work is subcontracted, but the exacting work is done by the firm's skilled craftsmen.

The renovation cost over $1.5 million and took about a year to complete. When it was done, I had a home that would have pleased Renoir.

Tony Aritta and I met for lunch at "21". On my only prior visit, I was ushered to the upstairs dining room where the nobodies are seated. This time, when I gave my name and said I had a reservation for two, Tony and I were seated downstairs. I think it was just by chance as it is unlikely that my new fame had spread to the maître d'. Or perhaps it was something in my bearing proclaiming I was no longer a member of the hoi polloi, but a Master of the Universe.

Tony ordered the "21" hamburger at $25.00. His judgment: Hamburger Heaven's burger at $5.00 was better. I ordered halibut at an outrageous price. It was, I thought, a good thing I was a rich man. Otherwise, I could not have digested my lunch.

As Aritta was chomping away on his burger, I told him of my plan to start an art hedge fund. "I'd like to have three partners. All well-connected in the art world and able to tell the difference between a picture and a painting. I'm hoping you'll be one, and the others, the two unhappy assistant curators from the Met and the Whitney."

"I'd like to join you and so probably would my friends. We need a change and your project sounds interesting. There's a problem. We don't have any money, and by no money I mean we live hand to mouth. Our three combined salaries, before taxes, are less than $100,000. Hedge funds are for the superrich."

"I'll contribute the initial capital of the fund at about five mil, of which two mil will be for my account. I'll lend each of my partners $1 million at 10 percent interest deferred, but compounded for five years."

"What do you mean 'deferred' and 'compounded'?"

"You three will not pay interest for five years. Your share of the profits is set at sixty percent, but they'll stay in the partnership. At the end of five years, if your share exceeds $1 million plus five years of deferred, compound interest, you have a positive equity equal to the excess. If it is less, we'll continue our operations or dissolve the fund. By compounded, I mean in year two, the interest rate applies to $1.1 million."

"You've got so much money, why don't you give each of us $1 million as an inducement to join you."

"Except for today's $25 hamburger, there's no free lunch. The success of the hedge fund depends on the work of my partners, who will use the five million to buy paintings of unknown artists. If you pick the right paintings and the prices go up, we'll make a bloody fortune. I want my penniless partners to have a million-dollar incentive. "

"In the meantime, what do we live on? I'm not married but Stephen Jefferson is married. He has no family. Alex Martin is married and has a family. "

"You'll be employed by me for five years at a salary of $50,000 per year. In addition to selecting art for the hedge fund, you will run my gallery. I'll spend my time painting and managing the art school. It's my contribution to society. Students will be admitted based on merit. No tuition will be charged. I'll pay the teachers. Everything else is profit driven.

"I purchased a building near Gramercy Park. It's being gutted and renovated by our very own classmate, Henry Greenberg. When it's completed, the art school will occupy the fifth floor, while the gallery and hedge fund will occupy the ground, parlor, and second floors. My living quarters will be on the third and fourth floors. The plans call for a swimming pool and gym in the basement. Greenberg estimates we'll be open for business in about a year. I'll keep you posted. I'd like to meet Messrs. Jefferson and Martin fairly soon. Not here. Maybe at Burger Heaven."

On the following Saturday, in front of my building, I met with my prospective partners and Henry Greenberg. He handed us a rendering of what the exterior and interior would look like when the building was completed. "As we walk through the building, I ask you to ignore the wreck you see and use my drawings to visualize how beautiful the structure will be when completed."

After the tour, my future partners and I adjourned for lunch at my club. They each had an opportunity to earn a million dollars, courtesy of Michael Angelo Lombroso, and, while they were waiting, that same generous fellow was paying them salaries of $50,000, more money than their present wages. If you think they showed an ounce of gratitude, you are wrong. Instead of being grateful, they raged war.

"The location of the gallery is all wrong," Martin said. "It should be in a neighborhood teeming with galleries. Like SoHo. Collectors like to make the rounds. Stroll from one gallery to another. You're in Siberia. Why didn't you consult us before you bought? I suggest you sell the building and start all over."

Jefferson agreed, but said we had to bite the bullet. "Michael made a grievous error. The location is all wrong. We're smart, and the fifty-million-dollar man has made a generous offer. My suggestion: we make a virtue out of necessity. We'll turn our gallery into a destination place. We'll provide inducements for visitors to stay. People will come to us not to hop, skip, and jump out the door and onward to the next gallery, but to savor our programs.

"At the Whitney, we attract flocks by holding monthly lectures. We'll hold sessions every weekend. We'll turn Michael's living room into a salon. We'll invite critics, art historians, auction house pooh-bahs, and even artists. They'll accept. We'll give them a small honorarium, a token, for devoting many hours of their time. These experts love an audience. The difficult part will be attracting people to attend. Will it work at the M.A. Gallery? "Probably not. The Whitney is a prestigious institution.

It's an honor to speak there, and experts appear for peanuts. We'll probably have to pay more than a nominal fee to get even second-rate players. Will people come to hear mediocre speakers? I doubt it."

"I agree with Stephen and Alex," Aritta said. "We'll need to provide inducements to attract crowds to this bourgeoisie neck of the world. Not a single museum, not even an art movie house or a top-flight restaurant. The area is known for its restrictive rules summed up in the words: 'Stay out of our park.' Gramercy Park is lovely, serene, inviting. What do the residents do? They build a high fence and declare: 'Gramercy Park is open to residents who alone have a key to the locked gate.' Nice, friendly neighbors you picked, Lombroso. Well, I, too, would like to ditch the project and start over, but we'll have to live with adversity.

"The Tate Modern attracts crowds, and it's a long trek from the center of London. One way it overcomes its geographical disadvantage is to lure kids. Each kiddie gets a Tate backpack containing cards with clues to paintings in the gallery. The kids race around trying to match the clues to the paintings. When they arrive at a solution, they write the answer on the card. Win, lose, or draw, each kid gets a prize. The beauty of the game: the kids come with their parents to the museum. The Tate doesn't have to worry about attendance. We do."

There were times during that session when I wanted to call off the deal and start all over again with a different team, one that would appreciate my brilliant plan. Who were they to criticize me? I'd made millions with one well-thought-out plan. They couldn't scratch two nickels together. I thought, *the problem is I can't do it all by myself. As much as I dislike these guys, I need them. We'll part company if they dump on the rest of my plan.*

I waited while they agreed with each other and disrespected me. At times, it was as though I wasn't there. They referred to me in the third person, insulting me by using sobriquets such as the "fat cat." I was patient. I absorbed the insults before bringing up a business matter.

"I hate to be crass, but I'm in this business to make money. Does that shock you? Well, it shouldn't. Art is business. A big business. The reason I selected you was for expertise in picking upcoming artists with the potential to become the next generation of superstars. I'm not at all interested in your views on real estate or gallery management.

"We're going to run a hedge fund for art. I say 'we' because I'm assuming you're with me. My idea, which I hope you will tweak, not slam, starts with retaining ten undiscovered artists. We agree to buy their output for five years. We pay them a fair sum plus what is unheard of in the business—a residual interest in an arm's length sale of their paintings. I stress arm's length for a reason. I anticipate that we'll arrange a series of phony sales, that is, we'll flip the paintings to nominees to create the appearance of activity at higher and higher prices. When a painting reaches a price equal to a predetermined fair value, we'll dump the painting on the open market. That is the arm's length sale in which the artist's residual is measured against. Our game is what stock manipulators call 'pump and dump.'

"As you can see, there are two elements: picking the artist, and manipulating the price of the paintings. I don't believe in euphemisms. I could have used a neutral word like 'promote' instead of 'manipulate,' but as I said I don't like euphemisms. If it works out, you'll be millionaires, and I'll own a successful gallery."

Aritta was the first to speak. He was subdued. "The part about selecting unknown artists and buying their output for five years is innovative. We should take an option for an additional five. It takes time before the powers that be declare an artist's works are entitled to a full price. Value is not decided on aesthetics, but is socially constructed. The critics, the historians, the art magazines, the dealers, auction houses, museum curators, and collectors determine market value. If we select well, our manipulative activities will hasten the process but only if the market-makers agree.

"I see where the gallery comes in. The paintings are displayed in the gallery. When we jack the price high enough, the M.A.

Gallery makes an arm's length sale. The gallery benefits as the owner, and for a change, the artist participates in the resale of his work. Too often in the history of art, the creative spirit gets screwed by selling his painting for zilch and the undeserving collector screams 'bingo' as he sells the painting for $50 million. No offense intended, Michael.

"Manipulating the price of art is as old as the Paleolithic engraver who etched his works on the walls of his cave. You're a lawyer. This sounds naïve, is this thousands-of-years-old procedure legal?"

"I talked with a hedge fund guru. He runs a six-billion-dollar fund. How did he get there? He and his cohorts traded back and forth undervalued stocks until they reached a fair price. Then they unloaded on an unsuspecting public attracted to the stock by the appearance of active trading at ever-increasing prices. They also used other tricks like planting bullish stories in the financial press. Their reputations grew with the profits they themselves created. In a short time, word that they were buying a stock was enough to cause it to rise."

I continued, "Was it legal? The securities market is policed by the SEC. Manipulation is a crime. Make no mistake about it. My hedgie called his crime victimless because the manipulated stocks were undervalued, and they left something on the table for the public. 'There are guys,' he said, 'who artificially inflate the price of worthless stocks. Those guys become targets of SEC investigations and wind up in jail.'

"Unlike the stock market, there's no cop patrolling the art market. I propose, however, you use your talents to help collectors. Pick the best artists, sign them to our hedge fund, and when it's time to sell, we'll sell at a fair price. Our paintings will maintain their value. The trick is to start with undervalued, not worthless, art. Let's not overreach. Any more questions?"

There were no more questions. We talked about how to "raise interest in a painter," a term they preferred to manipulation.

"We'll give paintings to MoMA, the Whitney, and the Met," Stephen said. "We know all the people there, and for free, they'll do us a favor and accept our paintings. 'Yes,' I can hear myself saying, 'It's true, Joe Jones is just recently being collected by the Met. Buy fast before the museum grabs everything.'

"There's a whole legion of guys who buy art like it was a commodity. Their interest is buying the next shooting star at a pittance, and then when he's launched, sell for big bucks."

Alex said his wife is an editor of *Artforum*. "She'll let us plant some articles provided we don't overreach."

"I tease my wife about working at Sotheby's," Stephen said. "I call it Suckerbees. We could put paintings in a modern art auction and buy them in. No better way to establish an inflated price than at an auction."

"An echo box is the metaphor I use for the way art prices are fixed," Tony said. "There are four sides to the box. They are: the galleries, collectors, art critics, and museums. If one of the sides is missing, there's no echo and the price drops like a rock tossed from the top of a mountain. We need to make sure the echo sounds loud, clear, and continuous."

Aritta urged that we start gathering our stable of artists. "We know their hangouts in the East and West Village, Dumbo and SoHo, and in Brooklyn. We'll get out the word that auditions will be held at the National Arts Club on Saturdays from 10:00 a.m. to 5:00 p.m. The winners get a five-year contract to sell their output to us. Michael, can you get us a hall?"

"I can't use the club for business, but an art contest is not business—it's, well, culture. That's what my club is all about. I'll speak to the manager on Monday. Let's assume we can do it. Each candidate should bring his portfolio and dress neatly. No jeans, tee shirts, or sandals."

I'm impatient. I was mollified by their adoption of the critical plan to manipulate prices and their readiness to begin. I decided to add some sugar to make the medicine go down.

"Since you're starting work, you should be drawing pay. Do you think $350 per week for the initial stage before we open is fair?" No one spoke, but all three smiled broadly. The day had started acrimoniously; it ended harmoniously.

On Monday, I spoke to the club manager and arranged to secure a meeting room on Saturdays until further notice. I told him who would be meeting and why. I also mentioned the voluntary dress code. He was accommodating and suggested coffee and muffins be served in the morning followed by sandwiches and soft drinks in the afternoon. "There's a charge for the room and refreshment, but I'll keep it at a minimal amount even though, Mr. Lombroso, I know that's not necessary."

Funny, I'm the same guy before I got $50 million, or am I?

The first Saturday only three painters showed, but as word spread, attendance increased. One day, we had twelve. Those we liked, we invited back for one-on-one meetings. As the year drew to a close and my building neared completion, we had signed contracts with ten artists and had acquired fifty-two paintings.

The building was renovated within the estimate of one year. The paintings were hung on the walls of the three floors. Next to each painting was a number, nothing else. Our philosophy: customers should view the painting without being influenced by the artist's name or the price. Once they fancied a painting, we urged them to pull up one of a dozen folding chairs stacked against the walls and sit in front of the painting for at least fifteen minutes. If, at the end of the period, a customer wanted to purchase the painting, information as to the title of the painting and the artist's name and price were furnished.

For the life of the gallery, our sales method remained unchanged, even when, in later years, some prices were as high as $50,000, and several of our artists had name recognition.

The opening celebration was a bust. Friends and relatives showed up, but none of the well-known collectors we were counting on. Lectures in my living room, children's days on Sunday, and articles about our gallery's approach to the sale of art began to draw people to our gallery. The gallery lost money for the first two years, broke even for the next year, and earned a profit for each year thereafter. It took ten years for Aritta, Jefferson, and Martin to become millionaires.

My partners and I became adroit at manipulating prices. We traded paintings to dummy entities and advertised the results as honest-to-goodness sales. We placed paintings at Sotheby's and Christie's and surreptitiously bought them in until they fetched a buyer at the predetermined market price we had set years earlier. Our gallery served as a neighborhood bell cow drawing two new galleries. We also took credit for the success of a wine bar, a French bistro, and a Japanese-fusion restaurant.

My partners criticized me for the King Louis IV spa, their name for my private pool and gym. I offered them access, but unlike me, they despised exercise. On the whole, we got along as well as could have been expected.

TEN

My dad had a business and social relationship with Eric Williams, the manager of the Federated Bank of Switzerland branch where he and I banked. I told Williams about my good fortune and my intention to keep half the proceeds in a blind trust in a Swiss bank. "The Swiss franc is the world's safest currency," I said. I made no mention of my real reason—to avoid taxes. I didn't have to. Williams understood. He suggested I take an intermediate step and transfer the money to FBS London and then to FBS Switzerland. "Our branch is subject to federal regulation. If asked, we would be compelled to say we transferred $25 million to our Swiss parent. Our London branch is under no such obligation. For maximum protection, it is best to keep your Swiss account secret from the fed's prying eyes."

When Cecil Ray's money hit my account, I transferred $25 million to FBS's London branch. I left $8.75 million in the bank's money market account to pay taxes. As advised by Williams, with the balance, I purchased a $25 million bank, ninety-day certificate of deposit.

I followed the $25 million transferred to London. Once there, I arranged with the bank manager to open an account at FBS's main office in Zurich and wire the funds there. The London manager introduced me by telephone to Ernst Goelen, a managing director of the bank.

I arrived in Zurich the next day and met with Goelen. He advised me to rent a PO Box in New York. "We Swiss like to keep our dealings confidential. I'll send monthly statements to your box. That way you'll pick up the reports, read them, and shred them. Only you will have access to your account, unless you make someone else privy. We've had lots of experience investing money. We invest principally in Swiss and German companies and US-based international companies. I hope you'll be satisfied with FBS's performance."

Although I opened the account to evade US taxes, I wasn't sure I'd follow through. The first year I thought about turning the monthly reports over to my accountant. Nothing wrong with having a Swiss account as long as you pay US taxes. When April 15 rolled around, I thought: *the money's in Europe, invested in European companies. The US has no ties to my money except for the noose around my neck. I'm paying taxes on my US income, includ-ing $8.75 million in capital gains. It's not relevant the tax dollars were paid to me and I'm using Ray's money to pay my taxes. Money is fungible. I'm giving the government enough money.*

As time passed, I added other reasons. The war in Iraq was a disaster. Why should I support it with my tax dollars? *Bush is an ignoramus.* I did not want to pay his salary or the upkeep on the White House, directly or indirectly. I knew I was wrong. I'm schooled in the law. No one's above the law. Taxes are the obliga-tion of every citizen. I was evading my obligation.

I thought about my Swiss account each year around tax time. And each year, the most I did was think about it.

Based on life's balance sheet, I should have been happy. I had twenty-five million in the US to spend and another twenty-five salted away in a Swiss bank. I love women and they are attracted to me. Why? I'm a kindred spirit. A man who talks about art and music, not about sports and the stock market. Delores, my girlfriend in our Music & Art days, claimed I was more Greek than Italian: "You're an Adonis." Delores was besotted, but objectively speaking, if one can be objective about one's self, I'm reasonably attractive, tall, thin and have regular features and wavy brown hair. I have a flair for fashion. I was well dressed when poor and now that I had millions was the veritable glass of fashion.

My lifestyle adds to my attraction. I entertain a lot at my home, a palace with attractions not usually found even in a palace. Openings at my gallery are frequent events, and for the fortunate few, there is dinner in my private dining room served by my butler and cooked by his wife. The pièce de résistance is an invitation to join me in my private swimming pool. There is no shortage of attractive, nubile mermaids.

The press pounced upon my unique lifestyle. Year after year, I headed the list of New York's most eligible bachelors and was featured in *Gentlemen's Quarterly*. The Style section of the *Times* ran a story entitled "Thirty-Six Hours with Michael Angelo Lombroso in New York City." Visitors from the outer boroughs, and other states asked for my autograph. My life, disguised somewhat, was part of a John Updike story, which appeared in *The New Yorker*. Because of my generous contribution to charitable causes and my wide circle of friends, I was named guest of honor at benefits ranging from the American Cancer Society to the Italian Anti-Defamation League.

Yes, there were periods of happiness, when I was thrilled with the joy of being me. There were also periods of depression when I found it hard to get out of bed. I knew the cause: I'm disappointed in myself. No matter how hard I try to put a shine on my life, I'm only a businessman and a crooked one to boot. I'm no closer to being an artist than when I enrolled in Music & Art.

Over the twenty years I've been painting, no gallery has offered to hold an exhibition of "the art of Michael Angelo Lombroso." Exhibition? No gallery would even hang a painting of mine.

Circumstances have changed. I own a gallery. I don't have to get down on my knees and beg. I can command my partners, "See here.

I'm an artist. Not like you, mere students of art. Here's a collection of my paintings. My oeuvre. Let's turn the gallery over to my works."

I have cojones, big cojones, but not that big. Self-dealing is for businessmen, not artists. The suggestion to show my works must come from my partners. I tried to give those nincompoops a shove in order to end my periods of depression. It didn't work.

The art school on the fifth floor was my baby. I selected the students and hired the teachers. My management was hands on. I was there in the morning and stayed there most days until late in the afternoon. I ate with and took coffee breaks with the young artists. On occasion, I invited a few to my quarters where we sipped wine and nibbled on artisan cheese and crackers.

One day, I selected the best works of my students, sprinkled in several of my paintings, and marched my partners to the fifth floor to see the exhibition. Aritta liked the work of one of the students, but dismissed the others with an aside to me, "all trash." The students were not much kinder. One appeared to admire a painting and said: "Your painting is good. Real good for an amateur."

The teachers were differential. What else would you expect? I paid their salaries. One commented on my work ethic: "You don't have to work, and yet you're the hardest working student in the school." The most flattering word I heard and that was only once by one teacher about one painting, who said, "that's nice."

An artist needs encouragement. I got none. The reason: I didn't deserve to be encouraged. I was a lousy artist. I'd have to accept that fact, live in the real world, and stop moaning over what I am not. I closed the chapter on Lombroso, the artist.

The art school was also a failure. The students, serious at first, treated it as a joke. There were days when none of the six showed. The two teachers talked too much with each other and instructed too little. Their attendance was sporadic. The art school was in operation for a year before I closed it. I needed a replacement and turned to chess.

My grandfather was an avid chess player. He played at the Manhattan Chess Club (Bobby Fischer's club) and at home with me. He had also played with the famous artist, Marcel Duchamp. He was a leading artist in the expressionist movement and a founder of Dada. His work, *Fountain*, is much maligned, but considered by critics as the classic example of Dadaism. It's a porcelain urinal decorated by Duchamp.

My grandfather often spoke of Duchamp, especially when we were playing chess. "Duchamp," Grandfather said, "said not every artist played chess, but every chess player is an artist." Grandfather endorsed Duchamp's view. He delighted in discussing the graceful moves of the bishops and the tricky hop, skip, and jump of the knight. He called the sixty-four squares of the chess board, the basis of every work of art, and analogized a game in progress to a painting. "You don't know how it will look until near the end."

I studied chess and played in junior tournaments. I liked the game and thought it might make me a better artist.

Paradoxically, when I stopped painting, I plunged into the chess world. The Marshall Chess Club was on West Tenth, walking distance from my home. After the art school closed, I went there almost every day. To play chess well, one must concentrate on the game and block out everything else. Day after day, I thought about the games I had won and the ones I had lost and not a whit about my failed career.

I became a believer in the miracle of chess, and through Chess-in-the-Schools, a not-for-profit charity, dedicated to teaching chess to inner city kids, I became a preacher and a proselytizer. I contributed a lot of money to the cause but also gave of myself.

I adopted Alexander Hamilton High School on West 145th Street, in the center of Harlem, as my very own. Twice a week I taught a class in chess. The principal remarked that attendance on chess days was higher than on any other day of the week.

I continued to instruct the entire class, but singled out the six best players and formed an after-school club "the Black Knights." At first we met at the school. Then with the approval of the principal and the parents, I took them to the Marshall. Afterward, I invited them to my house for dinner and my butler drove them home. My kids learned a lesson in life. Using the mind is fun, and thinking before making a move is essential. The Black Knights entered into statewide tournaments. They acquitted themselves with distinction, reaching the finals one year and winning the state championship another. What pleased me most was when they triumphed over a fancy prep school, Horace Mann. More important than chess were their victories in life.

In the history of Hamilton High, not one kid had gone on to college. The record was broken, not by one, but by all six of my Black Knights. They went to college and lifted themselves out of the ghetto. I helped with tuition and other expenses.

Meanwhile back in the art world, a singular honor was accorded to my forged painting.

ELEVEN

Aritta burst into my living room and shouted the news. "You'll never believe this! Cecil Ray had *The Blue Horses* appraised for a hundred million dollars, and then donated it to MoMA. He took a tax deduction in the amount of the appraised value. He out-traded you. You sold it to him for a crappy fifty million. A razor-sharp expert set the true value as twice that. You got hoodwinked. I'm not a lawyer like you, but even I know you can sue him for overreaching. There's more. He got a seat on the board for his wife, hot pants Sophie, who hates him."

Far from disappointed, I was overcome with happiness. A double victory for me. I sold my painting for $50 million, and now, according to an expert, it's worth a hundred million. To disguise my true feelings, I focused on Sophie. "How do you know she has hot pants?"

"I've got eyes and ears in high places. At trustee meetings she rubs against all the guys, even the old codgers. I've never met her, but I've seen her picture in the society pages with Cecil. She is never looking at him. Trophy wives hate their husbands and suffer. She's one sweet piece of ass."

Having provoked the comment about Sophie, I was ready to discuss Cecil. "We should get him to our gallery. He's a perfect client. No taste and plenty of money. Suppose we close the gallery to the public, except for Cecil and Miss Hot Pants. I'll even feed them dinner."

"Too obvious. Better if you tell him you're seeking his opinion on two painters. Make him feel like an expert rather than a mark."

I sent an invitation to our next opening to the Rays. Along with the invitation, I penned a note: "I'd like your opinion on a new artist we're thinking of promoting." Hedge fund managers are stock pickers and are always looking for a good buy. In art they want to find the next Jeff Koons. Ray made lots of money trading stocks based on inside information. Why not do the same in the art market? Ray considered me, a gallery owner, as an insider. He hoped and I encouraged his hope that I would tip him to the next sensation.

They came late to the opening. He was dressed in casual clothes—a blue blazer and an open-collar-striped shirt. Her outfit was eye catching. She wore a necklace with a diamond too large to be real, except I knew it was. The dress she was almost wearing looked like it was borrowed from a Puerto Rican whore. Cecil's Sophie was not a class act; she was closer to a floozy. He was proud of her. He took me aside and confided. "When you marry a gorgeous woman, you have an obligation to keep her happy in more ways than you can imagine. Sophie loves art, but wants to be Christopher Columbus. She's always saying, 'I want to discover the next Jackson Pollock.'

"I don't want Sophie to go crazy so I gave her a budget. She can spend on modern art whatever I sell the *Blue Horses* for. I asked sixty million, but the buyer wanted the painting tested. Infrared light, X-rays, microscopes, and other scientific tools. 'How do I know,' he said, 'the painting is not a forgery? No record of owner-ship for fifty years makes it a candidate for a forger.' What's your opinion, Mr. Lombroso?"

I ignored his question.

Ray continued. "One of my investors knows nothing about art, but a lot about life. 'Why take a chance? Who knows? The tests might damage the painting. If they disclose the painting is a forgery, you've bought a worthless piece of shit. Get the painting appraised for a hundred million, and donate it to a museum. It will be so grateful that it will allow you to keep the painting for as long as you live. The charitable deduction will save you almost as much money as you would net after taxes if you had sold the painting for sixty million.'"

He launched into a discussion over the expression "eat your cake and have it too." I nodded and murmured something like it always confused me. He explained how by giving the painting to the museum, he had eaten his cake and had it too. "Philanthropic organizations are flexible with taxpayers' money. Not the way a sound business is managed. *The Blue Horses* still hangs in my living room, and I got a $100 million-dollar charitable deduction for gifting it to MoMA. You've got to be clever to make the system work for you. If you're not shy and ask for it, they'll make you a trustee. I've collected enough honors for me. Sophie's involved in art. She's the trustee.

"Sophie's wild in the sack, but nothing like the night I told her she's a trustee of MoMA and has fifty million to spend on modern art."

Ray said he wanted me to place Sophie under my wing. "We've done business. No regrets on either side. You're knowledgeable and experienced."

I made Ray my chief occupation. He, or rather Sophie, had $50 million to spend, and I wanted to make sure they spent it at my gallery. They came every Saturday. They listened to the lectures and then left. Week after week they came and bought not a thing. Nothing I pointed out aroused their interest or, as Sophie put it, "It doesn't light a fire."

One weekday morning, after finishing my swim, I walked through the gallery on my way to the elevator to my apartment. There was Sophie. "Michael, you're all wet." She ran her hand through my hair. "I bet you look even cuter in the shower. Where have you been?" I said I was swimming in my pool. She insisted on seeing the pool. I thought maybe seeing the pool would make a buyer out of her. *I'm only human.* I wasn't just thinking about business. Her dress was cut low on top and high on bottom. It was also plain if there were something under the dress, it wasn't very much.

She took my arm as we took a back door to a staircase leading to the basement. "You do have a pool. I thought you were kidding. I'd like to go for a swim, but poor little me, I don't have a suit."

I pulled one of my suits from its hook and offered it to her.

"What will I wear on top? Besides I don't like the color. I don't look good in navy. Do you have one in red in a bikini size?"

When I said no, she untied my robe and said, "You put the suit on. Men look better with their you-know-what covered. God, what a physique. Pop into the shower. I'll join you."

After the shower, we slowly towel-dried each other. We were aroused before the drying episode, but during the course of it, we got so excited that we plopped down on my snooze bed.

I don't know what Sophie did to Ray when she learned she was a trustee at MoMA and had $50 million to spend on modern art, but it could not have been more than what she did to me.

We got dressed, went back to the gallery, and took the elevator to my apartment. I lathered my shaving brush in preparation for shaving when she announced she wanted to do the job. She held my chin in her left hand and with her right hand, gently shaved me. I couldn't understand it. We just finished making passionate love, and here she was trembling with desire. Her lust excited me. We made love again.

We returned to the gallery. I pointed to a painting and urged her to buy it. That was the first sale made to the Rays. Many sales followed. The Rays became our best customer until they stopped coming. I called Cecil and said I missed him. "That damn whore ran off with a carpenter working in the apartment. I hate anything and everything that reminds me of her. Be a friend and buy back all the paintings at a fifty-percent discount."

I did. I owed Cecil.

TWELVE

Basel, Switzerland hosts an annual international art festival. My gallery exhibited there. The major galleries have space on the ground floor, and offer for sale, grand masters at prices starting at a million dollars. Galleries featuring minor contemporary artists are assigned to an upper floor. One had to search very hard to find the M.A. Gallery. Those who succeeded in finding us were unimpressed. We sold no painting our first year, and over the next nine years, our record was unchanged. We did it for the prestige, both for our gallery and for our artists.

An advantage of exhibiting in Basel was an invitation to show at Art Basel Miami. We sold paintings there, not many, but enough to meet our expenses. There were lots of parties in Basel. The international art scene was vibrant and sophisticated, but no match for Miami.

Miami jumps with a South American beat. It helps to speak Spanish (I don't), but English is spoken everywhere. Unlike Basel, I blended in with the crowd. I liked Miami so much that I bought a condominium in the neighboring Key Biscayne. The condo was on the fourteenth floor of Tower Two of the Ocean Club, a luxury private club for owners only a few steps from the Atlantic Ocean. My three-bedroom, four-and-a-half bath apartment faced the ocean with views of Biscayne Bay from the back rooms. The complex was quiet, yet no more than fifteen minutes from Miami and the center of the festival. There was another reason for my purchase.

I live in fear. I obtained my fortune by fraud. If discovered, I could be sued and my property sold to satisfy creditors. Not my condo at the Ocean Club. Florida has enacted a homestead law. It provides that a man's castle is protected from the reach of creditors. If my house of cards were to fall, I'd be assured of a roof over my head.

Key Biscayne is a fine getaway in the fall, winter, and spring, but too hot in the summer. East Hampton, on the south fork of Long Island is a convenient summer retreat for New Yorkers. It had an additional attraction for me.

Beginning in the 1950s, East Hampton was home to the New York School of abstract expressionist painters. The section they favored was called the Springs, an area apart from the expensive oceanfront cottages. I thought about buying a home on Accabonac Harbor, the heart of Springs, and a shout from Jackson Pollock's home, now a museum, but rejected the idea.

Boyhood friends, Robert and Phil Bono run the Oceanside Inn in Montauk. It's a small hotel with a large beach, swimming pool and restaurant. If I'm stuck in the city on a hot summer weekend, I can always escape to the Oceanside.

While at the festival in Basel, I stopped in Zurich to meet with Ernst Goelen, my Swiss banker. He warned that the IRS was cracking down on US citizens evading taxes through private Swiss accounts. My bank, FBS, was the focus of an investigation. Goelen believed the bank would be forced to reveal the identity of its US accounts. "Your government has provided an amnesty period during which US citizens who have evaded taxes can pay their taxes in full with interest and avoid penalties and federal prosecution. I advise you to take advantage of the government's offer. My bank, as it has done for its other US customers, has prepared a worksheet detailing your income from the account since inception and the tax due plus interest at six percent."

Goelen handed me the worksheet. My tax hit was $8 million; my investment account initially $25 million had grown over the ten years to $52 million.

"I'll give consideration to making a deal with the IRS. I'd also like to consider other options. Are there any?"

"You can," Goelen said, "open an account with a family-owned Swiss bank. The legal owner of the account can be a Liechtenstein trust. Liechtenstein has banking laws similar to those in Switzerland. It's a crime in both countries for a bank to disclose the identity of its clients. That's about to change in Switzerland, but not in Lichtenstein.

"My bank is pressured by the US because it has branches there. Family-owned Swiss banks, such as Hottinger & Cie, have no foreign branches. One could erect an impenetrable wall by opening an account at Hottinger in the name of a Liechtenstein trust. In the unlikely event Hottinger were forced to disclose the owner of the account, the trust—not you—would be named. The US taxing authority would have to go to Liechtenstein, where it has no influence, to pry open the identity of the beneficiary.

"For one hundred percent protection, you might name a Liechtenstein lawyer as the beneficiary. You'd have to trust him. There are trustworthy lawyers who would conceal your identity and not touch your funds."

I said, "My first lover was an opera singer. Not a prima, but a member of the chorus. I went to all the operas. I still do; it's hard to break old habits.

"Puccini composed a one-act opera, *Gianni Schicchi*. I don't know who wrote the libretto. Like most librettos, the story is silly, but there's a moral.

"A dead man leaves his fortune to a monastery. His relatives read the will, and, with knowledge that tampering with a will is a crime, conspire to do just that. They remove the dead man from his bed and replace him with one of the conspirators. The imposter pledges to write a new will providing for an equal distribution of the estate. A notary is summoned and a new will is drawn.

"The new will gives everything to the imposter. The others, angry and aggrieved, are powerless to act. If they accuse the imposter of fraud, they implicate themselves in a crime.

"Moral: If you don't have to, you're better off trusting no one, especially when committing a crime. I'll consider a Liechtenstein trust, but I'll be the beneficiary. Alternatively, I may come clean and pay the back taxes plus interest. If I were to switch to Hottinger, would a record of my account remain at FBS?"

Goelen said, "Absolutely not. Once a transfer is completed, all your records are sent to Hottinger. Your past is scrubbed from our computer."

"I'm considering Hottinger. I'd like to meet with the bank. Would you provide an introduction to a banker there?"

Goelen called Sigmund Hottinger, the grandson of the founder, and asked him to expect a visit from a valued client of our bank and the owner of the M.A. Gallery. "The gallery is showing at the Basel Fair."

I went directly to the Hottinger bank. Sigmund was all business. He set up an account in the name of Gunther Gubich, as trustee, whom he said was among the leading lawyers in Liechtenstein. The account would remain dormant until funds were wired to Hottinger. "I know from our conversation that you are considering another option. Before you decide, I suggest you meet Herr Gubich. If you agree, I'll call Gubich. His office is in Vaduz, the capital of Liechtenstein. It is a short train ride from here. My bank will arrange transportation, but first, let's have lunch."

We ate a simple lunch in the bank's private dining room—a glass of wine, an omelet, and a croissant. After lunch, Sigmund called Gubich. He referred to me as a client of his bank and the owner of an important art gallery in New York. "Mr. Lombroso is representing his gallery at our fair in Basel."

Liechtenstein was founded in the fourteenth century. The two most important structures, the castle and the church, date from medieval times. The tiny country remained an independent principality until 1719 when it became a sovereign member of the

Holy Roman Empire. The country has changed very little since its founding. One change is a modern office building fronting the Rhine. Gubich's office was located in that building.

After we exchanged greetings, he showed me a form of trust instrument. It was the standard one used in the US and apparently as well in Europe. The beneficiary of the trust had the right during his lifetime to revoke the trust or withdraw all or part of the corpus. During the life of the trust, income accumulated at Hottinger unless otherwise directed by the beneficiary. Upon his death, the corpus and accumulated interest pass in accordance with the beneficiary's written direction. His right to the trust's funds is exclusive and absolute.

The document had two blank spaces, one for the name of the trustee and the other for the beneficiary. He offered to serve as trustee for the "nominal annual fee of $1,000." I asked how many trusteeships he held. "I do not disclose any information either general or specific about my clients. My arrangement with them is confidential. I will never breach the confidence they repose in me."

Gubich was that rare combination of a modern man imbued with the honor of an ancient monk. One could place him on the rack and he would never squeal. I agreed on Gubich as trustee and asked to be named as beneficiary.

The Swiss have a reputation for efficiency, which I can attest to. Within twenty-four hours, my account had been transferred to Hottinger & Cie, in the name of Gunther Gubich, trustee.

I silently thanked my father for persuading me to go to law school. I understood the ramifications of the new arrangement and believed I had made a sound decision by continuing to keep a large part of my fortune abroad and protected from the confiscatory US tax code. As a further precaution, I vowed not to touch the funds in my Swiss account except for an emergency. If caught I could claim I intended to pay taxes when I repatriated the money. I believed US corporations with foreign subsidiaries follow a similar procedure. They pay US taxes on foreign earnings only when they are turned over to the parent company. It even has a name: inversion. I knew my analogy was wrong. I was missing a crucial step, but didn't want to find out. Better to be in the dark and have a defense than to learn the facts and be defenseless.

Shortly after I returned to New York, I received a notice from the IRS. I was stunned. Had I been unmasked? Then I breathed a sigh of relief when I read the IRS's demand that I pay an estate tax of $27.5 million owed by my grandfather's estate on property received by me. The letter claimed that the painting I had inherited from my grandfather was worth $50 million. It was, the IRS claimed, part of my grandfather's estate at the time of his death, and that no estate tax had been paid.

My first thought was to tell the truth. I forged the painting. I got nothing of value from my grandfather's estate. That wouldn't work. I'd be confessing to a crime, a felony. I needed help. I called Max Zimmerman, a friend of my father's and a specialist in trust and estate law.

"The statute of limitations has run on the claim," he said. "At the time your grandfather died, I prepared and your father signed the estate tax form. Your grandfather's estate was valued at under $600,000, and therefore no tax was due. Unless the IRS can prove we knew the estate had a valuable painting worth $50 million, the IRS's claim is time barred. At the time of death, we reported the value of the paintings and other objects in the storage room as having a value of $10,000. Your father and I believed we had overvalued the contents. Your grandfather died without a will. Your father inherited all assets except the "junk" in the storage room. That was passed on to you.

"It's probably the publicity about the Holocaust victim's lawsuit and the subsequent sale of the painting that set this off. Perhaps a 'friend' complained to the IRS. The claim is bogus, but when the IRS has its sights on you, it digs and digs until it gets you. The best way to defuse an attack is to delay it. Maybe the world will end or a new fact will appear, changing or adding a new ingredient to the stew.

"I'm an old man. Bea and I winter in Florida. I'll call the agent and ask to put the matter off to the spring. We'll meet then. Resolve nothing, and put the matter over to the fall. Too much is happening at once. Let things cool down until another candidate steps into the IRS's crosshairs."

I had a carefree life until the recent succession of narrow escapes. I developed a tick along with some gray hair. I avoided social events, spending evenings wondering when the next shoe would drop. My doctor said I needed a change. "You seem depressed, anxious. Time to take a vacation. Develop an interest that will take your mind off whatever is troubling you. I play golf on the weekends. I get so involved in that silly little game, I forget everything else. There are great golf courses in Northern Italy. It's a beautiful part of the world. Even if you don't play golf, you'll have a change of scenery. Do you have anything keeping you in New York?"

I called my travel agent, Maria Carbono. I'm Italian, but she's a real Italian. She was born in Milan. Maria booked a room for two weeks at the Villa d'Este, a five-star hotel on the shores of Lake Como. "I've also arranged for seven lessons with the head pro. I told him you were a beginner. He suggested a lesson every other day and practice at the range on days you take no lessons. Depending on how fast you learn, you might be able to play a round near the end of your stay. Bring books along. The chairs along the shore are heavenly. They engulf you. You'll think you were back in the womb. The food is great. Well, it's Italian, what else would you expect?"

I cancelled my appointments and left for Italy. I brought three books with me, all by Thomas Mann: Buddenbrooks, The Magic Mountain, and The Holy Sinners. The books saved my life. I had no aptitude for golf. The food was too rich. Maria was right about the chairs.

When I returned to New York, I was as uptight as the day I had left. I had a presentiment of disaster, but never guessed the blow that would fall.

THIRTEEN

Although it was about midnight when I got home, my sense of disaster drove me to check my office before going to bed. I leaned over my desk and glanced at the papers. The worst possible event, short of death, had happened.

I sat down, took a deep breath, and started to read. A feature story in the *NY Times* blasted the news: "Major Art Forgery Exposed." The article reported on the opening of an exhibition, "Hidden Treasures of the Hermitage" at the museum in St. Petersburg. On the cover of the catalogue was Franz Marc's *The Tower of Blue Horses*. The *Times* story continued: "One of the last vestiges of Nazi rule was Hermann Goering's hunting lodge, Carinhall, nestled in a state preserve in the Schorfheide Forest, north of Berlin. There, Hitler's second-in-command stored the many treasures looted by him from German museums, and the institutions and citizens of conquered countries.

"As Soviet forces advanced towards Berlin, Carinhall, on Goering's orders, was to be torched. The Soviets' timely arrival preserved his purloined treasures. They were transported to Russia where they eventually found a home in the storage rooms of the Hermitage. Among the many works rescued was the famous painting by Franz Marc, considered among the most important works of German expressionism of the early twentieth century. That is only one part of the history of this painting.

"In the winter of 1996, another *Tower of Blue Horses* made its appearance. This time in an exhibition of German Expressionist paintings at the Museum of Modern Art in New York City. Michael Angelo Lombroso, the owner of the M.A. Gallery, loaned the painting to the museum. While still on loan, Mr. Lombroso sold the painting to Cecil Ray, the founder and CEO of Ray 2, for $58.75 million. Mr. Ray recently donated the painting to MoMA. For tax purposes, the gift was valued at $100 million.

"International art experts believe the Hermitage's *Blue Horses* is the original and MoMA's a forgery. A grand jury in the US District Court for the Southern District of New York has been convened to determine whether a fraud has been committed. Marvin Kaminsky, a retired federal judge, who has no connection with the case, said art forgery may invoke the federal crime of wire fraud if payment for the forged painting was made by wire.

"Mr. Lombroso could not be reached, and Mr. Ray refused to comment."

The article continued, but I stopped reading and turned to a memo from Aritta. He called me a "lying bastard," accused me of ruining his reputation. "MoMA blames me. I should never have believed you. Fool me once, shame on you. Fool me twice, shame on me. There will be no second opportunity. Alex, Stephen, and I, the holders of sixty percent of the partnership, are calling for an emergency meeting for tomorrow. We have retained an attorney who will be present."

I put aside the two-week accumulation of mail, retreated to my quarters on the fourth floor, took two sleeping pills, and went to sleep.

I started the next day with a long swim and workout on the exercise machines. After breakfast, I called Arlene Spiegler, the criminal defense lawyer I had met with more than ten years earlier.

"What took you so long to call me?" she said. "I almost called you, but I'm a closet-case ambulance chaser. I've been in touch with James Morrison, the Assistant US Attorney in charge of the case. He says 'conviction is a slam dunk.' Those macho guys breathe air and exhale confidence. Are you available this afternoon? You better be. Events are moving quickly."

I said I spent the past two weeks on the shores of Lake Como and returned yesterday. "It's a strange circumstance. The first day back from vacation, one would think a million different things were screaming for attention. Not so, at least in my case. I got a meeting in about thirty minutes with my partners who want to jump ship. I'm yours all afternoon."

I then went to the hedge fund's offices to meet with my angry partners.

They appeared along with a small, skinny lawyer who introduced himself as Seymour Gottlieb. He shook my hand, the others glared at me. Gottlieb said he was a litigator. He hoped litigation would not be necessary. "If it proves unnecessary, a corporate specialist at my firm will take over. I'll do the talking for my clients. I understand you're a lawyer, but if you want your own attorney, we'll adjourn for a few days to allow you to retain one and give him a chance to familiarize himself with the facts of the case."

I said I was not a litigator and that my experience was confined to real-estate closings. "I'm sophisticated enough to decide on my own. If my partners want to dissolve the partnership, I won't oppose."

"That's basically what we want," Gottlieb said. "That and the right to start our own gallery and hedge fund free of your claim, of appropriating an opportunity belonging to you."

I said I would not stand in the way of their new venture. "Why don't you have your corporate partner draw the papers? If they provide for the orderly liquidation of our partnership and an exchange of general releases, which allow me and Tony, Alex, and Stephen to engage in activities free from any claims we might have against each other, I'm sure we can wrap this up quickly. In the meantime, unless you or my former partners have an objection, I'd like to meet with them alone."

Seymour was big on handshaking. After his clients said they were willing to meet with me, he shook my hand and each of his clients' hands and departed—with a word of advice. "It's a good idea for you to retain an experienced business lawyer for your sake and the sake of my clients. With your own attorney, you'll have protection against overreaching on my clients' part—we won't anyway—and my clients will have protection against any subsequent claim on your part to void the agreement because you were not represented."

I asked Gottlieb for his card and said my attorney would call him. After he exited, the partners and I met alone. I said to them, "A bunch of rats you guys turned out to be. I saved you from poverty, and at the first sign of adversity, you jump ship. You don't care to hear my side. In your skewed concept of justice, there's no presumption of innocence. Aritta didn't know the painting was a forgery when he included it in MoMA's exhibition. Neither did the expert who testified at the Holocaust victim's trial. Maybe I'm no smarter than they? Maybe the Hermitage's painting is a forgery and mine Marc's true work? You have prejudged the case because you want to steal my business plan and grab all the profits. I'm going to let you do just that. I'm closing the M.A. Gallery until further notice. You can take the inventory and the artists committed to the hedge fund. I didn't need you when I started, and I don't need you now."

"This is confession time, Michael," Aritta said. "Do you swear on the Father, the Son, and the Holy Spirit that you believed your painting was genuine? Let me restate it. Did you have any basis for believing your painting was a forgery?"

"There are so many fakes and forgeries circulating in the art world that any good Catholic possessing a modicum of respect for his religion would decline to state under oath that even the Louvre's *Mona Lisa* was genuine.

"In every rich man's life lies at least one criminal act. Mine is none of your business. Look to your own crimes. You defrauded the art-buying public by manipulating the prices of hundreds of painting. When you start your own business, you'll continue to rig prices. You want to see a real criminal? Look in the mirror.

"We have important business to discuss. I love painting, not business, but let's get the business over with quickly. I'm agreeable to assigning all the artists on contract to the hedge fund to you, and likewise to consign the paintings owned by the hedge fund. I want nothing for assigning the contract, but forty percent of the profits on the paintings our hedge fund owns. I also want forty percent of the net assets of the fund. And one more thing. You can stay here until you get your own quarters provided you don't take longer than sixty days. I'm facing criminal charges. I've got my hands full."

Their attitude changed from hostility to concern. They wished me success in the criminal case and expressed sorrow that our relationship was ending.

After they left, I reflected on our ten years together. My business plan and money was an element in our success. In truth, however, it was the industry and intelligence of my former partners that made the gallery run. From the outset, I was the face, and they the brains, muscle, and sinew.

After many years of being the tail wagged by my partners, I was ready to turn the business over to them. My name was a liability; I was damaged goods. No one would buy a painting from an accused forger, even modern, contemporary art free from any possible taint of corruption. Would anyone buy a used car from an ex-convict? I thought, *not so fast, Lombroso. You haven't been convicted yet. It doesn't matter. If you beat the rap, it's because of a gap in the law. You committed a fraud. Your reputation is destroyed no matter what.*

In preparation for my meeting with Spiegler, I opened the safe and removed the tapes. Initially, I felt a jolt when I couldn't find them, but it was momentary. I wanted to play the tapes, but did not want to run the risk a court might accuse me of tampering. Safer to claim they have never been touched. I hopped a cab and was at Spiegler's office building at the corner of 59th and Lexington with an hour to spare. I walked a block north to Gino's, an old-fashioned, red-sauce Italian restaurant. I ordered a glass of Chianti and a bowl of fettuccini pomodora e basilica, a simple tomato and basil sauce. That was the sauce my grandfather preferred and so do I. What would Grandfather say about my choice in Spiegler? Was she the right lawyer? Now that I was rich, I wanted only the best. *Is Arlene the best?*

I arrived in Spiegler's office on time. It was on the sixteenth floor in a modern office building overlooking Bloomingdale's. When I consulted with her ten years ago, she had been practicing solo in an old building on lower Broadway. On the wall alongside the door to her office were three names, Spiegler, Harris & Marlow. When I was ushered into Arlene's corner office, I passed several cubicles occupied by young lawyers called associates. Spiegler had clearly come up in the world.

When I saw her, she looked even more luscious than she did ten years ago. She offered her cheek. I kissed her lips and slid my hand up and down her back until she brushed it away. "No games, handsome. You're in a serious jam. Also, I'm off men. Since we last met, I've been married and divorced. I have a son, age four. Let's get down to business. First, you have to sign a retainer and give me a check for $100,000. Don't look distressed. You're paying the bill in full, in advance. No further charges, except out-of-pocket expenses. You can call me all you want without fear of running up charges. In the event we lose after trial, the retainer covers my time on appeal. Besides, $50-million-dollar man, you can afford it."

I glanced at the retainer and signed it. I wrote a check, then handed it and the tapes to her. I said I hadn't played the tapes. "Good. In my hands not even that obnoxious young assistant will claim I tampered with evidence." She buzzed her secretary and then handed her the retainer, the check, and the tapes and asked her to transcribe the tapes.

While we were waiting for the transcript, Arlene brought me up to date on the grand jury proceedings. "I interpreted our meeting ten years ago as a nonbinding retainer in existence until you revoked it. Since I couldn't reach you, and you had no other attorney, I followed the grand jury proceeding. So far only your three partners have testified. I was not allowed in the grand jury room, but spoke to each as they left. Jefferson and Martin were in and out in a few minutes. They said they knew nothing about the painting other than the fact you had sold it for over $50 million. The third called you a 'bastard,' and testified for several hours. What's he got against you?"

I said the hostile guy was Tony Aritta and explained his role in the affair. I also said every conversation we had about the *Blue Horses* was on tape.

"Aritta and I met this morning. He was angry, but we parted on good terms. He was a friend from high school. I think he's over his hard feelings."

Arlene identified the other witnesses scheduled to appear. "There's a state court judge named Edelman. A judge's testimony for the prosecution is dynamite. His credibility is beyond attack because he's a goddamn judge who has no motive to dissemble. There's a hotshot lawyer named Bryant, two experts who tested your painting in their own lab. I looked them up. They specialize in the authentication of art. Their reputation is top drawer. Another witness against you is the philanthropist Jay Winston. Cecil Ray is the government's main witness. You remember Ray, he's the guy you defrauded-- or did you? Two executives of MoMA are also on the prosecutor's list. So far that's it. The government can add more. Morrison promised to alert me to the time and date of the scheduled witnesses and any others. Oh, by the way, Morrison intends to parade you before the grand jury. You'll plead the fifth. No sense giving Morrison a preview of our case. I'll prepare you before you have to testify.

"You know what's unusual? The government's witnesses are generally covering their own asses by getting immunity or cutting some other deal with the prosecutor. When we attack their credibility by referencing their criminal records, the prosecutors have a stock retort: 'We don't pick our witnesses, the accused selects his friends.' Not in your case. All the witnesses before the grand jury are highly credible, except, of course, when it's your turn."

I didn't appreciate her humor, but decided not to object. I needed her. I couldn't start all over again with a new lawyer; she had my check, and it was unlikely I'd find another lawyer as good-looking as Arlene. Why did looks matter? We would have to spend a lot of time together. All other things being equal, it's easier for me to spend time with an attractive woman than a man.

Arlene's secretary returned with the tapes and two copies of the transcripts. "Mary, please put the tapes in the safe. Make another copy of the transcript for the files."

We read the transcripts. "The tapes are good," Arlene said. "Not perfect, but good enough. There are references to faxes between you and Aritta. Where are they?"

"Sorry, I forgot to give them to you. Here they are."

"Your high school buddy tried to have you authenticate the painting. He was suspicious and should have been more so after your weaselly response. I have an idea which will become fixed only after I see the grand jury minutes. We'll meet again before it's your turn."

Three weeks later all the witnesses had testified. It was now my turn. Arlene briefed me on what she had learned from the witnesses. Winston and Judge Edelman refused to talk to her. The experts declared the painting a forgery. In their report, a copy of which Spiegler had, they dated the painting to 1995. They had examined the painting in the Hermitage and declared it to be the original painted in 1913. They also distinguished between my brush strokes and Marc's, finding mine to be "crude." I was disappointed to have my work disparaged; Spiegler was elated. "Don't you see? MoMA was complicit! If you're guilty, so is MoMA. If it had engaged in due diligence, the forgery would have been detected. MoMA, by exhibiting a painting that had disappeared for fifty years without any attempt at authentication, was an unintentional aider and abettor. It should have tested the painting before holding it out to the public. Poor Ray, he had a right to rely on MoMA. I wonder if he can sue MoMA and you for the return of his money?

"An unintentional aider and abettor is innocent of a crime, yet it makes an appealing argument to a jury. The culprit in this case is not Michael Lombroso, who did nothing more than return a lost work of art to life, but MoMA. It alone breathed life into the fraud. The argument is not bad in a civil action in which MoMA can be made a party, but is useless in a criminal proceeding in which MoMA is unindicted and could never be indicted.

"I have to stop dreaming and get back to our case. Tomorrow, you go before the grand jury. You'll answer questions as to your name and address. Nothing else. I mean nothing else. To all other questions even if you think the answer would help our case, you state: 'I invoke my rights under the Fifth Amendment and refuse to testify.' It doesn't matter how Morrison tries to goad you to answer, you just keep repeating your assertion of your rights under the Fifth Amendment.

"I told Morrison you're taking the Fifth, and by calling you, he's just wasting time. He smiled and said, 'Don't you know better than that?' He wants to create an inference of guilt before the jurors because you invoked a Constitutional right. It's a cheap shot."

"I'll have to testify at the trial, right?"

"You're our star witness. On trial, you'll be back-bending in telling the truth. We don't want to risk a charge of perjury. Often when the prosecution loses on the principal charge, it brings a new action based on perjury. Your case doesn't depend solely on the fact of forgery. You are charged with forging the painting, and fraudulently passing it off as the original. The government must prove both elements of the crime. The indictment sets forth facts so clear and convincing on forgery that if we were to contest you'd risk a perjury indictment. You will testify that you forged the painting. Your defense is based on a question of law: you did not represent your painting as the original; others drew that inference. Your crime, and it's not a crime in the sense that a wrong is a crime, is that you didn't bother to correct the false impression you created. Whenever you opened your mouth what you said was technically true—a half-truth. A half-truth creates a misleading impression, but it does not a crime make; an outright false statement is needed.

"This leads me to my next stroke of genius. We waive a jury trial and elect to have the law and the facts determined by the judge. Our judge is Frank Keogh. He's old-school Irish. His nomination to the bench was controversial. Most of the judges come from white-shoe law firms and were alums of Ivy League colleges and law schools. Keogh was born and raised in Hell's Kitchen, then attended parochial schools and Benjamin Franklin High School in East Harlem before graduating from CCNY and Fordham Law School. He spent his legal career as an assistant in Frank Hogan's office in charge of the homicide division.

"An assistant DA had never before been nominated to the federal bench. Keogh's patron saint, Senator Daniel Patrick Moynihan, knew Keogh from St. Raphael's church in Hell's Kitchen where they were both parishioners.

"The senators from each state take turns nominating judges to the federal bench in their states. An opening in New York City's Southern District arose in 1980 when it was Moynihan's turn. He recommended Keogh to Jimmy Carter. Keogh is not a member of the old boys' network, so the elite of our esteemed bar opposed him. Moynihan was adept. When the nomination came before the Senate Judiciary Committee, Moynihan didn't mince his words. His statement in support was reported in the *New York Law Journal*. I retrieved it:

"'The federal court in New York City is the most influential court in the land. Centered in the hub of the Financial District, it exerts influence upon the entire US economy. The judges, however, do not reflect the diversity of our country or even of New York City. Frank Keogh does.

"'He was born and raised in Hell's Kitchen, not on Park Avenue. His academic record is off the charts. Frank Hogan, in his letter in support of the nomination, referred to Keogh's twenty years of service calling him the 'best assistant who ever served under me.' What Keogh lacks in white shoe polish, he makes up for in street smarts and integrity."

Arlene smiled. "At the time, not being white shoe or even a male, I was overjoyed when Moynihan prevailed. His nomination was unanimously approved by the committee. No member wanted to risk alienating their Catholic constituency.

"Keogh never forgave the bar association for its opposition. While he decides cases fairly, the powerful receive somewhat less favor than the underdog. He likes people who have achieved success on their own over those born to the purple. We'll have to portray you as a self-made, $50-million man. You'll get points for Music & Art over Exeter or Andover."

"What makes you think he'll be good for our case?"

"It's an instinct. Nothing more. Keogh will not like Cecil Ray with his Harvard MBA and phony Boston accent. He may not like you either. He comes from a law-and-order background. His father was a longshoreman."

Over the course of mixing with lawyers, I had heard good things about jurors. In New York, the jury pool includes many poor, underprivileged whites and blacks. They see violence in their neighborhoods and associate it with criminal activity. Painting a picture might not fit their definition of a crime. Since a jury verdict must be unanimous, one juror could save me. "I hate to waive a jury," I said. "There's a human element there that may not be present in a former prosecutor."

Arlene said, "Under ordinary circumstances, I'd agree with you, but this is not the usual criminal trial. In the usual one, the jurors weigh ordinary everyday facts bearing upon guilt or innocence. In your case, the facts are technical. Was your remark a half-truth or an outright falsehood? There's no room for a juror's compassion."

"Why are we talking about abstractions? Let's talk about what I said. We got the transcripts in front of us. I was mindful that a half-truth was not actionable under the criminal law. I was careful not to cross the line between a half-truth and a false statement. Did I succeed?"

"When dealing with half-truths the issue is not cut and dry," Arlene said. "Every half-truth is misleading. In civil actions it's considered a misrepresentation. In criminal actions it's not, but the line is a fine one. The judge has discretion to draw the line. He'll take into consideration all relevant circumstances.

"Since the painting had been missing for fifty years should Ray have insisted on tests? In the criminal arena, the case is about the perpetrator. It is his conduct that is assessed. No money flows to the victim so he doesn't have to exercise care. But what if you sold Ray the Brooklyn Bridge claiming that you owned it? Your fraud is farcical, not criminal. The case of the too gullible buyer of the bridge would be tossed out of court. Our case differs from the absurd example, but we have to make it close to that case. What did Winston say? 'Only a damn fool' would buy the painting without subjecting it to rigorous tests? Could Ray rely on the fact that the painting hung in a MoMA exhibition and a leading expert testified it looked genuine? I don't know, but I have more confidence in a judge deciding the issue than jurors who might not be able to get over the fact you netted $50 million."

It was a delicate balance. I'd have preferred a jury, but Arlene was an experienced defense lawyer. I deferred to her and asked whether Morrison would have to agree.

"James will agree to waive a jury. He has to. Otherwise he's taking a slap at the judge. He's not going to insult Keogh. He believes Keogh's better for the prosecution than some bleeding-heart liberal jurors. If we win, what a defeat for a hotshot prosecutor. An open-and-shut case of forgery—all set forth in the indictment with a payday of over $50 million tried before a judge and he loses.

"There's another reason I don't want a jury. Jurors are not going to be sympathetic. You grossed $58.75 million by knocking off Franz Marc's work. Judge Keogh cannot take anything into consideration except the law. Keogh will follow the law, not bend precedents. The problem: This is a case of first impression. I've searched not only US law, but English law as well. There's no decision directly on point."

I said, "You told me a half-truth was lawful. Now you're saying you have no support for the position?"

"No fighting. I didn't tell you it's OK to forge a painting and pass it off as a genuine work. Take heart. Perjury is an analogous proceeding. It, too, involves a lie, but is a more grievous one than yours because the false statement is made under oath. There are cases dismissing perjury charges when a half-truth is involved. The courts reason that the examiner has a responsibility to uncover the truth by asking follow-up questions. If he fails to do so, the half-truth stands as a technical truth and the charges are dismissed. We have a chance to prevail by arguing by analogy from the perjury decisions. We'll know how good our defense is when we read the judge's decision."

FOURTEEN

Judge Keogh's courtroom, on the fifth floor of the US Courthouse on Foley Square in New York City was, like all the other courtrooms in the federal system, too large for the business at hand. Arlene and I sat at the defendant's table, large enough to seat eight persons comfortably. James Morrison, a young man whom I estimated to be in his early thirties, sat at an equally long table with an assistant at his side, an even younger man. Aritta sat between the two lawyers. We did not look at each other. In front of the lawyers' tables was a rail separating us from the space assigned to the judge and court personnel.

A judge sits behind an oversized desk referred to as "the bench." Two law clerks assigned to the judge sit on chairs below the bench to the left of the judge. The court clerk sits on the right of the judge, as does the court reporter whose task it is to record the testimony. Facing the reporter is an empty chair to be occupied by the witnesses. In front of the witness chair and forward of the lawyers' tables is the podium where the lawyer examining the witness stands. In back of the lawyers' tables stretched row after row of benches; it is enough seating space to accommodate a hundred spectators. For my trial, the benches were empty. From time to time, about five spectators took seats. They rarely stayed.

It rained on the opening day of the trial. I took it as a bad omen and mentioned it to Arlene. "I've got too much on my mind to worry about signs. Defense lawyers, however, agree with you. Rain is a sign God is against the criminal." She said it with a smile.

"Will you visit me in prison?" I asked.

Before she could answer, the judge and his clerks entered the courtroom. We rose. The judge, a tall erect man with a square jaw and a large head, motioned us to be seated. He stared at Spiegler for a few seconds before saying: "I've been on the bench for twenty-five years. This is the first bench-trial I've had on a criminal case. Ms. Spiegler, don't keep me in suspenders. Why for heaven's sake did you waive a jury in a case where the indictment accuses your client of being an out-and-outright forger, who sold the work for $50 million, net of taxes? Did you think I'd show your client mercy?"

I started to shake. *The judge has convicted me. Why did I let Arlene talk me into waiving a jury?*

She rose and said, "My client entered into a stipulation with the government admitting that he copied Franz Marc's work. He will not admit to committing a crime. There is nothing wrong with an artist copying the work of another artist. Go to any museum and you'll see young artists copying the work of old masters. A crime is committed when the artist represents his work as the work of the master. An essential element is that very representation. If it's not made, no crime has been committed. Mr. Lombroso did not say his work was Marc's work. Others did. He didn't correct them. Remaining silent when one has a duty to speak may lead to civil liability, but does not constitute a crime. The government must prove that the defendant claimed his painting was Franz Marc's painting. A misleading statement is not enough. Michael Angelo Lombroso may have made misleading statements, but he didn't make an outright false one. Whether what Mr. Lombroso said amounted to a false representation is a question of law for Your Honor to decide, not an issue of fact for a jury.

"Based on my knowledge of the state of the evidence, I believed it would be a waste of time to convene a jury, because it would have nothing to decide. The decision to waive a jury was confirmed when we learned Your Honor was presiding over the case. My client wants justice, not mercy."

"Flattery will get you lots of places, Ms. Spiegler, but it won't buy an acquittal." He then turned toward the prosecution. "Mr. Morrison, welcome to my courtroom. If it's true the defendant made no false statement, why is he on trial for fraud?"

"Judge Keogh, the evidence in this case will establish beyond a reasonable doubt that the defendant engaged in a scheme to defraud. He involved a close friend in the plot, who unwittingly assisted the defendant in the first stage: placing the forged painting in an exhibition at the Museum of Modern Art. He met with a philanthropist, and renowned art collector, who made an innocent remark which the defendant twisted and squeezed into a false statement damning as any strongly worded false statement could be. He used the false statement to convince an unsophisticated art buyer into purchasing the forged painting quickly or forfeit the right to own it. His statements as a whole created the impression the painting he alone painted in 1995, was, in fact, the great work of art created in 1913 by Franz Marc.

"In testimony before a state court judge, the defendant hornswoggled the judge into issuing a decision that lent creditability to the fraudulent scheme.

"The government will call five witnesses who will testify as to the fraud. The witnesses are credible, possess impeccable credentials, and enjoy outstanding reputations in the community. There is no basis whatsoever for Ms. Spiegler's assertion that the defendant made no false statements in conceiving and executing a monumental fraudulent scheme.

"The government is pleased to try the case before Your Honor. In fact, Your Honor's unquestioned ability to decide the case fairly is the only point of agreement between the two sides."

Judge Keogh said, "Ms. Spiegler, Mr. Morrison. That is what trials are all about. One side says one thing; the other says the other. Both of you can't be right. Mr. Morrison, call your first witness."

"The government calls Anthony Aritta."

Aritta, led by Morrison, testified that we were classmates at Music & Art, and that he was the valedictorian of our class. He said he graduated from Harvard and upon graduating started work at MoMA, rising to the position of assistant curator. He described our meeting at MoMA on a Sunday in July. Then Morrison got to the guts of Aritta's testimony.

Morrison: What, if anything, did you and Mr. Lombroso discuss about German expressionist paintings that Sunday in July?

Aritta: I said I'm working seven days a week to persuade collectors to lend the museum paintings for an exhibition on German expressionist art. I was in charge of the exhibition, and it was scheduled to open in January. Donors were wary because many feared Holocaust victims would make claims on the paintings. I said I was meeting that day with two potential donors and hoped to persuade them to loan their paintings.

Michael said he owned a painting for possible inclusion in the exhibition. He was with a young woman he had met that very day at the museum and I thought he was trying to impress her.

Morrison: What were the circumstances under which you learned he was serious about owning a painting for inclusion in the exhibition?

Aritta: Several months later he called me. He asked me to meet him outside his grandfather's former apartment house on Riverside Drive. When we met, he took me to a storage room located in the basement of the building, which he said had once belonged to his grandfather and had passed on to him upon his grandfather's death. I knew his grandfather. He was a cherished teacher and an icon at Music & Art.

He showed me a large painting which he said he had recently discovered among others paintings in the room. I was involved in the study of German expressionism in connection with organizing the exhibit. I recognized the painting as one of the great works of that period, one which had mysteriously disappeared after World War II, Franz Marc's *The Tower of Blue Horses*.

I said that if the painting was Marc's masterpiece, I'd be happy to include it in the exhibition. I arranged for a fine art's moving company to take it to the museum for further study. Lombroso and I waited for the movers. When the painting was crated and on the truck, I gave Lombroso a signed receipt.

Morrison: The painting has been moved from the storage room and is now in the possession of the museum. Was a decision made to include the painting, and if so, who made the decision?

Aritta: The painting was initially rejected. The curator, Howard Chin, said the circumstances were suspicious. "This is either a forgery or stolen property. In either event it has no place in the museum's exhibition."

I argued in favor of inclusion. I said our research uncovered that the painting was purchased by Goering in 1937, and last seen during the closing days of World War II in Carinhall, Goering's hunting lodge. Lombroso's grandfather was a member of the Monuments Men, an Allied army division charged with finding art looted by the Nazis and returning the stolen art to its rightful owners. Some folks at the museum surmised that Michael's grandfather had found it, couldn't return it to Goering as he was dead, refused to give it to Goering's heirs, on moral grounds, as he was legally obligated to do, and took it back with him.

They further assumed he kept the painting hidden in his storage room because he didn't want to disclose that he had, well swiped it. They thought he kept the painting in hiding hoping time would erase his crime. There is a well-documented history of stolen art kept underground for many years perhaps for the same reason.

I held Michael's grandfather in high esteem. I didn't think he would steal anything even from a Goering.

We now know Michael's grandfather didn't steal the painting, Michael forged it, and attempted to conceal his crime by assigning blame to his grandfather.

Arlene objected. Judge Keogh overruled the objection. "Why are you objecting? The defendant has admitted he forged the painting. I get it. You object to the inference Lombroso tried to pin the tail on his grandfather. Don't concern yourself. He's on trial for fraud, not for dishonoring his grandfather. I may take that into consideration, however, in sentencing him.

I thought my life was over. As if my crime was not bad enough, I'm going to spend time in the slammer for attempting to ruin my grandfather's reputation. Damn, I wish I could start all over again.

Aritta was silent for several seconds. I thought he regretted digging my grave even deeper. Judge Keogh asked Aritta to continue his testimony.

"I eventually prevailed but only by erecting several safeguards to prevent deceiving visitors to the exhibition. The museum would in no event authenticate the painting by claiming it was by Franz Marc. I was instructed to obtain Lombroso's representation that he believed the painting to be genuine.

When I told Mr. Chin that Lombroso refused, the curator said: "That ends the matter. If the owner refuses to authenticate the painting, there must be something wrong. Owners know more about their works than we can ever possibly know."

I argued for inclusion. "Lombroso," I said, "is acting to protect his grandfather who had a moral duty to return the painting to the world, especially since the prior owner, a Nazi, is dead." In the exercise of caution, I suggested the placard identifying the painting should say the work is "of the school of Franz Marc," a sign that the painting was not one actually painted by Marc. I also said the painting would not be discussed in the guide to the exhibition and it would be hung in a corner by itself. My boss reluctantly agreed, and after an exchange of faxes, so did Lombroso.

Morrison introduced the faxes into evidence and continued his examination.

Morrison: What was your reason for wanting the painting in the exhibition?

Aritta: Lombroso was a friend. I believed he was hoping to get the museum to somehow suggest that the painting was at least *possibly* the original. I wanted to do a friend a favor.

Morrison: Were the conditions attached to Lombroso's loan of the painting adhered to throughout the exhibition?

Aritta: They were and the painting was largely ignored by visitors to the museum. Then a Holocaust survivor claimed the painting was stolen from her grandparents' home in Berlin. The claim was frivolous, but we had a contractual obligation to defend. We defended vigorously, and the case was dismissed.

The lawsuit received a lot of attention in the media. The press discussed the testimony of a leading art historian who said the painting was the very one Goering, some fifty years ago, had purchased and hung in his hunting lodge. The buzz caused crowds to flock to the museum to see the exhibition and especially *The Blue Horses*. We moved the painting to the center of the exhibition and included it in the audio guide. We did not change the placard that said the painting was of the *school* of Franz Marc, a representation repeated in the guide.

Judge Keogh: Sometimes I get it and other times I don't. My wife and I were among the many who attended the exhibition after we had read about it in the *Times*. She knows a lot about art. She found the painting aesthetically pleasing and pronounced it "a monumental work." According to the newspaper reports, so did the art historian, Dr. Gruenfeld. Forgery is a crime not to be condoned. Let's put the law to one side. If a painting is aesthetically pleasing, why does it become worthless when it is discovered to be a forgery? I address this question to you, Mr. Aritta.

Aritta: Art is a part of history as well as a work of beauty. If the work is not authentic, the historical response will overwhelm the aesthetic.

Judge Keogh: I think I understand. If I owned a Gutenberg Bible, I would treasure it over a knockoff even though the contents of both were the same. Thank you, Mr. Aritta. Proceed, Mr. Morrison.

Morrison: What contact, if any, did you have with the defendant during the course of the exhibition?

Aritta: He called and said he had sold the painting and needed the museum's help to complete the sale. According to the contract of sale, the buyer's name must be substituted for his as the owner of the Franz Marc painting, and at the close of the exhibition, the painting must be delivered to the buyer. Lombroso said that if the museum agreed to the terms, the sale of the Franz Marc painting would close.

I was reluctant to agree until Lombroso threatened to withdraw the painting, if I did not. The museum had handled one brouhaha over the painting. I didn't want to subject it to a second so I told Lombroso to call the museum's attorney, Tom Bryant, and that the museum would instruct Bryant to comply, provided there were no legal complications.

Morrison asked whether Aritta had any further contact with me. He described our hedge fund, the interplay between the fund and the gallery, and then discussed how we promoted the artists in our fund and even went into details about phony sales to create an appearance of active trading. The judge was incredulous.

Judge Keogh: You've just admitted you engaged in market manipulation. If it were stocks instead of paintings, you'd be facing a prison term. I'm not sure that you haven't committed a federal offense. What do you have to say about that? Wait before you answer, I'm calling a recess to give you a chance to talk with Mr. Morrison, or another attorney of your choosing. We'll resume in half an hour unless Mr. Aritta wants more time.

I was nonplussed. At recess, I asked Arlene, "Why the hell did Aritta go into details about our hedge fund?" She said it was a foregone conclusion that the hedge fund manipulations would be brought up in my cross examination, so it looked better for Aritta to bring it up first.

"It's better," she continued, "if it comes out in direct rather than me pulling teeth on cross. By testifying to his sins, it dispels an inference that the witness was hiding something. Instead he appears forthcoming. Morrison has worked this out in advance. Aritta will have an answer to satisfy the judge."

Spiegler was right. When we reconvened, Aritta maintained that what we had done was beneficial to artists and not remotely like manipulation of the prices of equities in either means or ends. "Too often canny collectors have been able to buy art work for a pittance and resell it for millions. The artist has no residual interest in the resale. All the profit stays with the collector. I worked at MoMA before joining Mr. Lombroso. Stephen Jefferson and Alex Martin, the other partners, were assistant curators at the Met and the Whitney. Our taste and judgment in the contemporary art market was good. We spent a year viewing thousands of paintings from hundreds of artists before we made our selection. We told our artists that we would attempt to raise the prices until they reached what we and they agreed was a fair market price. At that point, they would receive sixty percent of the profit and our hedge fund the balance. I believe, and so do my partners Jefferson and Martin, that our activities raised the prices to the level the works would reach over time. The difference: we advanced the time and gave the artist the lion's share of the profits. In the aftermarket, collectors who purchased the art at the fair market prices we helped to create have been able to resell at a profit. We keep a sharp eye on the market. None have resold at a loss."

The judge said he believed in a free and unfettered market. He added that he was not unsympathetic to the plight of the artist who languishes in poverty while collectors pocket the profits of the artist's talent. "This case is not about you but about Mr. Lombroso. Mr. Morrison, do you have any further questions for Mr. Aritta?" When Morrison said no, the judge asked whether Aritta had any suspicion about the genuineness of the painting.

He said from the advantage of hindsight, he was too trusting. "We were high school classmates in a special school. We shared a love of art. I would never deceive Lombroso, and, if I even thought about it, it was inconceivable that he would deceive me."

Judge Keogh thanked Aritta and adjourned the trial for the day.

We went back to Spiegler's office. She explained her strategy on cross. "I want very little from Aritta, but the little I want will be decisive. It won't sound important until you and the tapes make their appearance. I want Aritta to admit that the meeting with you in your grandfather's storage room took place on Thursday, October 19, 1995. Then to prevent him from temporizing his testimony, I want him to reaffirm that you said you discovered the 'painting,' not what you actually said, the 'canvas.' I don't want to press the point too hard or he'll smell a rat. If I succeed, we'll show he misspoke when you testify. Morrison will have instructed him not to be contentious, but to answer what he has to answer in a pleasant manner. I'll prepare, however, for a difficult witness."

Spiegler's cross was not as easy as she had projected. Aritta refused to recall the day we met. Spiegler had proof that it was October 19, 1995, as Aritta had signed and handed me a receipt for my painting dated that very day. She toyed with Aritta before showing him the receipt. Even then Aritta said he may have given me a receipt a day or even a week later. Arlene snidely asked whether he might have given me a receipt the day before he took possession of the painting.

Judge Keogh interrupted. "I wrote the meeting in the storage room took place on October 19. I don't know the significance of the date, but you seem reluctant to admit the obvious and Ms. Spiegler is determined to draw the admission from you, so Mr. Aritta, did the meeting take place on October 19? If you say no and it turns out that the date is correct, I may refer the matter for a perjury prosecution."

A crestfallen Aritta admitted the meeting took place on October 19, 1995.

Spiegler then asked whether Aritta wanted to change his testimony that "Mr. Lombroso told you he found the painting in the storage room."

Aritta, softened by the battle over the date, said, "The meeting in the storage room took place more than ten years ago. If you have something to show me that reflects I misspoke, please show me."

Spiegler later told me she had thought to confront Aritta with the taped conversation in which I said I had found the "canvas," not the "painting," but didn't want to give Aritta the opportunity to say "canvas" and "painting" are synonymous. "Better if you on direct say 'canvas' is a piece of cloth and a 'painting' is the pigments applied to the cloth. I hate to argue with a witness especially when the result might lead to confusion."

She was silent for about ten seconds before saying, "No further questions. Thank you, Mr. Aritta."

Morrison called his next witness. "The prosecution calls Thomas Bryant Esq. as its next witness."

The judge greeted Bryant. "You've been before me many times as a lawyer, never as a witness. How can you possibly enlighten me about this situation? You weren't present at the scene of the crime. Don't answer. I'll let Mr. Morrison draw it out of you. We'll have to wait, however, until tomorrow as I have a preliminary injunction hearing scheduled in an hour. Court is adjourned for today. That means I'll have to spend a sleepless night wondering what Mr. Bryant can add to our record."

FIFTEEN

After court was adjourned, Morrison conferred with Spiegler. He asked a favor. Bryant wanted to whitewash MoMA by portraying his client as a victim, not an accomplice. It was important, he said, for the public to respect the integrity of its museums. The current scandal had tarnished MoMA's reputation. Bryant hoped to testify about the precautions taken by the museum to guard against forgeries and fakes. Morrison recognized his testimony was hearsay since he lacked personal knowledge, and that the testimony would be inadmissible if Spiegler objected. The favor: Spiegler not object. "His testimony won't affect the case, but will help the museum."

Spiegler spoke to me before responding to Morrison. "We've got enough enemies. It makes no sense agitating Bryant and the museum. If we think any answer may hurt our case, I can always object." I agreed and steeled myself for a long day.

The next morning Morrison informed Spiegler they had changed course. He said the judge's comments at the end of yesterday's session indicated his antenna was alert to the possibility of extraneous testimony, and he was likely to strike it on his own. Morrison would begin questioning on the Lemberg trial and not digress.

Arlene believed there was another reason: Bryant's firm had opposed Keogh's nomination. She believed Morrison feared

Keogh would resent Bryant for extending a favor to MoMA, a client of the law firm, which had opposed his nomination to the bench. Why risk offending the judge by aligning the prosecution with Bryant? Morrison had nothing to gain and something to lose.

Bryant's testimony stuck to the facts about which he had personal knowledge. He discussed the issues and the evidence that persuaded Judge Edelman to dismiss the case. He omitted any reference to the judge's bizarre behavior. He said I was helpful, crediting me with identifying the crucial document. "It had been pilfered by Heinrich Fischer, a British citizen, along with God only knows what else. He was serving at the time in a special Allied division during World War II called the Monuments Men. Fischer's widow donated the document to the Victoria and Albert museum, and the museum granted us access to the document. As a matter of interest, Mr. Lombroso's grandfather also served in the Monuments Men. His task was to return art looted by the Nazis to the lawful owners or their heirs."

Morrison: Did Mr. Lombroso testify in the Lemberg case?

Bryant: He did. As part of the museum's case, I had the painting moved to the courtroom. It created a sensation. I was curious as to how Lombroso got the painting. So apparently was the judge who declared he was going to unravel the mystery. The judge, on his own motion, called Lombroso as a court witness. He asked two questions. The first was how did the painting come into his possession? Lombroso said he "found the canvas in his grandfather's storage room." The judge's second question was how the "canvas" got to MoMA. Lombroso answered he "showed the painting to Aritta."

Morrison offered the pages containing my testimony from the Lemberg case into evidence. The judge was incredulous. "The transcript pages are thick. How could two such direct questions take so long to answer?" Morrison said Mr. Bryant will address the court's question.

Bryant: When I'm at trial, the adrenaline courses so freely through my body that at night I have to take a sleeping pill.

Lombroso's testimony was unusual; it almost put me to sleep. Right there in the courtroom. He discussed how his grandparents going back to 1925 went to artists' flea markets, garage sales, and yard sales. He said they bought so many paintings and artist's tools that they had to rent a storage room in their apartment building to hold their collection. He mentioned his grandfather had served in the Monuments Men and his task. He said he inherited the contents of the storage room when his grandfather passed. At first I thought his testimony was the paradigmatic example of double-talk. When he finished, I realized where he was going. He was planting the seed that his grandfather had stolen the painting, and that it had passed to him through the laws of inheritance.

Judge Edelman gave voice to the conclusion we had all reached: Lombroso's grandfather had swiped the painting and taken it back to the US as war spoils.

Lombroso denied that his grandfather had taken the painting. We thought Lombroso was lying to protect his grandfather's reputation. In retrospect, it was his one true statement.

Spiegler objected. The judge overruled it. "What's the difference? This is a bench trial which you asked for. I'll weigh the evidence and not the conclusion of the witnesses. For the record, I place no weight on Mr. Bryant's ipse dixit. No. I'm going to strike Mr. Bryant's conclusion. I'll draw the conclusions. No more conclusions, Mr. Bryant. Do you hear me? Proceed, Mr. Morrison."

I wrote a note to Arlene. *Here comes the napkin bit. Another way to make me feel guilty by inference.*

Nah, Arlene wrote back. *You are guilty of forgery. The only relevant question: Did you make a false statement? So far, we're ahead.*

Bryant drained every drop of blood from the napkin incident. He claimed that I had written on the University Club's property and then stolen it. You would have thought I was on trial for stealing a napkin. Morrison marked the Xeroxed copy of the napkin and moved it into evidence. Bryant read two passages. One where I recite I am selling "my painting in the MoMA exhibition titled in the museum's catalogue as *The Tower of Blue Horses*," and the other, the amount Ray had agreed to pay, $58.75 million. Bryant finished with a conclusion, despite the judge's warning. "By using a napkin instead of waiting for the drafting of a formal contract, Lombroso gave voice to his intent to defraud."

Arlene objected. Judge Keogh sustained the objection and added "by doing what I had asked you not to do, namely state conclusions, you have provided me with an opportunity to comment. The contractual recitals are accurate as far as they go. It was Lombroso's painting, and it did bear that title in the catalogue. I guess you hoped I would focus on the millions gained by Lombroso. In our economic system, it's not a crime to earn millions, unless it's obtained through unlawful activities. Suppose you sell the Brooklyn Bridge for $58.75 million? I'll have to think about that."

Morrison ended his direct. Arlene whispered in my ear she was going to take Bryant on. "The judge doesn't like him. Now's the right time and the right witness to unleash the tapes."

Spiegler: Mr. Bryant, since you represent MoMA, I assume you are more familiar than the average lawyer with the tools of the artist. Don't bother to answer. We'll find out by your answers to the next few questions. Do you know that canvas, the blank surface painted upon by artists, comes in rolls? Some as large as three hundred feet? Yes or no.

Bryant: I know artists paint on canvas. I know it comes in rolls. I believe the artists cut the canvas to the size of their paintings.

Spiegler: Very good, Mr. Bryant. You are so far passing the test. Do you know the finest grade of canvas is Belgian linen canvas?

Bryant: I don't have personal knowledge, but I have heard about Belgium linen being the preferred canvas for painters.

Spiegler: Good for you, Mr. Bryant. Now I ask you to assume that Mr. Lombroso found a roll of Belgium linen in his grandfather's storage room. Assume further he took the roll to his studio, cut the canvas to the size of Marc's painting then copied the painting, and returned the painting to the storage room. With those assumptions in mind, would either of Mr. Lombroso's statements to Judge Edelman, made under oath in a courtroom, that he found the "canvas" in the storage room and showed the "painting" to Mr. Aritta be perjurious?

Mr. Morrison: The defendant is charged with fraud, not perjury. Mr. Bryant is testifying as a fact witness, not an expert.

Judge Keogh: Mr. Bryant does not have to answer that question. I will. Mr. Lombroso's testimony was plainly misleading, but would not support a charge of perjury. It is the task of the examiner, in this case Judge Edelman, to ask additional questions to ferret out the truth. Does the same rule apply to fraud? Both crimes involve the spoken word. There seems an affinity between the two situations. There is, of course, a preliminary question: Did the defendant in his utterances cross the line between half-truth and false statement? I don't know yet. I will by the time I decide the case.

Spiegler: You criticized Mr. Lombroso for giving testimony which you characterized as being the "paradigmatic example of double-talk." Did you advise Mr. Lombroso to provide Judge Edelman with long-winded answers and to have fun? Yes or no, Mr. Bryant?

Bryant: I don't remember. The lawsuit was ten years ago.

Spiegler: I'm just curious about how selective your memory is. You remember impressions you formed, but not advice you gave? Let's see if I can refresh your memory by reading from the transcript of a tape recorded by Mr. Lombroso. "Nothing you say can affect the case. Give the judge long-winded answers. Have fun."

Bryant: Yes it does, but notice the context. Nothing that Lombroso could say can affect the case.

Spiegler: Was that your honest opinion then and is it your opinion today? Nothing Mr. Lombroso could testify to can affect the Lemberg case? Don't bother to answer. I don't want you to speculate. You are under oath. No further questions.

Morrison: Your Honor if Ms. Spiegler has tapes of conversations with other witnesses, I ask that they be turned over or she be barred from using them. Trial by ambush is not a fair tactic.

Judge Keogh: No, no. She has no obligation to turn documents over to you. If you wish to avert surprise, instruct your witnesses to testify truthfully and to sharpen their memories. Who is your next witness?

Morrison: My next witness, Your Honor, is Jay Winston.

Morrison explored Winston's curriculum vitae. Some of the high points: He served as chairman of the board of realtors for an unprecedented term of ten years—prior to his term the longest was five years; he served as an advisor to two presidents, one a Republican, George H, W. Bush, and the other a Democrat, Bill Clinton on federal programs to subsidize low and middle-income housing. He presently serves as chairman of the board of the Metropolitan Museum of Art, a director of the Metropolitan Opera and on the boards of philanthropic organizations ranging from the Boy Scouts of America to The Society of the Cincinnati.

I was impressed, so was Arlene, but not the judge. "Are you preparing to certify Mr. Winston as an expert witness?" When Morrison said no, the judge, dripping with sarcasm, said: "Even I have heard of Mr. Winston. Didn't you run for mayor of New York?" When Winston said he did, the judge, visibly annoyed, asked Morrison "to get on with Mr. Winston's eyewitness testimony."

Morrison: When, for the first time, did you meet Mr. Lombroso and what were the circumstances?

Winston: It was shortly after the decision in the Lemberg case. I've been active in seeking the return of Nazi-looted art and followed the case. My museum was interested in acquiring Franz Marc's great masterpiece. Once a court determined ownership, I called Mr. Lombroso and invited him to lunch. I suggested he give thought to donating the painting to the Met. He said he was not a rich man and the painting was his only valuable possession. We discussed Franz Marc, his work as an artist and printmaker, and the important place he occupies among his generation of painters despite his short life.

Marc died in his mid-thirties as a soldier fighting for Germany in World War I. Because of the time he spent in the army and his untimely death, there are not many of his paintings extant. *The Tower of Blue Horses* represents the high-water mark of his oeuvre. I said that the *Blue Horses* could sell for as much as $50 million, but because of the absence of provenance, the painting Mr. Lombroso owned would have to be authenticated by the most exacting testing standards. I don't recall anything more being said.

Judge Keogh: The painting you say is worth $50 million if authenticated. If it's not, what's it worth?

Winston: Nothing. Well, maybe a token sum.

Judge Keogh: I don't get it. The same picture if it's authentic is worth $50 million. If not, a subway token. Do aesthetics count for nothing?

Winston: Art does not have intrinsic value; value is socially constructed. In society's judgment if a painting is a forgery, it is worthless even if the forged painting is more aesthetically pleasing than the original.

Judge Keogh: Before meeting with Mr. Lombroso, did you see the painting in the MoMA exhibition?

Winston: Yes. The Met's curator and I inspected the painting. To the naked eye, it appeared to be the masterpiece.

Judge Keogh: How prevalent are forgeries?

Winston: As prices for art have skyrocketed, fakes and forgeries have become more common. Fakes are paintings made to resemble existing ones; forgeries are works passed off as the original. An example of a fake are the many Rembrandt paintings signed by him, but painted in his style by students working in his studio. Of the approximately six hundred and fifty paintings bearing Rembrandt's signature, only two hundred and fifty are believed to have been painted by him.

Here's another example, even more striking: In 1916, an artist R.A. Blakelock was the rage. In that year, one hundred paintings claiming to be Blakelock's flooded the market. Only one of the hundred turned out to be genuine.

It's not only works falsely attributed to important artists that turn out to be fakes or forgeries, fakes of unattributed works are numerous. Although I don't know who or where, the odds are that at this very moment some craftsman in Mexico is making a pre-Columbian relic. The odds are also good that the work will wind up in a museum, possibly the Met.

Judge Keogh: How foolproof are the tests? How certain are they to detect forgeries?

Winston: It depends. Take the present painting. We know it's a forgery. If we didn't, could tests unmask it? The dyes or pigments used by the German expressionists were of excellent quality. If Mr. Lombroso used modern paints instead of the pigments of the period, tests would find the painting inauthentic. German paints of the early twentieth century are still around, and as vivid today as the day they were made. If Mr. Lombroso used the paints at Franz Marc's time, the expert's task would be more difficult.

Canvas is another variable. If the forger used linen similar to that used by Marc, the expert's task would be made more difficult. Another variable is stroke. Great artists paint with different strokes. An expert well versed in an artist's style could distinguish between an original and a fake or forgery. As the expert moves from objective to subjective tests, the conclusion becomes less certain.

Judge Keogh: You purchased Claude Monet's Water Lilies and contributed it to the Met. Did you have it authenticated either before you purchased it or donated it to the Met?

Winston: I'd like to supplement my prior answer. There is one certain test of authenticity: an unbroken chain of ownership. In the case of my purchase of Monet's painting, there was an unbroken line of ownership from 1919 to the time of my purchase. Suspicion arises only when the line of ownership is interrupted. In the case of the *Blue Horses*, there was a fifty-year hiatus.

Judge Keogh: Mr. Morrison spent so much time developing your credentials as an expert, I decided to take advantage of your expertise. Thank you, Mr. Winston, for your help.

When Morrison said he had no more questions for the witness, Judge Keogh called for a thirty-minute recess "to provide for our needs and to allow Ms. Spiegler time to collect her notes."

During the recess, Arlene said, "There was one point we needed to put in the record, namely that Winston asked for a ninety-day option to buy your painting at $50 million. That's what you told Ray. What better way to get it in the record than through the horse's mouth. Otherwise there's nothing else to cross. He didn't hurt you."

When trial resumed Spiegler asked Winston whether he recalled telling Mr. Lombroso "in plain, un-adjectival language" that he wanted a ninety-day option to purchase his painting at $50 million? When he said he had no independent recollection, Spiegler read from the tape. "Now you must show your good faith and grant me a ninety-day option to purchase the painting at $50 million."

Winston said if it's on the tape, he said it, but he had no independent recollection.

Judge Keogh pointed his finger at Spiegler and said: "Mr. Winston does not recall asking for an option. Reading a truncated statement doesn't help him and doesn't help me. The use of the word 'now' shows that something preceded the offer of the option. Read it and see whether the complete statement refreshes Mr. Winston's recollection."

Arlene had no choice. She opened the door and Judge Keogh would not allow her to slam it shut.

Spiegler read: "Sold for $50 million dollars to Jay Winston."

She continued reading. "Not so fast. *The Blue Horses* has been missing for fifty years. Only a damn fool would buy your painting without first putting it through an authentication process. It consists of tests and expert opinions based on the results and subjective judgments. The procedure is expensive and time consuming.

It might take as long as sixty days. You should bear the cost since you as the owner are benefitted by a favorable outcome. To show my good faith, I'll pay all the expenses and turn over the results to you. Now you must show your good faith and grant me a ninety-day option to purchase the painting at $50 million."

Winston said his recollection was refreshed. He apologized to Arlene and the court for not recalling it on his direct or immediately on cross. "The conversation occurred more than ten years ago."

Arlene said she had no further questions. The judge thanked Winston. I was worried; so far Winston was the only witness the judge had thanked. Arlene said it was a courtesy extended to a rich and famous citizen.

The next witness was none other than Harry S. Edelman, the judge who had presided over Ms. Lemberg's case. Judge Keogh stepped down from the bench and shook Judge Edelman's hand. "Welcome to my courtroom. You were always welcoming to me when I appeared before you."

"You were the brightest assistant DA to appear in my court-room, and according to the record in your contentious confirmation hearing, possibly the most able ever. I liked having you appear before me. I sensed that if I followed your lead, I would not be reversed. I'm glad you were elevated to the bench, but I wish you had become a state court judge and stayed with us where you belonged and not crossed the street to the fancy federal district court. In fairness, though, if Senator Javits, whom I knew quite well, had suggested me for the federal court I would have jumped."

Judge Keogh returned to the bench and signaled Morrison to begin his direct.

When Morrison asked a question about the Lemberg case, Judge Keogh interrupted. "We heard all about the trial from Mr. Bryant. If I need more information, I'll order the transcript. Please move to the issue in this case. Frankly, since Judge Edelman wasn't asked to pony up $50 million for the painting, I don't see what relevance his testimony can have."

Morrison asked about the circumstances that caused Judge Edelman to take the unusual step of calling a lawyer representing a party as the court's witness and questioning him.

"Mr. Lombroso was not representing a third party, but himself. I would not otherwise have made him a witness. Additionally, the parties had concluded their presentation when I called Mr. Lombroso. The evidence established that the painting was in the possession of Hermann Goering in 1945 and then mysteriously disappeared for fifty years. It was now in my courtroom having been moved from the museum. A distinguished expert, a Rhodes Scholar, and a professor at Harvard had declared the painting to be the missing masterpiece.

"Where was it all these years? A judge, like Diogenes, searches for the truth. Sitting in my courtroom was the one man who could supply the answer. I put him on the witness stand and asked the $64 question: 'How did you come into possession of the painting?' He took almost an hour to answer.

"Judges are trained to listen. From his rambling testimony, I discerned he was covering up a theft committed by his grandfather. I announced my conclusion in open court, but softened it because I did not want to hurt his feelings. 'Mr. Lombroso's grandfather,' I said, 'saved the painting by bringing it home to America.'

"Mr. Lombroso fooled me. I hope he serves a long time in jail."

Spiegler objected, but before she could finish making her objection, Judge Keogh ruled he was striking all of Judge Edelman's testimony.

"This case is not about perjury in your court but about fraud in the marketplace. It's an improbable stretch from your courtroom to the market. I will not make that journey...Mr. Morrison, who is your next witness? I hope he has some connection with the issue before me."

"Cecil Ray, Your Honor, is my next witness."

"It's about time the central figure appeared. We've had a long day. Court is adjourned until ten tomorrow."

Judge Keogh exited from the courtroom without a nod to Judge Edelman who blurted out: "Damn. That smug Irishman is wrong. My testimony was relevant. I hope he gets reversed on appeal."

SIXTEEN

The judge criticized Morrison for delving into Winston's credentials. He did not repeat his error. He asked no questions about Ray's educational background or business activities, but went, without preamble, to the central issue. Ray testified that he became aware of my painting when his wife showed him a newspaper account of the Lemberg case. "She suggested we meet at MoMA, see the exhibition, and then have dinner at the University Club. 'It's Wednesday,' she said. 'The club has its seafood buffet which you love and I hate. Come with me to the museum and I won't say a single unpleasant word about the amount of food you gobble.'

"We saw the exhibition. To our untrained eyes, the painting seemed like the greatest painting we had ever seen. My wife said we must buy it. 'It would look great in our apartment. If it hung in our living room, I bet no one would look at the view of the park. If you can't afford it, we can sell our country home in Southampton, sell my jewelry, and forego trips to Europe and Asia. That's how strongly I feel about the painting. What good is money if we can't have what truly matters—art.'

"The next day I called Lombroso, and we agreed to have lunch at the University Club."

Morrison: What, if anything, did Mr. Lombroso tell you about the painting?

Ray: He said Jay Winston, a renowned art collector had offered to buy the painting for $50 million. He also said Winston would donate the painting to the Met. Winston holds the painting in such high regard, he would guarantee it would be on view for at least one month every year. Lombroso said if he sold the painting to Winston, he would not be parting with it as he could see it by going to the Met. "As the owner of the painting, the most I can do is look at it. If I sell it to Winston, I can eat my cake and have it too. I can pocket $50 million and look at Franz Marc's great painting during the hours the Met is open and the painting is on display. If I sell it to a third party, such as you, I'll never see the painting again."

I squirmed. *That lying bastard. My life's at stake and he's fabricating.* Arlene sensed my anguish. She wrote me a note. *We got the tape. The more he stretches the truth, the better off we are. Relax.* When she put down her pen, she stroked my knee.

Morrison: Did Mr. Lombroso say unequivocally that Jay Winston had agreed to purchase the painting for $50 million?

Ray: Yes.

Morrison: Did Lombroso refer to the painting as a work by Franz Marc?

Ray: Of course he did. My actions confirm his claims. I agreed to pay $50 million plus the tax on the tax. I agreed to sign a contract drawn by Lombroso on a napkin, of all things. I agreed to waive my lawyer's review of the contract. I also agreed to waive testing. Finally, I agreed to close immediately. Why? I didn't want Winston to buy the painting and then have to face my wife's wrath. I didn't want to act rashly, but felt I had no choice if I wanted the painting.

Judge Keogh: Were you aware that MoMA referred to the painting as being of the school of Franz Marc, and did you know what that designation meant?

Ray: I thought then the designation meant the painting is in the style of Franz Marc, but may or may not be by him. On the other hand, the painting was included in the exhibition, and an expert witness, an art historian called by MoMA, testified at the Lemberg trial that the painting was genuine. If MoMA had doubts as to the painting's authenticity why did it come forward with a witness who said it was genuine? The icing on the cake was Winston's willingness to buy the painting. I knew Winston was an expert in the field. If he wanted the painting, it must be genuine. I also didn't want to get into a bidding war with him and was relieved to close the deal right then and there.

Morrison: Do you still own the painting?

Ray: No. My wife, now my ex-wife, was the collector, not me. She declared the painting "old stuff." Contemporary art was now her main interest. "Sell the painting so that we can make room for what's happening today. The four old horses are jarring when hung anywhere near modern art. The world has moved on so should we." I tried to sell the painting for sixty million. The price wasn't a problem. Every potential buyer wanted to subject the painting to tests; none were willing to buy it as is, on trust as I had done. I contacted Jay Winston. Told him my wife was into modern art. He could now buy the Franz Marc painting. During my conversation with Winston, I learned, for the first time, he had not made an unconditional offer to buy the painting, but that his offer was subject to testing. He said the painting would have to be thoroughly tested, and if it passed the tests, he was not prepared to pay anything near the $60 million I was asking.

A good friend told me a test would subject me to a risk. "Suppose the painting failed the test? It would become worthless. You don't need the money. Get the painting appraised at $100 million and donate it to MoMA. You can then take a $100 million deduction that can be spread over five years. The museum might even make you a trustee. I know a master appraiser, Eric Goodwin. For a $10,000 fee, he'll appraise your painting at $100 million. Goodwin has a good reputation. The IRS will accept his appraisal; indeed it has employed him. All you have to do is get the museum to accept the painting. A no-brainer for any museum."

I got the appraisal and MoMA agreed to accept the painting and offered to make me a trustee. I declined. My wife's the collector, not me. The museum named her to its board.

Judge Keogh: The painting, whose authenticity had not been established and about which MoMA had doubts some ten years earlier, is appraised at $100 million. You, who couldn't sell the painting for a mere $60 million without tests, donate the painting and take a $100 million tax deduction. The winner is Michael Lombroso, but you're not the victim—the American taxpayer is. Did you tell the appraiser you were trying to sell the painting for $60 million, but there were no takers, at least no takers without tests? Did you tell the appraiser Winston would not buy the painting for anywhere near $60 million even if it passed the test?

Ray: Goodwin has forgotten more about art than I will ever know. If he didn't think the painting was worth $100 million, he shouldn't have appraised it at that price. As far as tests are concerned, what do I know? The appraiser is in the business. If a test were required before accepting my gift, it was up to the museum to suggest it. To answer your questions, I didn't think it was up to me to tell Goodwin or the museum what it should or shouldn't do.

Judge Keogh: The reason I ask, Judge Edelman said I should hang Mr. Lombroso for nondisclosure of facts, some of which you did not disclose when you unloaded the painting. Maybe the custom prevalent in the art world, not the law, should govern this case.

Morrison: There's a difference between the two transactions. Mr. Lombroso sold the painting to Mr. Ray for $58.75 million; Mr. Ray gave the painting to MoMA.

Judge Keogh: There is a difference between the two transactions, but Mr. Ray didn't just gift the painting to MoMA, he insisted on a quid, a $100 million tax deduction. There's another difference. Mr. Ray is not on trial for defrauding MoMA.

The judge's comment satisfied Morrison; he decided not to push the matter any further. He informed the court that his direct of Ray was concluded and turned the witness over to Spiegler.

Arlene had told me it was important to establish the obvious: Ray was a sophisticated investor, and we had dealt at arm's length. She delved into his educational background—a bachelor's in business at the Wharton School at the University of Pennsylvania and an MBA at Harvard Business School.

Judge Keogh interrupted. "Why is this necessary? More bluntly, what does Mr. Ray's educational background—and I suppose you intend to question him on his business activities—have to do with this case?"

She responded, "The level of Mr. Ray's business experience will affect the law to be applied. I believe when the trial is over, Your Honor will find Mr. Lombroso spoke truthfully as far as technical truth can be regarded as true. Some of his statements amount to what the law sometimes calls a half-truth because he omitted material facts. The law is not absolute in condemning half-truths. In perjury cases, a witness who testifies under oath in a misleading fashion cannot be charged with perjury. If his testimony is misleading or not responsive to the question asked, he has not committed perjury. Rather, it is the duty of the examiner to further interrogate the witness to obtain a responsive answer, an unambiguous answer, or a false statement, which will form the basis of a charge of perjury.

"The law on perjury has carried over to the law of criminal fraud. The courts will examine the relationship of the parties. Are they dealing at arm's length? Does one party bear a fiduciary duty to the other, arising from trust and confidence reposed by one in the other, or imposed by operation of the law? Are both parties sophisticated so that one cannot sit back and expect to be spoon-fed all relevant information, but must exercise due diligence in uncovering the relevant facts? Are there suspicious circumstances, red flags that should put a party on notice? A spectrum or continuum exists: where the parties fit determine the amount of disclosure required.

"On this point, I agree with Mr. Ray. He was under no duty to enlighten MoMA as to facts it knew or could have learned through the exercise of due diligence."

Judge Keogh said, "To my mind there is a difference between the two transactions: one is a sale and the other a gift. I'll allow you to develop Mr. Ray's business experience. I'm not ready to rule it's relevant or irrelevant."

Spiegler established that Ray was a managing partner at Morgan Stanley. He left the firm to start his own hedge fund, which currently had assets of $6 billion. His income last year as a general partner of the hedge fund was $200 million. He said he was also a limited partner of the fund and his account "when I last looked at it was about $100 million. It fluctuates daily so it could be more or less, but that's the range." He said he owned a penthouse on Fifth Avenue, a home in Southampton, and a home in Palm Beach. He was also a limited partner in real-estate syndications. He didn't know the current value, but said he had paid about $10 million for the interests.

Spiegler asked about his non-business interests. He was on the Board of Governors of the New York Stock Exchange, an adjunct professor at Columbia Business School, and an adviser to President Clinton on economic matters.

Spiegler had made her point. Ray was a sophisticated businessman who could look out for his own interests. She next turned to her examination in chief.

Spiegler: Were you aware that Mr. Lombroso taped the entire conversation you had that day at lunch?

Ray: No, I was not.

Spiegler: I, too, believed you were not, because your testimony is at odds with what was said.

Morrison: Your Honor, before we begin with the tapes, Mr. Lombroso is a lawyer. The law prohibits a lawyer from taping a conversation without putting the other party on notice. May I ask a preliminary question on voir dire limited to whether Mr. Ray was aware his conversation was being taped?

Judge Keogh: You may not. Mr. Ray has already testified he was not aware. Ms. Spiegler, I wondered when you were questioning Mr. Winston whether you had the right to use the tapes. Enlighten me nunc pro tunc.

Spiegler: The tapes, under present circumstances, may not be used to establish what was said. They can be used to refute what a witness said if the testimony is inaccurate. May I hand Your Honor a memorandum of law on the point?

Judge Keogh: Yes, you may. We'll take a brief recess. Please give a copy to Mr. Morrison. Your point, I take it. It's in your opening sentence: "The tapes can be used as a shield, but not as a sword."

After the recess, the judge ruled the tapes could be used to refute Mr. Ray's testimony. Spiegler offered the transcript of the tape of my lunch with Ray into evidence. In view of the court's ruling, Morrison did not object and the transcript was received into evidence.

Spiegler: You testified that Mr. Lombroso represented that Mr. Winston had offered $50 million for the painting. Now that you have had the opportunity to read the transcript, was the testimony you gave on this point truthful?

Ray: The conversation took place more than ten years ago. I testified to the impression I had formed at the time. I believed Winston had offered $50 million. Now I see Lombroso said Winston had asked for a ninety-day option at $50 million. An option and an offer are closely related. The impression created was that the painting was worth $50 million. It's a difference without a distinction.

Judge Keogh: There is a distinction. If Mr. Lombroso said Winston had made an outright offer of $50 million, the statement would be false. If he said, as he apparently did, Winston asked for a ninety-day option, the utterance is a half-truth. Misleading to be sure, but not an outright falsehood. The statement is misleading because Lombroso omitted an important qualifier: Winston needed the ninety days to have the painting tested. Whether half-truths arise to the level of criminal fraud is the very issue I will decide.

Spiegler: You testified that Mr. Lombroso referred to the painting as the work of Franz Marc. Was that testimony truthful when given?

Ray: Well, according to the tape, he didn't mention Franz Marc, but, he sure implied as much. Why were we talking about $50 million if the painting was not Marc's masterpiece? Look, I don't care what he said, he created the impression that the painting was a great work of art, not a forgery.

Spiegler asked Ray whether he harbored doubts about "Mr. Lombroso's good faith" at the time he agreed to purchase the painting. When Ray said no, Spiegler read from the tape: "I like you, Lombroso, even though you may be taking me for a ride."

Ray: I was being funny. That's my sense of humor.

Spiegler: Was it you, Mr. Ray, who offered to make Mr. Lombroso a "fast deal"?

Ray: Yes, but that was to protect myself against Winston tying up the painting either through an option or an offer.

Keogh: Mr. Ray, before you buy a stock, do you engage in independent research? Do you analyze the financial statements filed with the SEC? Do you meet with management? Would you buy a stock because you heard a competitor was buying that same stock?

Ray: We do our own analysis before making an investment. If, however, I had information that Warren Buffet was buying a stock, I might try to buy some stock depending upon whether the price had already moved. I equated Jay Winston in art with Warren Buffet in securities. I was offering approximately what Winston was offering.

Keogh: Except Winston was not making an unconditional offer. Forgive me, we're just going round in circles. Please continue, Ms. Spiegler.

Spiegler: Didn't you suspect the painting might not be authentic?

Ray: Not at all. Do you think I would have paid $58.75 million for a painting I thought might be a forgery?

Spiegler: I'll answer your question with a question. When your wife instructed you to sell the painting, didn't you make a conscious effort to avoid buyers who wanted to test the painting for authenticity? Please answer yes or no if you can.

Ray: I can't answer yes or no. I paid the full price for the genuine *Tower of Blue Horses*. I had nothing to gain from tests establishing the authenticity of the painting and a lot to lose.

Spiegler: Isn't it true that you thought the risk the painting was a fake was so real that rather than have the painting tested and sold for $60 million, you chose instead to give it away?

Ray: No. The tax benefit was almost the same as the net benefit from a sale and a lot easier to effect.

Spiegler ended her cross of Ray and Morrison rested his case.

It was now my turn to testify.

SEVENTEEN

Day after day, in preparation for trial, Spiegler and I worked on my testimony. She asked a question and I answered. Often she reworded the question until she got the answer she wanted. Only then did she dictate her question and my answer. "We could save time if I recorded the questions and the answers I wanted from you, but then your testimony might sound too structured. If the answers are in your words, what you say may sound natural, depending on your delivery. Also, there's less of a chance you'll forget."

When all my answers satisfied Arlene, she had the questions and answers typed and a copy given to me. "I can have the typed questions and answers in front of me; you can have nothing in front of you. Although it is common practice to coach witnesses, the law pretends their testimony is spontaneous. We have to play that game. So, memorize your answers. A slip could be fatal."

As trial neared, Arlene criticized my performance. I was either too emotional or too dry. She called in Robert McAdams, a drama coach. "Make Michael a Willy Loman," she told the coach. "He must sell his case to one tough customer, Judge Keogh."

McAdams advised me to go slow on some answers and quickly on others and marked on my script either andante or allegro. On some answers, he urged me to smile, and on others to look pained. Despite McAdams's efforts, my testimony sounded more stilted than before he had arrived on the scene.

"Arlene," I said, "it's not working. I know the overall plan. I have to tell the whole story, no half-truths, no false statements. I'm throwing my script in the circular file. Let me be free to roam."

We went through the questions again. I answered as though I was at a dinner party telling the story of my crime. Sometimes an answer covered an unasked question; other times, I repeated a previous answer. We liked the result and agreed no more rehearsals.

"I planned to cross-dress," Arlene said. "And pretend I'm Morrison in order to prepare you for his cross examination. You're good at ad-libbing. Instead I'll give you a list of possible questions and let you work out the answers."

At trial, I told my story about as well as my pitiful tale could be told.

The judge asked whether I had remorse for "cheating. I won't use loaded words like 'committing a crime' even though they might apply."

I said, "In the early stages, I weighed the ethics of my conduct but didn't believe I had one chance in a thousand to succeed. Like the thief who attempts to pick the pocket of a statue, my crime was doomed to fail. What were the odds MoMA would hold an exhibition on German expressionist painters, and that my friend and classmate would be in charge? I never could have planned for a Holocaust survivor to claim my recently forged painting had hung in her grandparents' home sixty years earlier. Until the lawsuit, my painting was an orphan, hung all by itself at the far end of the exhibition. After the lawsuit, my painting achieved celebrity status.

"Cecil Ray? In my wildest fantasies, I could not have conceived of a better candidate to buy my painting. A man worth billions of dollars, but lacking an ounce of common sense.

"As the plot unfolded, I was swept along and when it succeeded, well...to answer Your Honor's question, the millions in my bank account assuaged my remorse. Ray would never miss the money, and I planned to use some to help the poor. I thought of myself as a modern-day Robin Hood, not a scoundrel."

Keogh asked, "Did you help the poor? It's one of the privileges of being a judge, I can ask irrelevant questions."

"Yes, through a program called Chess-in-the-Schools, I helped about fifty black kids stuck in the ghetto to get out, go on to college, and become productive members of society. I did it more for myself than for them. I'm not married and have no family, not even a sister or brother. These kids became my family. They filled a gap in my life. None of it is relevant to the case so I'll shut up about my good deeds, unless Your Honor wishes to hear more about them."

"Not now, but if you come up for sentencing, I'll want to know more about your work with the black children."

There was something I read into the judge's expression. I thought he liked me, and the thought emboldened me. I said, "You didn't ask me nor is it, as best as I can recall, among Ms. Spiegler's remaining questions, but I rationalized my act. I wasn't a forger. I was returning a great work of art to the world. I was enriching not only myself, but the world at large."

I spotted Arlene grimacing, but it was too late. Judge Keogh pounced. "Did you still feel you had performed a public service when the Hermitage revealed it held the original?"

"I felt disgusted," I said, "but only for myself, and cursed my choice of painting. I had considered forging *War Cripples* by Otto Dix, before deciding upon the *Blue Horses*. I might have escaped detection if I had chosen Dix over Marc."

The judge asked whether it was difficult to forge a painting. "The genius," I said, "lies in creating the work. Any journeyman artist can copy a painting. What the run-of-the-mill painter can't do is what Marc and Dix and hundreds of other geniuses can do: conceive of the painting. Your Honor asked Mr. Winston how prevalent fakes and forgeries are. He said there are many. I'll supply the reason: it's not difficult for one painter to copy the work of another."

I finished my direct at the lunch break. When we returned I anticipated a grueling cross-examination. For lunch I had a bowl of soup and crackers. Nothing else. My stomach and I were ready.

In his cross, Morrison harped on my concealment of the forgery by making misleading statements. He read the half-truths from the tapes and then added the omitted facts. He followed with a question that pieced my heart like a dagger.

Morrison: As a first step in your scheme to defraud, you abused your friendship with Anthony Aritta. You led him to your grandfather's storage room and showed him the painting you had made several months earlier. In that dark, dank subterranean room, he thought he recognized the painting as a Franz Marc. In all innocence he asked, "Where did you get the painting?" You replied, "I found the canvas right here in my grandparents' storage room." Had you told your friend the truth as honor obliged you to do, you would have added: "It was a blank canvas when I found it. I reproduced the *Blue Horses* on the blank canvas."

Do you agree, Mr. Lombroso, if you had told your friend the truth, your scheme would have ended as abruptly as the attempt by the thief to pick the pocket of the statue?

It hurt to answer by admitting his proposition, and thereby, confessing that one truthful answer would have sunk my scheme. Spiegler, however, had warned against arguing with Morrison. "Keogh will side with Morrison who's doing his job of trapping a forger." I followed her advice and answered "yes."

Morrison was relentless. He went on to the second half-truth.

Morrison: Mr. Lombroso, you are a lawyer and a member of the bar. As an officer of the court, you have a duty to speak the truth. Your duty is heightened when addressing the court. You and your painting were in Judge Edelman's courtroom. The judge asked you: "How did this magnificent painting come into your possession?" You played fast and loose with the judge and replied, "I found the canvas in the storage room." Had you told Judge Edelman what you were obligated to do, to wit, that you had painted the picture on the canvas, the mystery of the origin of the painting would have been revealed in all its stark significance.

Once again, I had no choice. I bowed my head and answered "yes."

Morrison: Now we come to your critical meeting with Cecil Ray. To persuade him to buy your painting for $58.75 million, you claimed: "Jay Winston, with whom I have recently met, said the *Blue Horses* would likely sell for fifty million dollars. He asked for a ninety-day option to buy my painting at that price." What Mr. Winston said was much different from what you represented. He said: "*The Blue Horses* has been missing for fifty years. Only a damn fool would buy your painting without first putting it through an authentication process."

Do you agree your chances of selling the painting would have ended if Ray, like Winston, had insisted on testing the painting?

This time I wanted to argue with Morrison. Ray's wife instructed him to buy the painting. He was pussy whipped. He had to buy the painting or face his wife's wrath. Then I looked at Arlene. She sensed what I was planning to say and was shaking her head and glaring at me. What could I do? I answered "yes."

Morrison asked if I had forged Otto Dix's painting and the forgery had gone undetected, would my crime have been any less heinous? I answered my crime would have been equally reprehensible regardless of whether it had been discovered.

My defenselessness won some sympathy from the judge. He asked whether my namesake Michelangelo "would stoop to forge another's works?" It was a softball question.

"My grandfather and father were also named Michael Angelo. We were proud of the association. My grandfather owned a biography of the great Michelangelo. The book reported that Michelangelo tested his skills by sculpting an ancient Greek work. He then passed off the work as the original."

Keogh asked how much Michelangelo received for the sculpture and whether he suffered any consequences. I said the biography was silent on both points.

"Well then," the judge said with a big grin, "you can't cite Michelangelo's acts as a precedent. I'm sorry for the interruption. Please proceed, Mr. Morrison."

Morrison: You tried to adhere to a practice of speaking half-truths. But you, Mr. Lombroso, made a mistake. Mr. Ray asked a follow-up question to one of your misleading half-truths and trapped you. Your answer to the follow-up was false, not a half-truth, but a 100 percent pure fabrication deliberately made to turn Mr. Ray off the scent. Do you know what I am referring to?

I said I did not. Morrison said Ray asked what Winston had offered to pay for a ninety-day option and quoted from the tape:

> "Winston's a shrewd businessman. A ninety-day option on a $50 million object is worth about $5 million. What did Winston agree to pay?"
>
> "Nothing."

That, Mr. Lombroso, was a lie. Mr. Winston said, in exchange for the ninety-day option, he would pay the cost of the authentication process, an expense you should rightfully bear. Mr. Winston also agreed to turn over the results of the tests and the opinions of the experts to you without charge. Do you wish me to read the applicable part of the tape?

I said it wasn't necessary. "You have fairly summarized it. My legal experience is in real estate. Options are a common tool. The party seeking the option pays cash to the grantor. I don't recall a single transaction in which an option was granted for anything but a cash consideration.

"Mr. Winston wanted an option and offered to pay for it with an act having value to him, but not to me. I knew the painting was a forgery. I painted it. He needed tests to decide whether to purchase the painting. The authentication process was for his benefit, not mine."

Keogh: Throughout the trial, you have been skating on thin ice. One slip and you fall in the drink. From your perspective, tests were not only worthless, but were of negative value. If the tests disclosed the painting was a forgery, the game was up. I wonder whether your subjective approach to value is controlling. In answer to one of my questions, Winston estimated the cost at about $50,000. In his exalted world, $50,000 is petty cash; in mine, it is serious money.

Every law student learns about the "reasonable man test." He exists, not only in Academe, but in decisions in which the judge seeks an objective standard against which to measure a party's conduct. Would a reasonable man consider bearing the cost of testing to be nothing? That depends upon whether our artificial construct is a forger or an honest man? What Winston Churchill said about Russia I'll say about the issue you have posed: "It is a riddle, wrapped in a mystery, inside an enigma."

Shortly thereafter my testimony ended. It marked the end of the trial. The judge set a briefing schedule and suggested closing arguments would be more helpful if made after briefs had been exchanged. He set argument for two weeks after the last brief had been served. The judge thanked both attorneys for their excellent presentations. "My indecisiveness is a reflection of the odd circumstances of the case. The victim was not harmed. A fraud, however, was committed. The defendant forged a painting and passed it off as an original work. Does he escape liability if all his statements were technically true, but misleading, for the very reasons Mr. Morrison pointed out? I'll be in a better position to answer the question when we next meet.

"I am also troubled by the custom of the marketplace. Ray was tricky. He sought an appraised value of $100 million without disclosing he would have happily sold the painting for $60 million. He, too, was unwilling to sell to anyone who would insist on tests. Just as Lombroso found Ray, Ray found Goodwin. A painting the museum refused to credit to Franz Marc, and had doubts about its authenticity he appraised at $100 million. Is dishonesty part of the culture of the art world?

"Now you know what is troubling this judge. I hope your briefs and arguments will not only address these issues, but put a sharp focus on them."

EIGHTEEN

I read the briefs and was convinced I would lose. Morrison's brief convinced me that I had committed the crime charged in the indictment. The brief emphasized my acts and downplayed what I said. I forged a painting and passed it off as an original. "His acts constituted a willful fraud. His defense: he didn't commit a crime because his representations were merely misleading, not outright falsehoods. Even if one were to assume misleading statements are a complete defense to the crime—a preposterous assumption—the facts are at odds with the defense."

He then dissected each of what I claimed were half-truths and argued they were blatant lies. "In the art world, the word 'canvas' is another way of referring to a painting. If the defendant had said, he found the painting in his grandparents' storage room, he would have been convicted the second the trial ended. Should the result be any different because he used a word that has a double meaning?"

Morrison conceded that a perfect crime could be committed, but argued that this case was not one. "The defendant has admitted he reproduced Franz Marc's masterpiece and placed it in his grandparents' storage room. He sold it for $58.75 million. Is he to be exonerated because he called the forged painting a canvas and not a painting?"

Spiegler's brief was weak. Her principal argument rested on line drawing. "The criminal law," she argued, "must state with exacting specificity the acts comprising the crime. There is no room for liberal interpretation. If the act does not satisfy literally every element of the crime, a crime has not been committed. Criminal fraud requires a material false statement. If one was not made, the crime of fraud has not been committed." She analyzed my statements concluding each was a half-truth, a technically true statement.

She urged Judge Keogh to avoid the trap set by the government. "If the law should be amended then under the Constitution the task falls to the legislative body and not to the judiciary."

For eight years, I had spent two days a week teaching chess to students at Alexander Hamilton High School located in Harlem. The principal, Bradley Taitt, was a chess player and worked with me in developing student interest in chess. The stress of the trial made it difficult for me to keep to my prior schedule. I told Taitt that I had been indicted and the nature of the case against me. I asked for a leave of absence until the case was over.

Taitt called several times to encourage me to fight on. His most recent call occurred after the briefs had been exchanged. I predicted I would be convicted and sent to jail for many years. He asked for my lawyer's phone number. Arlene told me he called and wanted to fire off a letter to the judge. "I told him letters are helpful when it comes time for sentencing."

Taitt rejected her advice. "I'm a chess player. It makes no sense making a move after your king has been mated. I'm writing to the judge now." Arlene gave him the judge's name and address and asked for a copy of the letter.

Taitt's letter provided a lift to my morale. I was not all bad, although Spiegler claimed the letter was premature, I agreed with Taitt. The judge had introduced the subject of my work with black children during the course of the trial. Why wait until after he ruled to supply character evidence. The letter is set forth below:

Dear Judge Keogh,

I am the principal of Alexander Hamilton High School located at 145th Street in New York City. I have been principal since 2001. I write on behalf of Michael Angelo Lombroso. My purpose in writing this letter is to inform you of a part of Mr. Lombroso's life you might otherwise be unaware of.

When I arrived at Alexander Hamilton, it was among the lowest-rated high schools in New York City. Attendance was poor, the students disengaged and underperforming. More dropped out than graduated. In the prior ten years, not a single student applied to college, not even to a community or technical school.

I am a chess player and believe the fundamentals of the game can be applied to areas of life. Chess players are taught to think before they make a move, a process successful people automatically engage in, and one in which our students too often fail to consider. I chose chess as an extracurricular activity to introduce the students to the joy of using one's brain.

I called Chess-in-the-Schools, a not-for-profit organization that sends volunteers to inner-city schools to teach the game, and asked for a volunteer. Michael Lombroso was the volunteer. He agreed to teach chess two days a week.

At the end of Michael's fourth session, the students knew how the pieces moved and the rules of the game. By the end of the eighth session, they had played at least one game.

Michael donated the chess men, boards, and clocks. He requisitioned a room off the main gymnasium and furnished it with tables and chairs. His chess sets, boards, and clocks were stacked in the room, on open shelves. He encouraged the students to play chess during their free time. The basketball coach, who worked in the main gym, had an opportunity to observe students playing chess in the next room. He claimed more were playing chess than basketball, which was a sea change in student attitude. I attributed it to the influence of one man, Michael Angelo Lombroso.

Most of our students are disrespectful of school property. Anything that is not nailed down or placed under lock and key is likely to be stolen. Walls and desks are routinely defaced. The one exception: the chess room. At the end of the day, the chess pieces, boards, and clocks were returned to the shelves. Not a mark was made anywhere in that room.

Michael asked if the school were willing to field a team to compete statewide against other schools. He offered to hire, at his expense, Lev Alburt, an International Grandmaster and three time US chess champion to tutor for two hours twice a week the top six players. Michael said he had talked to the candidates who were eager to form a team, which they had already named the Black Knights. The lessons would take place in the chess room after school hours. All students could watch the lessons, but only the six would be tutored. Michael was present at all the sessions; I, at many. We assisted Lev.

The after-school lessons were well attended. The onlookers, like chess kibitzers throughout the world, suggested moves, but only after the games were over. After six months of training, the Black Knights entered the state competition. The first year they lost more games than they won. It took five years before a team reached the finals and two additional years until the Black Knights won the state championship.

Michael outfitted the team at Brooks Brothers. The uniform consisted of navy blue blazers with Black Knights embroidered over the left pocket, white shirts, gray flannel trousers, and black loafers. The first team was all boys. Later teams, including the championship team, had several female members. Brooks made matching uniforms for them. Being well-dressed, Michael believed, would stimulate a positive state of mind essential to winning.

On many weekends, Michael collected the team and drove them to the Marshall Club. After an afternoon of chess, he took the team to his home for dinner. I was a frequent guest on those weekend trips. The team reveled in a world outside the ghetto.

Of the original six members of the Black Knights, every single one went on to college. None could afford the expense. Each got a full scholarship awarded by Michael, plus a new wardrobe, and a generous monthly check to cover personal expenses. The tradition begun by the Black Knights continued through each successive team. All went to college, some to Ivy League schools, all at Michael's expense.

New York State grades each school. A "D" is the lowest grade; an "A" is the highest. Within five years, my school progressed from a D to a B. No other school had improved so quickly.

Michael was not the only one who made our progress possible. I believe, however, without Michael's dedication, my school might not have moved out of the rabbit's hole.

I hope and pray you will not imprison Mr. Lombroso, but if you do, may it not be for very long. Alexander Hamilton High School needs him.

Very truly yours,
Bradley Taitt

The night before the scheduled argument, I took two sleeping pills. The next morning I worked out in the gym, swam, and ate a bowl of oatmeal and two poached eggs. I arrived in Judge Keogh's courtroom at 9:30, a half hour before the scheduled argument. Spiegler and Morrison were already in their seats. Promptly at ten, Keogh and his two law clerks appeared and took their places. Morrison walked to the podium prepared to make his argument. The judge motioned for him to be seated.

"I received a letter from Bradley Taitt, which on my instructions, copies were provided to you, Mr. Morrison, and to you, Ms. Spiegler. I invited Mr. Taitt to my chambers. We talked for over an hour. Do you know Mr. Lombroso put fifty-four black children through college? He paid tuition, outfitted the young students, and provided a generous monthly check to cover expenses.

"Mr. Lombroso did not just write checks, although he did plenty of that. The average cost of putting a child through college is about $100,000. The cost of fifty-four students amounted to about $5.5 million. Mr. Lombroso gave more than money. He gave love, attention, and a part of himself. He was, Mr. Taitt said, 'a surrogate father to his kids, many of whom lived in homes without a father.' After our meeting, I was convinced Mr. Taitt's letter did not paint the lily, but rather understated the influence Mr. Lombroso had upon the students at Alexander Hamilton High.

"Mr. Morrison, in your brief you call Mr. Lombroso a 'scoundrel.' I think he's closer to a saint. It's not, however, only evil people who commit crimes; many times decent people violate the law. This case is the paradigmatic example of a man of fine moral character committing a crime.

"Ms. Spiegler, I reject your argument that half-truths are insufficient to establish the crime of fraud. When half-truths are deliberately uttered in furtherance of a fraud, they become an integral part of the scheme. More to the point, Mr. Lombroso's claim that he found the canvas in his grandparents' storage room is not, under the circumstances, a half-truth. Paintings are called canvases, and canvases are called paintings. Mr. Lombroso intended Mr. Aritta to believe he found the painting in the storage room, not a blank canvas. Further, Mr. Winston offered something of value for the ninety-day option he sought, not 'nothing' as Lombroso told Ray.

"I want this case settled by way of a guilty plea to a lesser offense. In that way, I can sentence Mr. Lombroso to a short term in prison and stay within the federal sentencing guidelines. You must, Mr. Lombroso, serve a term in prison. Our justice system is wrongly accused of sending poor people to jail, but not the wealthy. The guidelines were drawn to insure that like crimes are treated alike regardless of the criminal's means or race.

"Ms. Spiegler, now that your client's defense has been rejected, you should have no trouble persuading Mr. Lombroso to agree to plead guilty to a lesser charge than the one I have told you I will sustain.

"Mr. Morrison, be magnanimous in victory. Never forget you came close to losing an open-and-shut case.

"I have asked Magistrate Hollins to stand ready to assist both sides in reaching an agreement. He is available tomorrow to meet with you but suggests the attorneys work out some common ground before meeting with him.

"Nothing is scheduled for this courtroom, so if you want to meet here for a preliminary meeting, it is available."

We spent several hours talking. Morrison was not magnanimous. He started with five years in jail and ended with "my minimum three years and six months probation." Arlene contended that six months in jail was probably more than the judge wanted to give.

Morrison sought a fine of $50 million. His office, he claimed, would never agree to a penalty that made it appear that crime pays. We countered with $5 million.

My concern was not with money, but with time in the slammer. I had had the use of Ray's $50 million for thirteen years. During that time, the money had more than doubled, a factor Morrison had failed to calculate. If I paid the fine the government sought, I'd still be left with more than $50 million. I told Arlene "give in on the fine. Make Morrison a hero, but in return fight for six months in jail."

The next day we met with Hollins. He was short, bald, and nervous, biting his fingernails and jumping in and out of his chair. He met separately with Arlene and me and then with Morrison. He told us what we already knew, "Keogh is ready to convict. If I can get you two years, it's a lot better than the seven years under the guidelines for the degree of Lombroso's offense. As far as a fine, Morrison is correct. $50 million is the only figure that makes sense. If you're convicted, the fine will be $50 million plus thirteen years of interest."

I was shaking when we left the room and Morrison took our place. "Relax," Arlene said. "He'll tell Morrison the judge's decision will make Morrison look like a fool since the judge will write that Morrison hadn't pierced the defense. 'Morrison, you'll be the laughing stock of the office. A guy admits to forging a painting and selling it for $58.75 million and you almost lose the case. You'll be reassigned to immigration.' Now I know why they call Hollins, the hammer. Many judges use him because he's so good at forcing a settlement.

"Would you accept a sentence of two years and a $50-million fine? If I can get it, I recommend you grab it. I'll meet with Morrison alone in an empty room after he leaves Hollins's woodshed. He'll be wounded and pliable. Wait for me in the cafeteria. Have a cup of coffee and relax."

Arlene looked drained when she met me in the cafeteria. "Morrison's supervising attorney, John O'Malley, joined us. Since it wasn't his case, he wasn't as hardnosed as Morrison. He agreed to fifteen months and six months of probation. With good behavior, you'll be out in ten months. He refused to hear a counteroffer to jail time. 'The fine is a given,' O'Malley said, 'and fifteen months is the lowest we'll go.'"

"I think we have to take it or leave it. There's no more give on the government's side. My advice? Take it."

"How much time do I have to consider."

"A reasonable time. That means a day or two. Bernie Madoff was sentenced to 150 years. He stole billions; you stole millions. Michael. Take the deal. It's good enough."

The judge was hearing oral argument on a motion to dismiss a complaint. He nodded at us. We took our seats and waited. When the argument was over, the judge asked Spiegler and Morrison to step forward. Morrison outlined the agreement. The judge said if I pleaded guilty to the charge, he would honor our agreement. The judge called in a court reporter. With a push from Spiegler, I pleaded guilty. The judge accepted my plea, waived a presentencing report as unnecessary, and imposed a fine of $50 million, a sentence of fifteen months in prison, and six months' probation.

"Let's see where you are going to spend the next fifteen months," Keogh said. He called the US Marshal's Office. A young man armed with a gun and dressed in a policeman's uniform said there was room in medium security in Butner penitentiary. "Isn't that where Madoff is spending the next 150 years?" Keogh said. "Maybe you'll be lucky and bunk with him. I'll call the warden and put in a good word for you."

The judge ordered me released on my own recognizance, and further ordered that I could self-surrender at Butner. "How much time do you need, Mr. Lombroso, to put your affairs in order?"

"About fifty years?"

The judge did not take kindly to my attempt at humor. "You may have a week, provided you turn your passport over to the Marshal's Office today. Today is Wednesday, August 12. You'll report on August 19, 2009, at 8:00 a.m. at the reception center at Butner. The Marshal's Office will provide directions. A violation will be dealt with severely, including resentencing you to a much longer time in prison.

Arlene was upbeat. I wanted to weep. Was my life over? I thought so.

"A medium security prison is bearable," she said. "No violent prisoners to rape you. I'll arrange for Thomas Thompson, a prison consultant, to meet with you. He has advised celebrities on how to survive in prison. He'll help you."

Thompson came the next morning. He said he was a sociologist who has spent years studying and writing about prison life. He handed me his book *The Family in Prison*.

"Ms. Spiegler said you're not married. That's one less stress point. Statistics reflect that fully thirty percent of wives of inmates have affairs. Do the inmates get agitated about the possibility that their wives are playing around while they're serving time? You bet. When they're released, they go after their wives. Those who can afford it get divorces; others engage in domestic violence and wind up back in jail.

"I like art and would like to go through your gallery, but that will have to wait. Right now you have a lot of preparation to do and only a week in which to do it. You probably could have gotten a month if you hadn't been a wise guy and asked for fifty years. You'll be out in ten months if you keep your nose clean. Here's some basic rules of behavior on how to survive and avoid trouble."

He paused and stared at me for a few seconds and then said, "Before we discuss proper prison decorum, I advise you to have a thorough medical and dental checkup. There are doctors and dentists servicing the prison population, but nothing to compare with private care. Get vaccinated for everything possible. Every disease, every illness is there and at close quarters.

"There's a prison rule book. You'll be given one when you enter the reception area. If you're not handed it, ask. Study it and make sure you observe all the rules."

Thompson turned to the unwritten code governing prison life. "Integration is not a way of life. Whites stick to whites, blacks, Hispanics, Latin Americans, and so forth to their own kind. Neighborhoods are another source of allegiance. Inmates from Chicago will hang together, provided they are of the same race. You can nod or even smile at blacks, etc., but don't try to be friendly. It will be taken as an insult."

He advised against staring at another prisoner. "It may be interpreted as showing sexual interest. And while we are on the subject, when walking to the shower, keep your shorts on. Don't take them off until you're inside the shower."

He continued, "Don't stare into another inmate's cell. It's considered an invasion of privacy."

Thompson remarked on behavioral traits, such as being polite to guards and not snitching on what I may have seen or heard other prisoners do or say. "Be like the three monkeys who see no evil, hear no evil, and speak no evil. Stay as much as possible in the background. Don't call attention to yourself. Always remember the guards are not your friends. They are powerless to help you. The rules are the rules. The guards can't and won't change them.

"The Constitution does not apply in jail. Your mail and phone calls will be monitored. Be careful about what you say and write."

I asked about money. Thompson said cash would be confiscated. A postal money order of not more than $290 per month is "all you're allowed." He suggested I buy two or three books of stamps. They are used as currency, but are discounted.

Thompson advised me to bring plenty of reading material and get my favorite magazines and newspapers mailed to me. "You'll have plenty of free time. You'll work four hours per day. After that you'll have nothing but free time. Speaking of work, you'll be assigned a job. Let's say sweeping the cafeteria floor. If a guard asks you to empty the garbage pail, don't say 'that's not within my job description.' There are no unions in jail. You're a slave. Do what the guards ask you to do.

"Your cell will make the most ascetic monk's quarters look like a luxury suite in a five-star hotel. The cell is about eight feet by ten. There is a double-decker bed, a porcelain sink, and toilet. In your section of Butner, there are windows, not bars. Your cell is unlocked, so you can walk the hall. There's a library, gym, volleyball court, and pool tables.

I asked about work, particularly whether I would have a choice. "You're a painter. Ask for a job painting in the prison. After a few months, you might get work release. With a trade, you can be assigned to a local painting contractor. You'll be paid thirty-nine cents per hour, but you'll work outside the prison. It'll help to pass the time, and you'll get a non-prison lunch and two coffee breaks."

I made medical and dental appointments, put my regular bills on automatic payment, and gave a power of attorney to my accountant to pay other bills. I made a roundtrip plane reservation to Raleigh, NC with an open return. I bought a lot of books from Amazon with instructions to ship to Butner. I ordered a supply of sleeping pills, gastric medicine, and anti-depression drugs—all as prescribed by my doctor.

On August 18, I boarded a flight for North Carolina. Upon arrival, I took a cab to Butner and spent my last night of freedom in a Holiday Inn. The next morning at 7:30 a.m. I arrived at the prison.

NINETEEN

Butner was expecting me. When I arrived at the reception room, I was issued three pairs of khakis and three brown shirts with my name and prison ID number glued to the pocket. The guard told me that there were 756 inmates in the medium-security section, my home for the next fifteen months. "You are the 757th. Another arrival came in several months ago from your part of the woods. He's here for 150 years. Perhaps you've heard of him. His name is Bernie Madoff. He's your roommate. Two wise guy con artists, a match made in heaven or hell, depending on one's view of swindlers. I'll show you to the penthouse you two big hitters will share."

The tiny room was empty when I arrived. I put my things away and lied down on the upper bunk. I was exhausted from the trip and a sleepless night. I don't know whether I dropped off before Madoff made his appearance. He looked like death. Pale, stooped, and grimacing in pain. From the pictures in the papers and on television, he had a rich-man's belly. Now he was gaunt. His long-flowing hair was cut short. Although his body seemed wasted, he was alert and in our conversations was frequently amusing.

"I heard through convict.com that you had arrived. Being an artist of renown, with impeccable logic, the powers who rule over us have assigned you to plaster and paint the walls of this hellhole. You'll get paid nineteen cents per hour. You know how long it will

take to make $50 million? I worked it out. I'm a genius with fig-
ures. Ready? Two trillion, six hundred billion hours plus change.
Michael, look how far you have fallen in only thirteen years.

"After the fine of $50 million which you agreed to pay, do you
have anything left? If so, I'd be willing to take you on."

I remembered Thompson's advice to trust no one. Even if I
weren't in lockup, I wouldn't trust Madoff. Who would? You'd
have to torture me—say waterboarding—and even then I wouldn't
tell him about the millions in Switzerland waiting for me. Instead,
I resorted to my trademark, the half-truth. "I traded a stiff fine
for a lighter sentence. You got millions, maybe billions stashed
away. They're never going to do you any good. Even if you live for
another 150 years, the ravages of inflation will render your hidden
fortune worthless. Tell me how I can get my hands on your cache,
and I'll give you an Otto Dix to decorate our magnificent duplex."

"How is this simplex a duplex?"

"We have a double-decker bed."

"I like you, Lombroso. I read about your case. You didn't help
Ray recover his money. OK, you gave back the fifty million, but
what about the money you earned off it?"

"I lost it all. I turned it over to a guy named Bernie."

"Yeah sure. Contrast your case with mine. I rendered invalu-
able assistance to the trustee of my bankrupt estate. I helped him
locate assets, which believe me, he never would have found. So far
that skinny little bastard has recovered billions. My so-called victims invested $16 billion. They stand to get their money back plus
a handsome return. There's a big difference between them and
me. I've been stripped of everything, including life itself. Even my
collection of antique watches—all two hundred of them—were
seized and sold in a fire sale for a pittance of their true worth.
Now, are you ready? I'm seventy years old. What's my sentence?
One hundred and fifty years. You know what that is? It's a life sentence. It exceeds the sentencing guidelines. We challenged it on
appeal. An open-and-shut case. No way for me to lose. You know
what the dumb bastards on the Court of Appeals said? 'Affirmed.'

"So here I am. I'll spend the rest of my life in this shithole, while my so-called victims play golf in Palm Beach."

Madoff claimed he never solicited accounts. "People threw money at me. Hedge funds, banks, charities, folks I hardly knew. Almost everyone I ever met, they begged me to take their money. Why? The greedy bastards wanted more.

"You're Italian. I assume you're Catholic. I'm a Jew. Many of the victims were Jews and Jewish charities. In synagogues all over the world they blame me. Not for just plain thievery, but hurting Jews. I don't feel any worse for a Jewish victim then for a Catholic. And there were plenty of them too. Religion had nothing to do with it. They voluntarily turned over their money without me saying anything. All I did was take it. Many of my investors made a bloody fortune. That brings to mind a funny story.

"An old bitty came up to the office and screamed: 'I want my money back!' She was disturbing the office. She had these long false fingernails and was threatening to poke them in my eyes. I wrote out a check for the full amount in her account and handed it to her.

"She looked at the check and gasped. 'That's twice what I gave you.' She handed me back the check and said, 'Keep on investing for me.' Now she's spewing venom every second of every day. 'I planned to play canasta around the pool. Because of that thieving bastard, I have to sell my condo and freeze all winter long in New York. Madoff should be hung by his balls and his dead body drawn and quartered.'"

It took months for Madoff to get past denigrating his victims and revealing how his Ponzi scheme worked. My constant prodding paid dividends.

"No reason for you to remember this, but I can never forget it. My downfall began on October 19, 1987, a day that will go down in history as Black Monday. Up to that time, I was doing a little worse than the market, but the market was moving up smartly. It didn't matter what stocks I bought; by and large, they moved up. Not a lot. As I said I was doing worse than the market but making some money. As long as I wasn't losing money, my clients didn't complain. On Black Monday, the Dow Jones dropped more than five hundred points, the biggest one-day decline in history. I knew what caused it: program traders."

I was skeptical about everything Bernie said. Although he was represented as some sort of an evil genius, in my opinion, he was an uncommonly common man. I asked how he knew what caused the decline and what was program trading.

He said his principal business was running an over-the-counter trading firm, Bernard Madoff Securities. "We made markets in stocks not listed on the New York or American Exchanges. It was not an exciting business. If someone wanted to sell a given stock, you matched it against someone who wanted to buy the stock. The names of the brokers who had orders to buy or sell were listed in the pink sheets. Don't look at me that way; they were pink. They listed the bid price—that is what a trader is willing to pay for a stock—and the ask price, what another trader is willing to sell. All my traders had to do was match the bid with the ask and pocket a small differential, our commission. The firm made money, but it was dull. The adrenalin didn't flow. I turned the business over to my brother Peter. Back to your question, through our trading desk, I knew what caused Black Monday. It was computer trading, or program trading, that triggered the crash.

"C'mon Bernie, computers can't buy and sell stock even today. Someone has to operate them."

"True, but only in part. Computers can be programmed to automatically sell or buy at fixed price levels. Institutional investors, mainly insurance companies, programmed their computers to sell stock at or below a fixed price. When a stock falls to say $10, the computer program dumps the stock at the best price it can get. If the market is falling, the dumping of stocks causes it to fall more.

"The stock market decline began in Hong Kong. Spread west to Europe and on Black Monday hit the US markets. When you sense a market is collapsing, you hold on and wait for it to stabilize. I didn't sell a share on Black Monday, but the computer programs did. They flooded the market.

"The supply seemed inexhaustible; demand for stocks infinitesimal. We couldn't match the many sell orders with nonexistent buy orders. Orders took hours to fill. The New York Stock Exchange halted trading until it could catch its breath. Three hours passed before the exchange resumed trading. When it did prices were so low only the guys seeking bottom fish were active.

"I was managing some money. Not much but some. My accounts took big losses. I didn't want to tell my clients I lost money. So instead, I sent false statements showing that I made money. I announced a ten percent gain when other managers were showing declines of fifty percent or more."

"Hold it right there. Your investors are losing money, and you tell them they're making money. What do you do if your clients decide to cash in? Take an account of $50,000. You did have accounts that small?"

"At that time, yes. There were accounts as small as a few thousand dollars. I couldn't afford to impose a minimum limit. I was still small potatoes, and so were my clients. I took whatever I could get. Mostly from relatives and friends. I had no reputation as a money manager and didn't deserve one. I had no training as a securities analyst and didn't have a clue as to how to analyze a stock."

"Let's get back to my question. A guy puts $50,000 into your hands. The market bottoms out. His account is worth half of what he put in, or say $25,000. You tell him his account is worth $55,000. He says, 'You're a fucking genius. I need the money to buy a house. Give me my $55,000.' What do you do?"

"That happened. There was only $25,000 in his account. I liquidated his account and took $30,000 from other accounts. That marked the start of my Ponzi scheme. Using other people's money to meet withdrawal requests. It was my only source of cash."

"Did you have any big winners like Apple, Amazon, Google, or Walmart?"

"No, Michael. I'm like you. You're an artist who can't originate; I am a deaf and dumb money manager who can't spot a winner. Others thought I was as good as Warren Buffett. Why? I was the only manager who made money during Black Monday and its aftermath.

"There were other steep declines throughout the early nineties, then the dot.com bubble burst at the turn of the century. Throughout all those turbulent times, I reported profits each year of about ten percent, even though I had stopped investing money.

"My well-publicized success when others were losing money gained me a reputation as a genius. When asked for the secret of my success, I put it down to arbitrage. 'I'm on both sides of a transaction. I make money on the upside and money on the downside. In true arbitrage transaction, you can't lose. The profits are small. I keep costs down by using my trading desk.' Not only did I not engage in arbitrage, I didn't know how to spell it.

"My apparent success was all people cared about. No one, not a single investor, asked to examine my records. The SEC, in an act of bureaucratic blindness, examined my books and found nothing amiss.

"As word of my success spread, people with vast amounts of their own money, or in control of pools of assets, pleaded with me to take their funds. 'Please Bernie, take my life's savings. I want more and more. I want to live like you.' It wasn't just Jews or Jewish charities, although there were plenty of them. There were also banks in Europe, hedge funds in Connecticut, sophisticated business tycoons, socialites, and Harvard MBA-investment bankers. These guys understood the stock market. They thought I had found a sure thing: the way to make money regardless of the direction of stock prices. Super smart guys got down on their knees and pleaded with me to invest for them, me a financial nincompoop. I was the biggest name in the investment world. A hero to all the people who turned over their money to me.

"What nobody understood, even if I had some secret method, I couldn't invest the vast sums thrust upon me. I held billions of dollars. Maybe I could have invested a few million, but of course, not well. If anyone examined the custodian who held my assets, they would have discovered that I had $24 million in boring old blue chips. Where was my client's money? In savings accounts and money market funds, readily available to meet withdrawals.

"There came a time when even the billions in ready-cash accounts were inadequate to meet the multibillions of dollars in artificial profits."

"I know when that happened. The Great Recession struck. I lost about a third of my net worth. I panicked. I wanted to withdraw my money and stuff it under my pillow. For the first time, I read the financial section of the *Times*. Pundits were advising 'keep your money in cash, or if you want, to take a risk buy treasury bonds.'

"Why were you affected? Your funds were in cash or cash-like investments. You were insulated against loss."

"Right," he said. "But on my books, I had $50 billion of fictitious profits. That's $50 billion more than the $16 billion in hard assets. When the Great Recession struck, everyone reacted like you. They wanted to withdraw the full amount of the account. In other downturns, I paid Peter with Paul's money. In October 2008, there was no Paul's money. It was as though a spigot, perpetually flowing, was suddenly turned off. Investors were frightened. They feared a depression. They wanted their money in cash. Bear Stearns and Lehman Brothers had failed. Fannie Mae and Freddie Mac, US government-backed agencies, had to be shored up. AIG, the largest insurance company in the world, was going belly up. It looked like Goldman Sachs was washed up."

He paused. "I knew the dance was over. Everybody, except for me, was running for the lifeboats. My sons turned me in. Not fair. I told them to. By turning me in, they saved their own skins. I shielded them until it was over. I was trapped. My sons were talking to the SEC. So I started talking too. I confessed to the FBI. I was fingerprinted, handcuffed, photographed, arrested, and treated like a common criminal."

"You lived a sultan's life. A penthouse in New York, an ocean-front home in Montauk, a palace in Palm Beach, yachts, fishing boats, cars, jets. Did you use your clients' money to pay for all those things?"

"When I wanted to buy a home, jet, yacht, or car or pay for upkeep on my homes, I used whatever funds were available. The chauffeurs, maids, pilots, gardeners were all on the office pay-roll. The money to meet the payroll came out of one big pot. The entire Madoff family, children, grandchildren, in-laws, relatives fed from the same trough—my clients' funds."

"Did you ever refuse to take money?"

"Never. Well, there was one occasion. I liked to fish. It was a form of escape. One day in the early 1970s I was out fishing off Montauk in my own boat. The fog was rolling in. I could barely see, so I followed some other boats that I hoped were heading for the harbor. My motor conked out. I was alone. I thought I'd drown. A shortwave radio saved my life. I called for help and was rescued by the Coast Guard. They towed me to a boatyard in Montauk. The mechanic, who came to service my boat, looked familiar, but I didn't recognize him until he called me Bernie. Then I knew who he was, Andrew Machowski. We went to high school together in Laurelton, Queens. Because our names began with 'ma,' we sat next to each other. We both liked the water. We were lifeguards, and we fished off the beach. He was Polish, one of the few Christians in the neighborhood. I asked him what he was doing in Montauk. He said he had quit his job as a boat mechanic in Sheepshead Bay in Brooklyn. 'Not a good place to raise a family. I bought a home and got a job in the yard. My boss has promised to sell me the business when he retires.' I asked whether he fishes. 'Whenever I have free time. In the off-season, I'm a commercial fisherman. My dream is to retire in the Florida Keys and bone fish.'

"I decided I would never fish alone again. In short order Andy agreed to be the captain of my boat. He'd continue working at the boatyard, and we'd fish together whenever he and I were free.

From that day on, whenever I wanted to go fishing, my captain-mechanic came with me.

"Andy, with my help, bought the boatyard in August of 1996. In 2008 Andy called it quits. He was my age, 69, and ready to retire. He sold his home and the business. He used part of the proceeds to buy a home in the Keys and a boat.

"In early December, he came to my office. He handed me a check in the amount of $970,000. 'It's my life savings. Please invest it for me.' I told him to hold onto his money. I said, 'Now's not a good time to invest. Keep your money in a savings account. When the time's right, I'll invest your money.'

"I heard from Andy one more time. After the scandal broke, I got a two-word note from him saying 'thank you.'"

Bernie asked me lots of questions, not about my scheme and none about art. He wanted to know about the sex life of a "handsome bachelor with a $50-million-dollar bankroll and who's knowledgeable about art. Women love culture, even more than money. They cozy up to novelists, poets, artists. Broads go nuts for intellectuals."

We had lots of time together trapped as we were in a small cell. I thought about Scheherazade. To tell the tales took a thousand and one nights. I had a fantastic sex life, but not enough to fill a thousand nights. I rationed my tales to one a month. I said my hallmark was never to pay for sex. I admitted I treated my women generously, but money never changed hands.

"What's the difference," Bernie said, "between wining and dining a broad, giving her expensive gifts, and an outright cash payment?"

"The difference can be summed up in one word: seduction. To me the art of seduction is all-important. Being young, rich, and in the art world gave me access to exotic women. I offered an event, not a night in the sack. I referred to it as a 'sexual happening.'

We'd spend a few days together, sometimes as long as a week in a romantic place.

"You're a fisherman. When you catch a fish, you know it. When I had a long-legged, slim, gorgeous dame on the line, I reeled her in."

I began my tales with Marge Wilson. "Marge was a ballet dancer, a transplanted New Yorker from Wisconsin. I met her at a dinner at the National Arts Club. I was alone; she was with a gorgeous young man. It didn't take long to learn they danced together in the New York City Ballet Company. She said to me, 'It's a shame Robert is gay. Almost all the guys in the company are. My instincts tell me you're not.'

"It was a dark, cold January day. 'I'm planning a trip to the Caribbean. My yacht is waiting for me in St. Croix. You're the one person in the world I'd like to have join me. It's no fun traveling alone.'

"'Will there be a chaperone on board?'

"I said there would be two. One to protect me and one to protect her. She laughed and said mine would have the tougher job. We agreed to leave the next day. At the end of the evening, I took her and Robert to their apartments in my chauffeured limousine. I dropped Robert off first. She moved close to me, but I made no advance. I walked with her to the building's front door, squeezed her hand lightly, and said I'd pick her up at ten the next morning.

"When my car arrived, she was waiting in front of her building. My chauffeur placed her bag in the trunk. I greeted her, opened the car door, and slid in next to her. Three hours later, the chartered jet landed in the St. Croix airport. A cab took us to the Christiansted Harbor where my chartered yacht was waiting. The captain piped us aboard, and under a clear, blue sky we set sail for Antigua.

"We unpacked. Changed to bathing suits and sat on the deck and talked. She about dance; I about art. After a suitable interval, I asked the captain to find a quiet cove. He did. We dove into the clear blue water and swam. We got back on the boat and went to our cabin to change. With our bodies damp and salty, we made love. Screwing a dancer is a treat. She was acrobatic and graceful. She was on top of me, below me, and on the side with poised and elegant movements.

"We dressed. The boat anchored at Caneel Bay in St. John. We had dinner at the hotel, walked along a flower-lined path, and returned to the boat. We were tired. Spoke lovingly to each other. The next day, we sailed around St. Thomas, swam in Magens Bay, and lounged on the beach. After we returned to the boat, we showered and screwed and screwed and screwed. The next day, we took a taxi to the custom-free shopping district. We went directly to H. Stern, a chain of jewelry stores that originated in Brazil and sprouted all over the Caribbean. There's even an H. Stern in New York. She selected a necklace. I placed it around her neck. We kissed lightly on the lips and returned to the cab and the boat. The trip was nearly over. Soon we were back in dreary, old New York."

Bernie said, "Just what I thought. You paid her for her services. There's no difference between cash and a necklace. How much did the necklace cost?"

"I don't remember...a few thousand dollars. The difference between an after-the-event gift and a prepayment of cash is significant. I was under no obligation to buy a bauble, and she didn't expect a gift. We fucked because the circumstances were compelling. Two naked bodies, dripping wet, alone in a cabin, what else would you think would happen? Money played no part except that I paid for the outing."

Bernie argued there was no difference. He asked why I bothered to buy an expensive necklace if there was no obligation to do so.

"The gift," I said, "was a parting gesture. My way of saying thanks and farewell."

"If she was so great in the sack, why did you want to end the affair almost as soon as it had begun?"

"Bernie, short-time romances are part of my DNA. My mother died when I was six. My father never remarried, but had many affairs. He said he was having lots of fun without having an entangling relationship. In that respect, I'm like him except he had a son, me, and I have no family. Some days I think freedom is a fair trade for a family. Other days I think not.

"The ballerina was perfect in bed, but she wasn't smart. Some dancers have their brains in their feet, and that was the case with Marge Wilson. When we weren't screwing, I was bored."

I related a tale about a married woman I took to London to view an exhibition at the Tate. I added I purchased a Schiele drawing for her in a gallery in London. I told Bernie about an older woman, a widow, with whom I had spent a weekend in Paris eating, drinking, walking, and fucking. Bernie's face came alive when I said "older women know how to please a man, better than their younger sisters." To his question about the gift to the widow, I said I got her a box of macaroons. "French macaroons are sumptuous, nothing like the New York brand."

I told about a famous actress, a sex symbol whom I took to Cannes for the film festival and another actress to the Oscar awards. Bernie asked for their names saying he would keep it confidential. "My word is good. You run no risk. If I wanted to broadcast it, nobody would believe me."

I laughed. Sometimes Bernie could be funny.

Thomas Thompson, the consultant who had advised me on how to survive in prison, had cautioned against associating with prisoners of another race or ethnicity. I followed his advice.

Carmine Persico, the boss of the Colombo family, is another celebrity prisoner at Butner. He is like me, white and Italian. I approached Persico in the cafeteria, introduced myself, and asked to join his table. Persico shook my hand and congratulated me for committing the almost-perfect crime. "But for those no-good commie Russians, you'd have gotten away with it. I'd like to talk with you but not at meal times. I only eat with members of my family because we discuss confidential matters. Do you play bocce?"

"My grandfather was an ace at the game. He taught me how to play on the bocce court in Riverside Park. If the US had fielded an Olympic bocce team, I'm sure my grandfather would've been on it. Nobody in the park could beat him except for me and only on rare occasions. I haven't played in years, but I'd be happy to beat you. I've seen the bocce court in the yard. Do you have a set of balls?"

He said he did, and if in the standard round of twelve I came within five points of his total, he'd give me one of his prized Cohiba cigars. We agreed to play that afternoon during "rec" period.

A bocce game is started with a flip of a coin. The winner gets to roll the *pallino* ball. Persico won the toss and smiled when I said I wanted to inspect the coin. "Who rolls the *pallino* is of little moment. If you'd like to, go ahead."

I rolled the *pallino*. It hit the pin set in the middle of the 13-by-90-foot, rectangular court and rolled to a position in the back third of the court. The *pallino* was in a proper position to start the game. Carmine asked me to choose my color, and when I said red, he handed me four red balls. They were large, professionally sized balls. He played with the green.

Since I rolled the *pallino*, I bowled the first ball. He then rolled. His ball was closer to the *pallino*, so he got to roll his remaining three balls. Then I rolled mine. The goal is to position your balls close to the *pallino*. If all four of your balls are closer than all four of your opponent's, you score four points. If two of your balls are closer than all four of your opponent's balls, you score two points. If a ball touches the *pallino*, it's called a *baci*, or a kiss, and it's worth two points.

I was no match for Carmine. He won in a walk.

The next day, we played a team game—Carmine and I against two of his cronies. We won, but it was a close game. Over the following months, weather permitting, we played bocce twice a week. I became friendly with Carmine and his "family," but not friendly enough to dine with them.

Once a week, the commissary is open to prisoners. They are allowed to buy candy, fruit, and toiletry, provided they have a credit balance in their account. The maximum balance is $290, which can be replenished each month. Spiegler kept mine at the max. Too often big black thugs laid in wait for me and seized my purchases. I remembered Thompson's advice, "Don't complain to the guards. They won't help you, and those who have wronged you will retaliate."

At mealtime, I was also hassled. Inmates at the end of the line pushed me aside and took my place. I meekly stepped out of their way.

Attacks ceased after I began to play bocce. My association with the mob gave me status. No one dared to steal my purchases or push ahead of me in the chow line. Even the guards were deferential. Within the prison walls, in Mafia language, I was a made man.

Who to sit with at mealtimes was a problem. I spent enough time in the cell with Bernie. In the cafeteria, we avoided each other. Carmine and his "family" had refused me a seat at their table. I tried other cliques, but being an outsider, I was uncomfortable. My search ended one day at breakfast. I spied a soulful male, about sixty, with a full beard and a partially bald head sitting alone in a corner. I asked to put my tray down, and when he said, "yes, please do," we introduced ourselves. He was the notorious Jonathan Pollard, the American convicted for being an Israeli spy. He was serving a life sentence for disclosing classified information to Israel. From that breakfast on, we took our meals together.

He inveighed against the system. "The indictment charged I provided classified documents to an ally, Israel. My acts were not claimed to have hurt our country, a claim that could have been made, if, in fact I had endangered our security. You know what it is for aiding an enemy—a death sentence

"The guidelines provide for two to four years for passing information to a friendly country. What country on Earth could be friendlier than Israel? Moreover, snooping on allies is a common occurrence. The US employs a whole network to spy on its allies, including Israel.

"In my case, there was an ameliorating factor. The information I gave Israel concerned military movements of Arab nations hostile to Israel. Israel was entitled to this information under an agreement with the US. By not providing the information, the US was dishonoring its obligation. I did no more for Israel than what our country was obligated to do.

"Rather than try a case that would have exposed our country to embarrassment, I entered into a plea deal. By its terms, I pleaded guilty, and in return, I was to be sentenced to a year in jail. Instead, I was sentenced to life.

"My lawyers have been trying for years to void my plea bargain, and for me to stand trial. I'm willing; the government is not. It hornswoggled me into making a deal and then didn't live up to its end. A fine way to treat a citizen. I've been confined for twenty-two years."

Although Pollard professed his love for Israel, he was motivated, not by altruism, but greed. He sold the classified information to Israel and to three other countries. Some of the information got passed along to the Soviet Union.

Despite the fact that Pollard sold secrets, his plight had aroused support from a diverse political spectrum. He showed me letters from senators, congressmen, cabinet members, heads of US intelligence services, petitioning every president from "Bush the first" to "Obama" for a grant of clemency. The presidents refused. Pollard's need of a presidential pardon is no longer urgent. Under the law, a prisoner sentenced to life is automatically released after thirty years. At his release in 2015, Pollard will be sixty-one.

TWENTY

My fifteen-month sentence was reduced, for good conduct, to ten months. On August 1, 2010, I was released. On the morning of that day, I went to the prison's administration wing for processing. The procedure was straightforward. I was shown a receipt I had signed for my personal items and clothing. They were returned to me. In a small dressing room, I exchanged my prison uniform for the civilian clothes I wore on admission.

The ten months at Butner seemed like ten years. My civilian clothes hung loosely on my frame, confirming what I had already known—I had lost ten pounds. Arlene Spiegler was there waiting to take me to New York. The gate swung open, and Arlene and I walked to her rental car. Her face spoke as loudly as her words. "You look like shit. You lost too much weight. You're pale, and you have aged. Let's get back to New York. Stuff some good food down your gullet, expose you to fresh air and sun, and get back the old Lombroso good looks."

Adjusting to civilian life was difficult. I was unsure whether my time in jail was tattooed on my face. Did everyone, even strangers, know I was an ex-con? The doorman at the National Arts Club sure did. "Please wait here, Mr. Lombroso. I'll alert the manager." I was on the board with the power to fire the manager. In times past when he saw me, he bowed. Not this time. In a voice, loud enough for everyone in the lobby to hear, he said: "Mr. Lombroso, the club charter provides for the automatic expulsion of a member convicted of a felony. You may apply for readmission (it's rarely granted), but until you are readmitted, you can't enter the club without being accompanied by a member."

I wanted to curse, call him a pompous son of a bitch, but I was too embarrassed to say a word. Members gathered in the lobby stared at me as though I was an extraterrestrial being. A few of them I knew. One, frightened by the word "felony," abandoned the open lobby for the safety of the men's room. I followed the flunky's order and left the club, formerly my club, but now a hostile place. I walked several times around Gramercy Park before returning home. I sat at my desk and contemplated my future.

Money was not a problem. After paying the $50 million fine, I had, in my name in the US, about another two and a half million. And then there was the $52 million in my Swiss account. I started to shake. *What if the IRS uncovered my account? How much time would I have to spend back in the slammer? Put it out of your mind. If the account is discovered, the holder is a Liechtenstein trust. What if I withdraw money? The IRS can ask, where did you get the money? No need to touch the Swiss account until you retire. Then you'll renounce your US citizenship and find a new home in an exotic European city. Perhaps Florence or Paris or Rome or London. Once you're a resident in a foreign country, you can spend your money and live like a sheik. It's only fitting. I made my money from oil too. Not the kind you pump into your car, but oil as in oil paint. As long as you don't touch the account when you're subject to federal tax, you'll never be detected.*

I had to stop ruminating about something not likely to happen. I had an immediate problem, though. What to do? I couldn't sit around and do nothing. I'd fall deeper and deeper into depression. I had to start a new venture. I owned an art gallery. *Yeah sure. Who's going to buy a painting from a convicted forger? Why not if the painting is labeled a forgery and the price is right?* I got it. I'd be upfront. I'd change the name of my gallery to Fakes and Forgeries. I'd sign and date each painting to eliminate the possibility that a buyer might pass the painting off as an original. I'd hire other painters to work for me.

Before beginning my new venture, I called Arlene and invited her to dinner. "It's social in that we'll be eating, but it's business as well. I need to vet a business idea." I had a second motive. I was horny as hell after ten months without sex. Arlene was the only woman with whom through letters and phone calls I had maintained contact. While we were talking, I thought about her two battleship-sized thighs. Arlene must have suspected my second motive, because she turned down my invitation. "I'm a lawyer specializing in criminal defense. If it's truly business you want to discuss, I suggest you call another classmate of ours, Sam Hertling, he's a top-notch corporate lawyer. Remember Sam? He was editor of the *Law Review*."

"I remember Sam, and if my project was straight business, I'd call him, but I need advice on whether my new venture, although legal, might constitute a violation of probation. I don't want to start all over again with another lawyer." I got tough. "I probably have some credit left over from the hundred grand I paid you."

It worked. I sensed a less resolute Arlene.

"The retainer was a one-shot deal. It covered the criminal trial, an appeal if we took one, and that's all. There was no appeal so I feel I owe you something. On a personal level, even though you're an ex-con and I'm an uptight Jewish lawyer, I'm fond of you. I'll help, provided the new venture is legit. If it's crooked, I can't help you."

Her response emboldened me, so I decided to change dinner to a weekend at a seaside resort. If it worked, even if we didn't have sex, in her bathing suit, I could gaze upon her thighs. Sound strange? Try to imagine your average heterosexual male locked up with Bernie Madoff for ten months and think about what that might do to his libido.

I said, "It's not a crime I'm planning, but I'm worried about restrictions on my activities while I'm on probation. I can't engage in certain legitimate activities—at least that's the way I read it.

I'm a lawyer too, you know. A violation and I'm back in jail. I'm not certain whether my proposed activity violates probation.

"Dinner won't give us enough time. Also there's the problem of privacy. Our conversation is privileged as long as others don't overhear us."

"What do you have in mind?" she asked.

"If I can book a two-bedroom cottage at Oceanside Inn overlooking the ocean with a connecting sitting room, we'll have private sleeping quarters and a room in which to work. If you'd feel more comfortable in separate rooms, I'll try that too, but we'll either have to work in a bedroom or in one of the inn's public rooms. The inn bustles in the summer. It will be hard to find a peaceful spot. A suite works. "

"Well, it is hot and sticky. Don't be offended, Michael. If my bedroom door has a lock, a cottage is OK. Otherwise, book separate rooms. It's not you alone I fear, although I don't trust you, but I also don't trust me. The code of professional responsibility prohibits a lawyer from having sex with his/her client. A well-known divorce lawyer violated the code and got disbarred. I wonder if there's an exception if the client is also a lawyer, but you're not a lawyer anymore. A lawyer convicted of a felony is automatically disbarred. How do you know you can get a cottage in August for a weekend?"

I was encouraged until she mentioned felony and disbarment. I lost my club and now my profession. What she said wasn't all bad. She was thinking about sex and added she didn't trust herself. In responding, I ignored her sexual comment and directly answered her question.

"Tony Bono, the nephew of the deceased owner, Nick Bono, is Italian as was his uncle. My grandfather and father were friends of Nick's. They used to take me there when it was a plain old inn. Now it's a spectacular seaside resort and spa. I played with Tony and his younger brother Joey. They're my age and friends. Tony is in charge of rooms at the inn; Joey runs the restaurant and bar. I'll call Tony and see what's available."

"All right, but I reserve my right at any time to change my mind."

Tony said all the cottages were booked "except the Bridgedeck, but it has three bedrooms, not the two you're looking for. We require a week's stay. It's the best we have to offer. For you old buddy, I'll let you have it for the weekend at the rate we charge for a two-bedroom cottage. We make deals for VIPs. You're a VIP. Through the grapevine, I heard you played bocce ball while you were away on vacation. Nick, bless his soul, liked the game, and so did your grandfather and father. Remember the matches we played? There'll be a basket of fruit and a bottle of champagne in the fridge. I'll reserve a table for dinner on Friday. Don't forget to say hello at check-in."

We left New York at nine in the morning and arrived at Oceanside three hours later. A carhop took the car and a bellman our bags. When Arlene looked around the cottage, she thought there was a mistake. "It has three bedrooms. I hope you're not planning a ménage à trois."

"There were no two-bedroom cottages available. The extra bedroom is for your protection. You'll have a hiding place."

After we unpacked, I suggested a walk on the beach. I changed to a swimsuit and a golf shirt; Arlene looked trim in shorts and a sleeveless blouse. Had she lost weight and all of it from her thighs?

As we walked along the beach with our feet in the water, I unveiled my new business plan. "There are some people who, for example, would like to buy the *Mona Lisa*, but the price is out of reach and besides the Louvre would never sell. What about if I forged—no, I don't want to hear that word again—what if I reproduced the *Mona Lisa* like I did the *Blue Horses* and offered it for sale, say for $25,000? I'd put my initials on the painting and a current date. No one could possibly be fooled. Anyone who has $25,000 to spend on a painting would know the original was in a museum in Paris. Also, if you thought it necessary, I'll write in indelible ink on the back of the painting 'this is a reproduction.' I intend to rename my gallery 'Fakes and Forgeries.'

"I don't plan to reproduce the old masters, but rather the five hundred odd works of German expressionist art missing after the Entartete Kunst exhibition as well as some of the works confiscated and destroyed by the Nazis in the fire at the main fire station in Berlin. It should keep me busy for the rest of my life."

"What makes you think you have a problem?

"The terms of my probation as incorporated in my order of parole states: I can't forge paintings."

Arlene laughed. She reached down and splashed water on me. "You are a cutie, Michael Angelo. You'll have the whole art world seeking your head. The proposed name of your gallery is terrible. Let's relax for now. I'll think about it, while we're having fun and games. You need the sun and time to rejuvenate. We'll talk some more about your new venture later or maybe tomorrow. Tell me about those dark, dreary days in prison." She took my hand and we continued our walk.

I told her about Bernie, Carmine, and Jonathan. I embellished the stories, but omitted my sex tales to Bernie. One more half-truth wouldn't matter to St. Peter.

When we got back to our cottage, it was time to shower and get dressed for dinner. We went to the bar, had a drink, and then were showed to our table. It was the best table in the house with a direct and unobstructed view of the ocean. Our waiter called me "Mr. Lombroso" and said Tony was comping me. "He said you can even have the $68 stuffed lobster." First Tony and then Joey came to our table. They stayed and talked.

Arlene was impressed. "It's fun to be in a place where my host is treated like royalty."

"The brothers regard me as an old friend, which indeed I was. I was here with my father and grandparents when John Gotti was staying at the hotel. He had a table right up front as close to the ocean as one could get without getting wet. A waiter was assigned exclusively to his table. Nick filled his glass with wine.

"Well, I'm glad your treatment is different from Gotti's. Still I'm impressed with the way you're treated."

What did I think? Among my people, being convicted of a felony is no disgrace.

After dinner, we kicked off our shoes and went for another walk along the moonlit beach. As we ambled eastward, we passed others strolling westward. We smiled at them and they smiled at us. At Oceanside, unlike Butner, everyone seemed happy.

After our walk, we returned to our cottage. Standing close together in the sitting room, I held Arlene's hands in mine. I dropped them and held her face. She put her arms around my shoulders, and we kissed.

"I hope you won't lock your door."

"Lock it? I'll leave the door wide open."

A lamp light was glowing dimly when I entered her room. It was, however, casting enough light for me to see Arlene in bed with bare shoulders. I hopped in next to her. She was naked. As we kissed, she removed my night shirt. I've been told that I'm a good lover but never have I displayed such talents in the sack as I did that night. I was out of practice but not out of vigor. My prowess overwhelmed Arlene.

"After being made love to by you, I think I've never been made love to before. Hey, my Michael, until you crossed the threshold I think I was a virgin."

The next morning we went for an early morning swim in the ocean, took steam baths, and relaxed in the Roman bath. We had breakfast at John's Pancake House. We drove to the lighthouse, then to the dock and shopped at the Montauk mall. When we returned to our room, Arlene was all business.

"I'll call Judge Keogh on Monday and make an appointment for an in-chambers conference. I'll notify Morrison that I'm asking for a meeting and give him a copy of the supplement to the orders of probation and parole. It will state that you are permitted to paint works of art attributed to others provided they are clearly labeled reproductions and bear your initials in the right hand corner and the date the painting was completed. Stamped on the back of each painting shall appear the legend 'Purchased from the Michael Angelo Gallery of Reproduction Art.' That, by the way, is the new name of your gallery.

"If the judge insists on giving notice to the public—in reality the art world—your start will be delayed during the notice period, probably thirty days from the date of the order. I'll inform the judge that you will begin your work during the notice period but not sell anything until the order becomes final. If it does not become effective, you will destroy any completed or partially completed paintings. As a fallback position, may I say you will restrict your work to replacing the art lost or destroyed by the Nazis?"

I agreed. "Sure, but tell the judge that and also disclose that I intend to hire other artists to help me. Before I open to the public, I'll need to collect an inventory of works. I plan to hire about six artists. It will take us about a year to produce enough paintings to open the gallery. Also, I'd like to come to the conference."

"Keogh likes you; he doesn't like the art market. It's a good idea for you to be there. I'll let you know when and where."

We had dinner at Salavar's, an old-fashioned, rundown, seedy fish restaurant smack on the Montauk commercial dock. The fish come directly off the boats to the restaurant and are simply prepared, either grilled or fried. When we got back to the inn, we joined other guests at the bar. We sipped brandy and returned to our room. Arlene said she didn't want sex, but did want me in bed with her. "We'll read in bed. When we're ready to sleep, we'll turn off the light and go to sleep."

I agreed, but knew once the lights were turned off, not sleep, but sexual delights awaited me. I was right. I knew the cause of my passion, but not that of Arlene's. When I discovered the reason—she was in love—I decided this was the last weekend we would spend together. Like my father after my mother's death, I was unwilling to exchange freedom for the ties that bind.

Federal courts are unusually slow during the dog days of August. Judge Keogh set the conference for Monday at 3:00 p.m. He greeted me warmly, and with a wry grin asked whether I planned to return to a life of crime. I assured him that chapter in my life was closed. The fear of another stay at Butner had reformed me. I planned, however, to spend the rest of my life painting. He laughed and quipped, "That's what got you into trouble in the first place. It doesn't seem to me you've been rehabilitated. Now if you said you wanted to be, for example, an auto mechanic then I would agree prison had worked. Let's get on to business. I can conceive of no legitimate ground for you, Mr. Morrison, to object to Ms. Spiegler's supplemental order. I'm ready to sign it, but I'll give you an opportunity to be heard."

Morrison said he lacked experience to determine the effect reproductions of German lost art might have on the art market and suggested notice be published and an opportunity be accorded to members of the public.

Judge Keogh ruled, "Mr. Lombroso's plan as described in the supplemental order, is legal. He can engage in it after the probationary period ends and begin his activities immediately. I can conceive of no legitimate reason to give notice or to restrict his activities any further."

Right there in chambers, Judge Keogh signed the order. I was free to start my new business.

TWENTY-ONE

My grandfather had an aversion to throwing things out. He held on to all kinds of junk. He rationalized his action in a variety of ways. The most common: "Someday I'll need this widget. I'll stick it in this drawer." I inherited his form of thing-constipation and find it difficult to discard objects long after their usefulness has ended.

Although I hadn't used nor even thought about the photos I had taken fifteen years earlier on my journey to London, I was sure they were not discarded. After a quick search, I found them in the bottom drawer of my desk. They were in the original envelope from the Golders Green film shop. The photos were essential in 1995, but times had changed. Acting against a well-ingrained habit, I tossed them.

Google was a gleam in Larry Page's eye when I started my research leading to the forging of the *Blue Horses*. Now it was the consummate search engine locating in seconds information on the World Wide Web. When I typed "Reich ministry V&A," out popped a reference to the gift of Elfriede Fischer to the Victoria and Albert museum of the two-volume document kept by the Reich Minister of Propaganda. The museum had digitized the document, and it was available for downloading. I downloaded both volumes and printed them. From the material, I searched for the five hundred missing paintings—many of which my new venture would reproduce. Deep in the bowels of the Web were scanned pictures and descriptions of most of the missing works. Since I'd be reproducing the works and selling them as new, pigments dating from the period were unnecessary.

I hadn't painted in years and wondered whether I had lost the skill. I had rust in my brush, but with intense concentration, I started reproducing the missing Otto Dix painting *War Cripples*. Shortly after I had started, I stopped. Dix's strokes were refined, distinct and clear; mine were clumsy. I realized it would take a better painter than I to make a good reproduction of this work.

There was a second reason. The task was exacting and too much like work. Even if I were still able to do a credible job, I did not want to go back to work. I'm rich and middle-aged. It would be better if I hired young artists and supervised their work. I was eager to resume my prior life of fun and games.

After being down in the depths for ten months, my spirit had returned. The weekend spent with Arlene had started the transformation. Judge Keogh's swift approval of the changes in my order of probation put the imprimatur of the law on my new business. The information tracked down in seconds by Google made the task feasible. My next chore was to find a handful of artists to paint the reproductions. Finding them would be easy; I'd ask my former partners for candidates.

Their gallery was close to my home. The next morning, I stopped by. They were delighted to see me.

"You look great," Aritta said. "Not a trace of prison pallor. We're doing well operating your business plan. There's room for you. Would you care to join us? We'll use both galleries. We'll be a chain store. "

It's easy to tell when an offer is sincere as opposed to polite. Aritta was insincere. Even if he had meant it, I would have declined. "I'd be an albatross. My reputation would spook sales. I've decided on a new business plan. One that's right in the face of the art world." I then revealed my plan to reproduce the missing art that Hitler had confiscated in 1937. Martin asked whether it

was legal. I showed him the supplemental order. "I'm not taking any chances. I got an advance ruling my new business is legal. What I need is about a dozen starving artists (are there any other kind?) to do the work. I'll pay a decent wage for talent. Can you supply me names and contact info?"

My former partners were relieved; I had declined the obligatory invitation. Jefferson jumped up and came back with an index of artists hoping to be represented by their gallery. With comments from Aritta and Martin, they prepared a list of a dozen artists. I thanked them and turned to leave when Aritta interjected, "How about lunch at your club?"

I said I was no longer a member and told him about what had happened with the manager.

"To hell with him," Aritta said. "I'm a member and so are Stephen and Alex. We'd be honored to have you as our guest."

Lunch was pleasant. It felt good to be back in my club even though it was no longer my club. The one discordant note was when I asked for an accounting. "Business has been good," Jefferson said. "Your share for the past ten months comes to about $350,000. Our accountant, Seymour Steinberg, who was your accountant and maybe still is, will give you a formal reckoning.

"Since you have rejected our offer to return to the fold, we'd like to buy you out. It will take time to pay, but you waited patiently before. Would you be willing to wait again?"

The payout, I said, could extend over five years. They agreed. I said a buyout price of five times this year's cash flow would be fair. Again, they agreed. I left the club in good spirits.

I walked to the DArcy art supply store on East 24thStreet and made its day. I ordered twelve easels, several rolls of linen canvas, palettes, brushes, and paints. I paid with a check. The owner, Richard Eisenberg, with whom I had dealt with for many years, came out of his office, greeted me, and thanked me for my order. He asked whether I was in a hurry to receive the supplies. "Is there a problem with my credit? I'm paying with a check, and yes, I'll need the supplies right away."

"It's not your credit; it's our delivery man. He's away and won't be back for two days."

I sensed the bastard was lying. In the fifteen years we've done business, there was never a delay. In those days, I had an account and didn't pay until I had received a statement—sometimes a month or more later. It was a reaction to my status as a convicted felon. "I'll wait for the easels, canvas, knives, and palettes, but I'll take the paints and brushes with me. You know my address, same as before I went to prison." I wrote out my check while the clerk wrapped the brushes and paints. Isenberg tried to shake my hand, but I refused.

I hopped a cab to B&H on 34th Street and 8th Avenue, a high-tech superstore. I explained my need to John Bottington, the store's resident genius. "I have twelve students who will be painting twelve different images from the web. I want each student to have his image on his own screen. Visualize the scene. The student stands in front of an easel with his brushes and paints within easy reach. On the side of the easel is a screen reflecting the image. How do I do it?"

"Easy," Bottington said. "You buy twelve memory cards. Download the twelve images from your computer to the memory cards. Insert the memory cards into twelve digital picture frames, which you will have to purchase. The total cost is about a thousand dollars."

"I'll select the images, but I want you to handle the technical stuff."

"There's no need for me. It's simple. If you want me, I'll come, provided you live in the city and agree to pay me $100."

I agreed. I gave Bottington an extra $20 to cover transportation and delivery of the equipment. The next day, I selected the twelve paintings. Bottington arrived at about 6:00 p.m. with the cards and frames. In about thirty minutes or less, each digital picture frame was working and displaying a different image. I was ready to interview the resident artists.

I called the artists on the list made by my former partners. I explained the project and the pay. Each painter would be paid

$500 per week. I'd provide the supplies. I turned on the picture frame and asked each one whether he thought he could make a perfect reproduction of the painting. When the painting was completed, the painter would affix his initials to the bottom right-hand corner along with the month and year the painting was completed. The paintings, on the back, would be stamped with the following legend: "This painting is a reproduction painted in the Michael Angelo Gallery of Reproduction Art."

I told each artist that quality, not time, was my only concern. If I became dissatisfied with an artist's work, he would be fired with a week's severance. "It is my plan to have an inventory of a hundred paintings among the five hundred lost through Hitler's seizure of modern German art."

Some of the artists were good, others bad. I dismissed the bad ones and encouraged the talented to recommend others. It took three months to assemble a staff of twelve. A spirit of camaraderie developed, helped no doubt by the free lunches and wine and cheese served at the end of the day. Painting is solitary work, uninterrupted by telephone calls or meetings. At the communal table, on the third floor of my home where we ate and drank, the thoughts bottled up poured forth with the wine.

It took a year before I had thirty-six quality paintings, enough to fill the walls of my ground floor gallery.

To breathe life into the exhibition and give it historical perspective, I hired a young woman, Anne Kritzer, an art history doctoral candidate at Columbia to prepare a biography of the original artists and a history of their works. Anne wrote a pamphlet about the Munich Entartete Kunst exhibition and attached a catalogue of the exhibition. The pamphlet was available to all who came through the door. The history of the original paintings was affixed to the wall next to the reproduction.

When the walls were full, I looked over the gallery with pride. Without a word having been said, the exhibition proclaimed: lost art has been brought back to life—a noble and honorable cause.

Opening night was a gala event. The title of the exhibition was "Lost Treasures Brought Back to Life." Champagne flowed and hors d'oeuvres were plentiful. I was in black tie, and so were many of the guests. I mingled freely and received many compliments, yet I sensed undertones of disapproval. I did not, however, anticipate the extent of the harsh feelings.

The *New York Times* review was headlined: "A Rose by Any Other Name." It read:

> Michael Angelo Lombroso, a felon, convicted of swindling $58.75 million for a forged painting is back to his old tricks. Prison is designed to rehabilitate the criminal and return him to society as a useful, law-abiding citizen. Lombroso, who spent ten months in a medium-security federal prison in Butner, North Carolina has returned unreformed. Small wonder. At Butler, he roomed with Bernie Madoff and socialized with Carmen Persico, the boss of the Colombo crime family.
>
> Lombroso's modus operandi has only slightly changed. In defrauding Cecil Ray, he forged Franz Marc's *The Tower of Blue Horses*, pretending his grandfather had stolen the painting while serving in the Monuments Men unit during World War II. When the Hermitage unveiled the original, Lombroso was unmasked, fined $50 million and sentenced to fifteen months in jail.
>
> The only difference between Lombroso's prior fraud and the present show is that Lombroso admits his paintings are forgeries. Give the devil his due. The paintings are clever forgeries, many very good, but in the end whether open or concealed, a forgery, like a river, cannot rise above its source.

New York Magazine blasted me in harsher tones than the *Times*. *The Post* on Page Six headlined "A Forger Strikes Again." I was castigated on TV news stations and on National Public Radio. If, after my exhibition opened, there was someone in the US who didn't know I was a forger, that person must have been living on Mars.

The news stories created a reverse excitement. Seeing the exhibition became a must for the in crowd. People came from all over—residents, tourists, and foreign visitors. Day after day, the gallery was jammed. I had to hire security guards to prevent my gallery from being overrun. Some people waited an hour to see the show. In the first month, however, not a single painting was sold. I was distraught. I had priced the paintings at an average of $15,000, hoping to clear $500,000 when all were sold. Now I was concerned with stopping the bleeding. I had hired attractive young women to handle sales and assist customers. All had to be paid. My team of twelve artists was hard at work reproducing paintings to replace those purchased, only none were. I kept the "no sale" facts from the painters, but they sensed the venture was a failure

The ice broke when, not a man on the street, but the famous collector, John Schlossman, purchased two paintings. He told me, "I'm not a snob. The paintings represent works conceived by geniuses. The reproductions have been competently executed. They'll mix with my collection. And the price is right. If the paintings were originals, they'd sell for millions. They're bargains based on prices paid for insipid modern art. What do you get for five times what I paid for the reproductions? Sperm from a white-and-black man mounted on canvas. Or a single piece of chocolate with bite marks similarly mounted. They're not works of art. Your reproductions are. Congratulations on a brilliant idea."

I asked if he would be willing to be interviewed by *Artforum*. "Much as I hate publicity," he said ironically, "I'd be happy to speak with *Artforum*. Here's my card."

Midge Martin, the wife of my former partner Alex, was the managing editor of *Artforum*. I called her and told her that Schlossman had bought two reproductions and his comments on the contemporary art market. I added he was willing to be interviewed and gave her his phone number. "Schlossman is always eager to be interviewed; *Artforum,* on the other hand, is not always eager to interview him. He does have a fine collection. I'll give him a call. No promises that I can get it in the magazine."

Midge not only got it in the magazine but combined it with a feature story on my gallery. There was, of course, the obligatory reference to my conviction, my time in prison, and my association with Madoff. There was positive stuff too. In addition to Schlossman's favorable comments, the reporter discussed a new meaning of reproduction. "The gallery features reproductions of works that no longer exist. It is making a positive contribution to art history by recreating lost art."

The article did not presage a tidal wave, but it did produce a trickle. Two more paintings were purchased.

The art market reacts to fads. I waited for the craze to turn to reproductions. It did not happen, but by the end of the year, most of the paintings had been sold and replaced by others. The gallery was moderately successful, but not my life.

I was unmarried and alone on too many occasions. My social life had been active and exciting before my vacation at Butner. I received many invitations to dinners, benefits, openings, and parties. Some days, I wished I could be like the amoeba and by binary fusion split in half or even clone myself. That way I could attend all the pending events. After my release, I received no invitations, and by no, I mean none at all. My mental state was borderline depression. I needed help. My internist recommended a shrink named Martin Perkins.

He recommended marriage and a family. "You live only for yourself. While you were famous, you were surrounded by friends, toasted and hailed. Once your fame turned to infamy, you were deserted. Your friends were all fair weather. You need a bond, a tie you never had before. Most of us find a loyal companion in a spouse. One who cares for us and sticks with us through times thin and thinner. Michael, rescue a woman with children who is struggling to raise them. She will need you as much as you will need her. That's a good basis for a long-term relationship."

When life is not working well, it's a good idea to change. I ran through my short list of contacts. Arlene Spiegler kept coming up. She had been married and divorced. She had a son whom she was trying to raise and had commented when he got older he would need a dad. Being married to Arlene would not be as exciting as my former life, but a lot better than my present circumstances. I called Arlene at her office.

"Well, hello stranger. You make me think about the ape who rapes a woman who complains he never calls or writes. To what do I owe the pleasure of this call? Wait. I've got some good news. I married a lawyer I've been seeing on and off for years. His name is David Stein. He's a well-known criminal defense lawyer. We've joined our practice as well as our lives. The firm is called Stein and Spiegler, and our offices are at One Rockefeller Center. How's your business going?"

"I'm happy for you and sad for me. I called to propose marriage. I hope you won't be available in the future, but if you are, call me."

"You're sweet, Michael. Call me if you need help. Legal help that is."

Arlene was prescient.

Within six months, I needed help.

TWENTY-TWO

A dark cloud hung over my head. For fifteen years, I had evaded the tax law. A news story sent a chill coursing through my body. Switzerland changed the rule governing the secrecy of its bank accounts. Banks were now ordered to cooperate with US enforcement officials in uncovering crime. As one paper reported, "The change is not radical. The FBI, for example, cannot go on a fishing expedition to search for US citizens evading taxes. Identity of the owner of an account need only be revealed if there is a suspicion that a crime other than tax evasion has been committed."

Despite the caveat contained in the report and the shield I had added in the form of a Liechtenstein trust, I was anxious. I must have been crazy to reject my FBS banker's advice to accept amnesty, pay back taxes, and put my unlawful activity behind me. Everyone pays taxes; nobody is happy to. Why did I think I was entitled to an exemption? The penalties for tax evasion are draconian—back to prison.

At the time I had sheltered part of my money from taxes. I had not experienced prison. Now that I had, I didn't want to experience it again. I checked on whether amnesty was available. I didn't care how much it might cost in interest and penalties; I needed a release from the tension plaguing me. I called the IRS from one of the few remaining pay phones in the city. After being put on hold for what seemed like an eternity, I was told amnesty no longer existed. I hung up and dashed away from the booth.

I had a fallback position. I had no reason to stay in the US. I had no family, no devoted friends, and no allegiance to the US. It put me in jail and fined me fifty million. Love the US—not me.

I reflected on the strange course of Italian immigration. Between 1880 and1920, four million Italian immigrants left their families behind and poured into this country. There was no work in Italy, but plenty of work in the US. They toiled in unskilled labor jobs. They saved their pennies, and when they had enough money stashed away, many returned to the country they loved. It was a well-documented course of reverse immigration. Other immigrant groups, such as the Jews who emigrated from Eastern Europe, did not return to the old country. Unlike the Italians, the Jews were persecuted in their homeland.

My great-grandfather emigrated from Naples to the US. My grandfather was a first-generation American; I'm third generation. My return to the mother country was a mere skipping of three generations until I had put aside enough money to live like a Medici. Like other Italian immigrants, I'd start a new life in the old country.

I swung into action. I put my home in Gramercy Park and my condo in Key Biscayne on the market. Real estate is illiquid; it would take months for sales to close. Time was of the essence. My fear of impending doom was so great that I decided to leave before the real estate had been sold. Sleep had never been a problem. Now it was. When I did sleep, memories of prison haunted my dreams. I had no appetite for food. My mental health would benefit from an early departure. I booked a flight to Rome with an open return.

I checked in at the Alitalia desk at Newark Airport. On request, I handed my passport to the agent. She screened it while I waited and waited. The people in the line behind me were impatient and grumbled. They feared they would miss the flight and urged the agent to move on. A supervisor arrived and opened a new line. I tried to remain calm, but my stomach was churning and my head aching. A security guard appeared. My luggage was removed from the check-in station, and it and I were escorted to a room off the main concourse. I sat in there for more than two hours. I tried to read the *Times* and the *Wall Street Journal* on my iPad. I asked for the return of my passport. The guard said someone would arrive soon and I should ask him about my passport. I also asked to use the bathroom. I did have a need, but that was not my primary motivation. I thought about escape. I'd give the guard the slip and run. I didn't know where, but I couldn't stay in the room anymore. My idea of fleeing was squelched when the guard showed me to a rest room and locked the door on the outside. "Knock when you're finished."

There was no window, only a fan that went on when I turned on the light switch. When we returned to the room, a tall, broad-shouldered man in a shiny blue suit was waiting. "I'm agent George Stearns of the FBI." He showed his badge and continued. "You are under investigation for tax fraud. My office considers you a candidate for flight. You've booked a ticket to Rome with an open return and have placed your homes on the market for sale. I have a court order temporarily restraining you from leaving the country. Pending the expiration of the order, your passport will be withheld. You are free to leave now." He showed me the court order and gave me a copy.

I was trembling as I put my luggage on a cart and pushed it to a waiting cab. When I returned home, I went directly to a bathroom and threw up. I took off my clothes, showered, got dressed, and called Arlene. She was out of the office. My call was transferred to her husband, David Stein. I told him what had happened at the airport.

"I was chief of the criminal division of the US Attorney's Office for three years" Stein informed me.. I've worked closely with the FBI. I'll make a few calls and find out how far the investigation has progressed, that is, if you authorize me. Arlene will be back this afternoon. I suggest you come in and meet with us. Tomorrow around three is good for us."

I arrived at their office at 3:00 p.m. and was shown into a conference room with an oval table and eight Marcel Breuer chairs. Arlene and David sat across from me. He took over the meeting. "The FBI is working with the SEC on insider trading cases. The securities agency, with the backing of Congress, is determined to stamp out insider trading. When corporate fiduciaries buy stock prior to a public announcement that will affect the stock price, it makes for an uneven playing field in which the fiduciaries have an unfair advantage over members of the investing public. To level the field, the SEC has embarked on a campaign to punish insider traders. The fiduciaries, greedy for the large certain profits stemming from insider trading, have gone underground. They use, so the SEC suspects, Swiss bank accounts to hide their illegal trading activities. The basis of the agency's belief: heavy trading occurs in Swiss accounts prior to merger announcements. One such instance occurred in the Mittal-Arcelor merger. Prior to the announcement of a takeover offer by Mittal Steel for Arcelor stock, Swiss banks heavily purchased its stocks. When the offer was announced the price was double the market price of Arcelor stock, the acquisition was a record-setting $33 billion merger. "

I said, "I never heard of either company. I know US Steel and Bethlehem Steel, but Mittal and Arcelor, what are they? And $33 billion for a company I never heard of? Further, what does anything like this have to do with me?"

"It should have had nothing to do with you, but it provided the means for detecting you. Mittal is the largest steel company in the world. You don't know about it because it's based in India. The combined company Arcelor-Mittal is a super company. I, too, never heard of either one. I'm going to check on Bethlehem Steel and US Steel. I'll be right back."

When he returned, David said, "Bethlehem went belly-up, and US Steel has been downsized and has fallen from the largest steel company to number thirteen."

He continued. "It was an accident that your Swiss account was discovered. FBS purchased, prior to Mittal's publicly announced offer for Arcelor, a shitload of Arcelor stock for its accounts. You were one of the lucky buyers. The SEC demanded to know the names of the holders of the accounts purchasing Arcelor's stock prior to the public announcement to determine whether any were officers or directors, i.e., corporate insiders. Of the forty-nine accounts purchasing Arcelor, one was an insider, a Mittal board member.

"Your account was held by Hottinger & Cie. It took a big push to get the bank to identify the account, and then it named a Liechtenstein trust. The investigation hit a dead end until, while searching a FBS-scrubbed computer, it discovered that $30 million had been transferred from your account at FBS to Hottinger, and that very account named Gunther Gubich, a Liechenstein attorney, as trustee for an unidentified beneficiary. Gubich refused to identify the beneficiary. The investigators were dumb, but not that dumb. They reasoned that unless you gave $30 million dollars to someone other than yourself, you were the beneficiary.

"The SEC decided that no action should be taken against you, a passive investor, not a corporate insider, but because you are American, referred your case to the IRS. It checked your tax return and found you had paid no taxes on the Arcelor investment either when it was sold on the stock exchange or purchased directly by Mittal. Further, you had failed to disclose the existence of the Swiss account.

"There is a missing link. There's no positive evidence linking you as the beneficiary of the trust, except for logic, and common sense."

My hands were covering my face to hide the fact that I was weeping. I could not hide my trembling body. Arlene came over to me and put her hand on my shoulder. "David has figured out a way to help you, but you must pay strict attention. You will have to make a crucial decision. Please, Michael, listen to David."

He said, "The way the criminal law works, the Assistant US Attorney will get the grand jury to indict you. Grand juries are putty in the hands of the prosecutor. An adroit prosecutor can get an indictment against a monkey for eating a banana. April 15 is around the corner. The IRS likes to make a large splash around tax time to strike terror in the hearts of taxpayers thinking of avoiding taxes. Your case and two others have been selected as the chill factor."

I rose, paced back and forth, and said, "What if I denied I was the beneficiary and claimed Gunther was both trustee and beneficiary?"

"Gubich has denied that he is the beneficiary," David said. "If you testify, we must advise you to tell the truth. If you reject our advice, we cannot represent you."

"Michael," Arlene said, "you'll be destroyed on cross. You'd have to admit the $30 million was yours. You'd also have to admit you directed the transfer from FBS to Hottinger. Now comes the zingers. 'Mr. Lombroso, Mr. Gubich is not a relative of yours, is that correct? You met Mr. Gubich on one occasion only, at his law office, is that also correct? Are you asking the jury to believe you made a gift of $30 million dollars to a total stranger you met once?' Michael darling, forget it. To tax fraud will be added a new charge: perjury."

"Well, what do you suggest I do?"

"Michael, David has a plan. It's not all good, but it's the best strategy."

I stared for a few seconds at Arlene before turning to David.

"The IRS does not know the full amount of the taxes you owe against which to assert taxes and penalty. My idea is to turn over all your Swiss bank account statements to a forensic accountant. He applies the IRS formula used when it offered immunity to taxpayers. We offer to pay that amount in full. The IRS would have a public example to chill taxpayers, and you would be punished financially to the same extent as those who obtained amnesty. There would have to be a jail sentence too, but maybe I could negotiate one as light as three years. You'd be out in two years." I said, "David, I can't go back to jail again. I don't want money; I can't face jail. It's hell, pure hell. Let's assume back taxes plus interest and penalty come to $30 million. There is presently $52 million in the account. Suppose I was to give the balance of $22 million to charity, could we trade that for probation or house arrest?"

"It's an interesting idea, but it won't work. The media would scream: 'Only the poor go to jail; the rich buy their way out.' It won't work. Even if I persuaded the US Attorney's Office, a judge would never buy it. You have to gather your strength. You'll have to spend time in jail. I'll negotiate as hard as I can, but at a minimum, you'll get fifteen months. Is the difference between three years and fifteen months worth $20 million? You survived one incarceration. What makes you think you can't survive another?"

I said, "When you're worth millions, millions on top of millions has little significance. In the US, I have close to $5 million in liquid assets. I paid taxes on that money, so it's all mine. That doesn't include real estate. I've put my real estate up for sale. I expect to clear $15 million. The balance in my Swiss account is surplus. What I need is not more money, but time to enjoy life. When this mess is over, I plan to live abroad, most likely in Italy. Would I trade twenty-one months in jail for twenty million? Of course."

"I got my work cut out for me. I'll leave you to Arlene to work out the financial arrangements."

David left the conference room. I opened my checkbook and asked Arlene, "How much?"

"The usual $100,000. If anybody can cut a deal, it's David. He's the best, trust me."

I had no one else to trust. *I'm almost forty-six and the only one in the world I can trust is Arlene Spiegler, a law school classmate? What does that say about my life?*

Three weeks later I was back in the law offices of Stein & Spiegler. David was all smiles. "The accountant, Morris Gerstein, using the bank statements and applying the IRS standard formula for interest and penalties, determined you owe the IRS $32

million. Coincidentally that was remarkably close to your estimate of $30 million. That leaves a balance of $20 million. Who do
you want to give it to?"

"How about Columbia University? It's engaged in a fundrais-
ing campaign to pay for its expansion into Manhattanville. I'm a
Columbia alum so it makes sense to me."

"It might not appeal to the judge. By donating $20 million,
you would undoubtedly receive honors from Columbia, in addition to a tax deduction. The gift has to be to a neutral agency, one
unconnected to you and one in which no benefits accrue, not even
a tax deduction. I suggest the International Committee of the
Red Cross. Donations to it are not deductible in the US. I further
suggest we roll the dice and make the donation before you are
sentenced."

"What if the judge disregards the donation and sentences me
to five years? Then I'm out twenty million and lose five years of
my life."

"Unfortunately Michael, I can't give you a guarantee. Certain
judges routinely approve plea deals. Your proceeding has not been
assigned to a judge because you haven't been indicted. The prosecutor can control the timing of a true bill or indictment. Until it
issues a judge will not be assigned. It's hard to know which judge's
turn is next, but an educated guess is better than no guess at all.
We'll time the indictment for a judge disposed to approve deals.
It's far from a guarantee, but it's the best we can do."

It was a Hobson's choice. There was one option available and
only one. I took it. A month passed and nothing happened. "We're
waiting for the right judge. The US Attorney has accepted the
deal. Your anxiety is matched by the IRS. It wants a done deal
before April 15, and we're getting close."

On March 25, I was indicted for tax fraud. The story made
the front page of the *Times* and was on the evening news program. The next day I appeared with David and Arlene before
Judge Oscar Bittman. He looked like a kindly old man. He questioned me about whether I understood the charges made in the

indictment and asked how I pleaded to the charges. I said I was a graduate of Columbia Law School. I had read and understood the charges contained in the indictment and plead guilty to the charges.

The judge asked if any promises were made to me and said he alone will determine whether to accept my plea. He asked how the International Committee of the Red Cross had been selected. I said I wanted to donate to a cause unrelated to me, one of impeccable reputation and from which I would receive no benefit, directly or indirectly, including a tax deduction. To the judge's question as to when the gift was made, I said, "$20 million was irrevocably transferred on March 15."

The judge adjourned the hearing until he received a presentencing report. "Since your passport is held by the US Attorney's Office, I will release you on your own recognizance. While you are awaiting sentencing, you are instructed not to leave the jurisdiction of the court."

Three weeks later, Judge Bittman accepted the plea agreement and sentenced me to fifteen months in prison. I was assigned to Butner and instructed to begin my term on May 16. On instructions of Arlene, I neither thanked the judge nor made mention that my forty-seventh birthday fell on May 16.

On the appointed day, I entered the prison hall.

The guard on duty greeted me. "Welcome back, Lombroso. We're expecting you only because we've been notified. I never thought I'd see you again."

I changed to prison clothes and returned to my old cell. After stowing my gear, I walked with bowed head to the rec room. It looked different. There were balloons hanging from the ceiling and red, white, and blue banners attached to the wall.

When I entered the inmates broke out in song. They sang "Happy birthday, Michael." I read the signs on the wall. They wished me a happy birthday and welcomed me "back home." In the center of the room was a table with a cake and candles.

I cut the cake and handed the first piece to Carmine.

"No, no," he said, "the first piece is for you."

For the first time in months, I smiled.